"Just who the hell *are* you?"

Ginny studied Matt's face for a long moment. She was going to have to trust him. "I didn't lie about my name. I *am* Virginia Carney, though in the past four years I've had four different names and lived in four different states. I've lost everyone I love.... I'm scared all the time, always looking over my shoulder. I can't live like this anymore." Ginny's bruised body ached. She was hungry, exhausted and soul-weary.

"Listen, all I need is a few days' rest, some decent food and clean clothes, then I'll be on my way."

Matt's lips twisted in a cynical smile directed at himself. He couldn't believe how quickly this woman's request for a temporary haven had turned into visions of an orderly household, of hot homemade food, clean clothes.... But he was a cop—*ex*-cop—and old habits died hard.

"I think you'd better tell me everything."

ABOUT THE AUTHOR

Evelyn A. Crowe worked for twelve years as a media director in an advertising company before turning her hand to writing in 1983. Her decision to change careers was certainly a stroke of good fortune for Harlequin readers, as Evelyn's bestselling books are favorites with readers around the world.

An avid nature lover, Evelyn makes her home in Houston, Texas.

Books by Evelyn A. Crowe

HARLEQUIN SUPERROMANCE

Evelyn A. Crowe
FATHERS & OTHER STRANGERS

Harlequin Books

TORONTO • NEW YORK • LONDON
AMSTERDAM • PARIS • SYDNEY • HAMBURG
STOCKHOLM • ATHENS • TOKYO • MILAN
MADRID • WARSAW • BUDAPEST • AUCKLAND

ISBN 0-373-70667-7

FATHERS & OTHER STRANGERS

Copyright © 1995 Evelyn A. Crowe.

All rights reserved. Except for use in any review, the reproduction or utilization of this work in whole or in part in any form by any electronic, mechanical or other means, now known or hereafter invented, including xerography, photocopying and recording, or in any information storage or retrieval system, is forbidden without the written permission of the publisher, Harlequin Enterprises Limited, 225 Duncan Mill Road, Don Mills, Ontario, Canada M3B 3K9.

All characters in this book have no existence outside the imagination of the author and have no relation whatsoever to anyone bearing the same name or names. They are not even distantly inspired by any individual known or unknown to the author, and all incidents are pure invention.

This edition published by arrangement with Harlequin Books S.A.

® and TM are trademarks of the publisher. Trademarks indicated with ® are registered in the United States Patent and Trademark Office, the Canadian Trade Marks Office and in other countries.

Printed in U.S.A.

FATHERS &
OTHER STRANGERS

CHAPTER ONE

RUN! RUN, GINNY, RUN!

Virginia Carney chanted the words as her feet slapped against the asphalt highway. She ran until she thought her heart would burst, then slowed to a walk, cooled down, then began running again.

Run!

Don't let them catch you.

The Texas sky was clear, the stars bright, the moon a huge globe that lit the way, showing her where the potholes were so she wouldn't fall. The moon was her own night-light, keeping the creatures that stalked the darkness away. Whenever she slowed to a walk she could hear the quiet scurry and rustle of animals over her harsh breathing, and she realized just how much a city girl like her was out of her element here. In the distance a cry of terror and pain would rent the silence, and all her fears would come flooding back, setting her off again.

Run! For your life.

How long had she been free? How long had she been running and hiding? As she jogged along the side of the highway, she tried to work it out in her mind. Two days? Could that be right? There was the car wreck and her chance to escape. Yes, she thought, that was two days ago. She'd awakened to find herself uninjured. Free. Some command from deep inside her had forced her numb body to move—fast—across an empty field towards the distant lights of another highway.

She'd run at night and hidden during the day, trying to find shelter, water and food. The shelter and water had proved easy. All she had to do was make her way off the side of the highway, climb over a fence or two and crawl as deep as she could through the thick stands of scrub oaks or cedar, never once allowing herself to think about snakes or spiders or other such creatures that might be there. The trees couldn't keep her dry from the rain that had poured down both days, but she had quenched her thirst by drinking like an animal from a water-filled depression in the ground.

Food was another thing. She'd found some berries she'd recognized along the roadside, and once she'd come across a peach orchard that ran right up to the highway. She'd scurried through the barbwire fence and eaten her fill of the sweet, almost ripe fruit, even filled her jacket and tied it around her waist. She'd managed. She'd survived.

Ginny laughed aloud. City girl she might be, but she'd outsmarted them all. She was free for the first time in four years, and she had no intention of being caught. Like the animal she'd become, she had acquired an instinct for survival. Sooner or later, she told herself, the hilly, winding road would lead her to a town, a house, someplace she could find help. But could she trust anyone?

She was daydreaming as she ran, not paying attention to where she was going, when suddenly she stepped into a hole. Unable to stop, she found herself propelled forward and tumbling in a free-fall down the incline at the side of the road, bumping against rocks, snagging her clothes and flesh on small thorny bushes. When she finally came to a halt, she was on her back, dazed, winded, staring at the sky. With great care she slowly tested each limb. Everything seemed in working order. She sat up, realizing as she did that the morning light was quickly stealing away the darkness. She needed to find shelter for the day.

It was when she tried to stand that she realized her ankle was sore, not broken or sprained, just incredibly tender. She could walk, but she needed to stay off her feet and rest if she was going to resume her nightly jog. Ginny pushed her dirty hair away from her face and glanced around to take stock of her position.

Across the highway was a wide stretch of cleared land and, beyond that, rough, rocky terrain. In front of her was cultivated land with long rows of what appeared to be some sort of thick-leafed vines. She glanced over her shoulder and sighed. She knew she'd be better off if she went that way, but the mere thought of civilization, just a peek, was too tempting to pass up. Somewhere beyond those beautifully manicured vines had to be a barn, a house, somewhere she might find food, dry shelter, maybe some clothes.

The morning sky was turning purple as the sun began to peek above the horizon. She had to get moving, and she gingerly hobbled over to the four-rail cedar fence and slipped through, every muscle in her body aching. It didn't take more than a few steps for her to realize the vines were grapevines, dense with bright green leaves and clusters of red grapes not yet plump from the sun. She was going to have to walk between the long straight lines and that would limit her movements and expose her to anyone passing on the highway or up on the slope. Squatting down, she measured the distance between the ground and the thick strands of wire and secured black plastic tubing that the vines were trained to grow on. Only about a two-foot clearance. She didn't like jeopardizing her position by being hemmed in between the rows and so decided to follow the edge of the vineyard as far as it would take her.

The going was slow, rough, and for the millionth time she glanced at her watch, only to remember that it must have been dislodged when she was thrown from the burning car. But she figured she'd been walking about twenty or thirty minutes when she came to the end of the rows of vines. An engorged, fast-flowing river bisected the vineyard, and Ginny decided to follow its course for a while, then cut across when she found the right spot.

As she moved along, the sound of the river became louder, the going rougher over the rocks and small boulders. She wasn't sure she'd made the right decision, and she stopped, debating whether to return the way she'd come or go on.

Suddenly, from the corner of her eye, she caught sight of a shadow moving toward her. She strained to see, her gaze darting around wildly as she wondered if her eyes were playing tricks on her, but no, something was stealthily sneaking among the vines.

Over the roar of the river, Ginny heard a low growl and imagined razor-sharp teeth and a jaw dripping with saliva. The morning light caught and held a pair of shining eyes. Ginny gasped, frozen to the spot. Then, as silent as the creature that was stalking her, she turned and walked away as quickly as she could. *Stay calm,* she told herself. *Don't run.*

She could hear it behind her, the crunch of claws digging into the ground, the whoosh and swish of its body rubbing against the wire and vines. She could hear the fierce growl. Then there was silence. Once again Ginny's feet froze to the ground, her skin icy with fear, her heart pounding as she strained to listen. Nothing. But she knew whatever was out there hadn't given up. The quiet scared the hell out of her.

All of a sudden she heard a twig snap no more than a few feet away. Panic set in and she was running recklessly over the rough ground, heedless of her now throbbing ankle. She stumbled and fell, bruising her knees, scraping her palms, but she frantically pushed herself up again.

Run, Ginny! Run for your life.

It was almost completely light now, but there seemed to be dark shadows everywhere. Ginny kept running. She knew that the creature chasing her was just playing with her, a game before it pounced, but she was out of control now and couldn't stop if she'd wanted to. Either the beast was going to kill her, or her overworked heart was going to explode.

She made the fatal mistake of taking her eyes off the terrain ahead of her to glance over her shoulder. In that split second her foot caught on a tree root, and before she could even scream, her body slammed to the ground. Her head connected with a rock and she felt the blackness engulf her. She was going to die, she knew it. God, she'd been so close to freedom. So close. But the beast, this time a four-legged one, had won.

MATTHEW BOLT stood hunched over the kitchen sink, tears running down his cheeks like a river of sorrow. He sniffed, squeezed his eyes shut, sniffed again, then tried to wipe his face with a bare shoulder. The tears just kept coming.

"Peel the onions under the water, Matt. Everyone knows that way they won't burn your eyes."

At the tone of his son's voice, every muscle in Matt's tall body went taut. Sarcasm seemed so alien coming out of the mouth of a ten-year-old.

Matt glared at the boy's retreating figure and flinched as the back door slammed shut hard enough to make the decorative, antique plates on the wall rattle dangerously. "Dammit, don't slam the door," he growled to an empty room. Empty—like so many of his threats, he thought. Like his life.

He sniffed loud and noisily, then gave a rumbling laugh. He didn't know if he was crying from the onion fumes or for himself. Shoving his hands, the knife and onion under the running water, he continued to work at putting together an edible dinner. He wasn't going to let a smart-mouth kid get the best of him. That would be playing right into the boy's hands. But then the kid—his son—hadn't had an easy time of it, either, he reminded himself. Maybe he was willing to let things slide because he knew all too well how Austin felt.

Life was a roller-coaster ride of ups and downs, and Matt figured this past year he'd been cruising straight down to hell. He'd been one of Houston's top homicide detectives before he'd made one almost fatal mistake and ended up with a bullet in his chest and one in his leg. He was a hero. He'd tracked a criminal of the worst kind—a child molester and a killer.

He was a celebrity. The standoff and hostage situation with the killer had been covered by a local news crew, but what they hadn't expected was a shoot-out when the ex-convict finally gave up, then changed his mind and tried to kill his hostage and the two cops he'd been negotiating with. What followed made headlines, even the national news—The Wild West Is Alive And Shooting Straight In Texas.

He was a star. He'd saved the lives of the child hostage and his partner—and saved the state and taxpayers from an expensive trial—but he'd paid a price by receiving two bullets. His fifteen minutes of glory lasted about three days while he hovered between life and death. Once he was out of danger and back among the living he was forgotten. Oh, everyone had been damn sympathetic, but it hadn't changed the fact that he was forced into retirement. Hell, he thought, it was as if he'd died. He might as well have. After months of painful recuperation, still weak, he'd decided to leave the city and go home.

Home. That was a dark word with darker memories. But home was the only place he could be alone, lick his wounds and wallow in self-pity. Home was Two Rivers, a small town in the Texas Hill Country. A place of rich farmland and ranches, of rolling hills and pure spring-fed rivers—and the family vineyard that had been left to him when his father died three years ago.

Home was supposed to be a place of peace, of quiet. A place to heal. All he'd found were painful memories, a younger half brother he'd never really gotten to know and a failing wine business. Then the final blow. His ex-wife had been killed in an airplane crash, and his son, a child he'd seen only twice in ten years, was now in his care.

Matt didn't know how long he'd been standing at the sink, his mind wandering down passageways he thought better left alone, but his fingers were now white and wrinkled. He quickly finished peeling the onion, quartered it and dropped the pieces into the bowl of water with the peeled potatoes and carrots then carried the bowl to the refrigerator.

Later in the afternoon he would put the pot roast on to cook, then about thirty minutes before it was done, he'd add the vegetables. Pot roast was his single culinary accomplishment and that was only because it all went in one pot. He was carefully gathering up the vegetable peelings to take outside to the compost pile when he heard Austin screaming his name.

Matt shook his head. The kid had cried wolf a few times too many lately. First there were the rats he'd seen in the barn, then the spiders. The last straw had been when the kid had cried bloody murder at the sight of a grass snake. It wasn't so much that he was afraid of the rats, spiders and snakes. He just enjoyed seeing his old man come tearing to the rescue. But Matt wasn't about to fall into the same trap again, only to be met with that smirking grin.

He picked up an oversize wooden spoon and tested its sturdiness by smacking it against the palm of his hand. A good spanking was what the kid needed. Then a picture of his own father holding a paddle, testing it against his palm, his face stony with anger, popped into Matt's mind. He dropped the spoon as if it had bitten him, watching it bounce on the floor with a feeling of horror.

The back door was jerked open. A disheveled young boy with dirt smeared on his face and clothes barreled in, knocking over a chair in his clumsiness. Sweat from the summer heat had plastered his brown hair to his forehead in spikes, and his dark eyes were wide with shock. Austin opened his mouth to speak but nothing came out. He took a couple of huge gulps of air.

"The...the...there...there's a dead woman in the vineyard."

Matt almost believed him, then reminded himself that Austin was a certified genius with an IQ of 180 plus, a child prodigy, and he was also a damned good actor.

"Dad, please. I'm not lying. There's a dead woman. At least I think she's dead. Down by the stream. Please, Dad."

It wasn't the urgency in his son's voice, the scared look on his face or the fact that this usually meticulously clean boy looked as if he'd been rolling in the dirt that convinced him. It was the sound of Austin calling him Dad that made him believe this was no prank.

"Show me," Matt said, and he suddenly had to struggle to keep up with his son as they made their way around the side of the house, past the barn, down the slope and through the long rows of grapevines. He could hear the river now, swollen and running fast from the rain they'd had the past two days. He could smell the sweetness of the wet earth as the sun beat down on it.

Suddenly Austin skidded to a stop, and Matt had to brake fast to keep from running into him. His breathing was loud, harsh, and he strained to hear what his son was saying. He hadn't exerted himself this much in months, and he shook his head, trying to clear the spots before his eyes. Austin stepped aside and at last he saw what the kid was pointing at—a woman sprawled facedown at the edge of the vineyard, her feet barely out of the river.

"Is she dead?" Austin asked. "She's dead, isn't she, Dad?"

Matt stared at his son, saw the stony expression, the sad eyes, and gulped. He could never explain what hearing the word "Dad" had done to his insides. Something to ponder later when he was alone. Poor kid, poor little soul, he thought. Too much death.

His gaze returned to the woman. After a moment to mentally prepare himself, he squatted beside her and reached out to touch her. He hesitated. She didn't look as if she was breathing, and death wasn't exactly pleasant to touch. With his index finger he gently flipped a thick strand of damp hair aside. Fighting back a growing revulsion, he forced himself to relax and placed his fingers on the artery at the side of her neck. The pulse was slow, steady and strong.

"She's alive, Austin." He heard the giant sigh of relief and its echo in his own mind. "She's damp and cold, though."

Austin was at his father's side, his hand gripping the strong bare shoulder when he heard a noise and jumped. "What's that?"

Matt heard it, too. A low, throaty rumble, like a growl. He jerked his head up and quickly glanced around, then relaxed. "It's just Dog," he said, pointing. At the sound of his name, the animal lifted his head. He was big and ugly, a mongrel with a patchwork of brown, tan and black hair, spooky light blue eyes and a set of vicious teeth he habitually showed to anyone who glanced his way. Dog lay crouched a few feet from the woman's side, as if guarding her. But that was ridiculous, Matt thought. Dog didn't take to strangers. Hell, he didn't take to the people he knew. Besides, the mutt was old Jericho's hound, if he was anyone's—at least he'd taken up with Jericho this past year. Strange that he should be here with the woman.

"You think Dog hurt her? Maybe attacked her? She's bleeding, Da—Matt. Look." Austin pointed to the torn shirtsleeve shirt and the streak of red staining it. "What're we gonna do?"

After ascertaining there was no injury to her neck or spine, Matt gently rolled the woman over and sucked in a deep breath. He'd seen injuries like this and there were only two explanations. Either she'd been in a car accident or someone had beaten her up pretty good. One eye was puffy and black, and a red welt and bruises marked the opposite cheek. Her lip was split and swollen, and there was a lump on her forehead. Matt leaned closer to get a better look and frowned, suddenly doubting his conclusions. Her clothes were ripped and filthy, and she was covered with scratches. This woman looked as if she'd been running over the local terrain like a fox running from a pack of dogs.

"Dad!"

"We need to get her up to the house, son." Matt glanced around as if he hoped help would pop up any minute, then he looked at Austin. "I don't know if I can carry her by myself. Maybe you should run up to the house and call for help."

"There's no 911 in this backwater, godforsaken, Podunk hick town."

"Call the sheriff's office."

The words were no sooner out than a cold hand clamped around his own. Matt nearly jumped out of his skin and fell backward from his squatting position onto the hard wet ground. He didn't much notice the dampness or the fact that Austin was on his hands and knees, patting the woman's other hand. What snagged his attention was a pair of soft brown eyes filled with terror. He knew that look, had seen it on too many faces throughout his police career.

"Please, no sheriff," she whispered.

The eyes closed. She was out. Matt found his son staring at him with that pleading, questioning look. "She's scared, isn't she, Dad? Real scared. What're we gonna do?"

Dog began to growl, and Matt was surprised to see the animal move closer to the woman, eyeing him at the same time. Animals and kids, he thought. "I'll take her shoulders. Do you think you can get her feet and legs?"

"Sure," Austin said. "I'm stronger than I look, you know." Then he asked, "You're not going to call the sheriff, are you? She asked you not to."

"We'll see." Matt cursed under his breath as he lifted the woman up by her shoulders, jostling the limp body for a moment until he managed a more secure hold under her arms. She was light enough, but the pull on his weakened muscles burned like fire. He straightened and stood panting like a thirsty dog, waiting for Austin to step between the woman's legs and lift them before he started walking backward up the slope of the vineyard.

By sheer willpower and a steady determination not to show any weakness in front of the boy, Matt made it to the house with only three rest stops. He and Austin deposited the woman on the couch in the closest room, his study. For all her fragile appearance, she'd been damned hard to carry, Matt thought as he slumped against the wall. Huffing and puffing, he forced himself to straighten and head for the kitchen. He needed water—lots of it. The boy followed him, and to Matt's surprise Austin pulled out a chair, gave him a gentle push until he sat, then rushed to the refrigerator. He yanked out the water bottle and handed it to Matt. Of course Matt broke the cardinal rule and drank right from the bottle, instead of using one of the two glasses Austin had set on the table.

The kid was grinning at him. Matt slowly lowered the half-empty bottle from his lips, then held it out to Austin. His son smiled at him, a genuine smile, then lifted the bottle to his mouth and drank deeply. Matt knew a thousand questions were coming, and he leaned back in his chair to wait.

Austin wiped his mouth with the back of his hand and shoved the bottle back across the table. "What're we gonna do, Matt?" he asked for the third time. "You won't call the sheriff, will you? She asked you not to. Maybe we should talk to her. You know, find out—"

Matt held up his hand. "The first thing I'm going to do is sit here until I start to breathe like a normal person. Then I'll sit here some more while I decide if my body's going to work like it's supposed to." When Austin started to get up, Matt grabbed his arm and gently but firmly pushed him back in the chair. "And you'll sit your butt right here with me until I've rested. Then *we'll* decide what's to be done."

Austin thumped his elbows on the table, rested his chin on his cienched fists and glared at his father. "She might be dead by then, or maybe she's in there dying now."

"No. She's all right. Bruised and battered, but she's alive. Hopefully she'll be in a talkative mood when we go in there."

"But she's unconscious." Austin's eyes, so like his father's, narrowed, and his voice rose to an indignant squeal. "When did you get a medical degree? How do you know she's not dying?"

"Because I just know." Matt realized the answer was a typical adult-to-kid response, a way to shut him up, but things like that didn't work with his son. "Believe it or not Austin, she's not unconscious—she's asleep.

I've seen it happen before after a shock or trauma. The body just shuts down, and the person goes into a deep sleep."

Austin had read of such things, but he didn't want to admit his father could be right either. He shied away from Matt's probing gaze and glanced at the back door. "What's Dog doing here?"

Matt yelled at the animal to scat, but the dog didn't move. "Crazy mutt," he muttered. When Austin rose as if to walk over to the screen door, Matt grabbed his arm. "Leave him alone, son. He's a mean one and could bite. I'll have to talk to Jericho." Matt struggled to stand. Every muscle in his body felt locked, but after a series of contortions, he made it to the sink and managed to get a pot of coffee together and set it on the burner. When he sat down again, he was trembling with fatigue.

Reluctantly Austin returned to his chair and picked up the bottle of water, but all the while his eyes were focused on the dog. The animal slowly stretched out on the porch, his head facing them, his spooky blue eyes staring past them as if he could see into the next room where the woman lay.

GINNY'S EYES opened slowly. For a moment she was confused, then her mind cleared and she sat up—and immediately wished she hadn't. She was stiff and sore all over, but alive. The last thing she remembered clearly was being stalked by some monstrous animal. After a quick check of her extremities, she frowned. Then it came back to her—a man and a boy. The feeling of being lifted, then a swinging motion that had lulled away all her worries.

She was worried now, though, and quickly glanced around. The room she was in was obviously a man's office or study. The furniture was masculine—big leather couch and chairs. Not the supple, soft leather a woman would pick but the stiff, durable stuff that outlasted its owners by generations. There was an ornately carved desk, piled high with papers and ledgers. A coffee cup and drinking glass sat on the desk beside a banker's lamp, its green glass shade covered in a layer of dust. Yes, definitely not a woman's room, she thought.

She quickly tucked that tidbit of information away in her mind. It was a habit of hers to memorize both the people and objects around her. That way she could spot anything out of place. She was good at it, too, they'd told her. Ginny lay back down and sighed.

She could hear the deep rumble of the man's voice and the high-pitched sound of the boy's in the next room. The sounds were soothing, familiar, and she wanted to drift away and wake up in another time, another place. But that life was over and there was no going back. The voices rose and lowered as if they were arguing. She couldn't understand what they were saying, yet she knew they were discussing her. Pretty soon she was going to have to let them know she was awake. But first she needed to think of a plausible story about why she was wandering on their land, injured and disheveled.

As she tried to compose a believable lie, she began to take a more complete mental inventory of the room. When she came to the photographs on the wall, she sat bold upright. Oh, God, she thought.

The framed photos, awards and certificates were testimony of one man's career—a cop's career. There were photos of a fresh-faced, smiling young recruit and a sober, more mature plainclothes cop and, last of all, in a spot of prominence among the other mementos, a framed gold detective's badge.

Well, she thought, she'd jumped from the frying pan right into the fire. Then again, maybe not.

She cleared her throat and called, "Hello. Is anyone there?" She lay back, listening to the scrape of chairs and the sound of feet pounding across hardwood floors. Then a small whirlwind flew through the door and to her side. Suddenly she was staring into a pair of wide dark eyes. "Hi," she said, and smiled.

Austin blinked. He'd been so worried, but she was smiling, so she wasn't dead. His mystery lady was alive. He wanted to jump and shout it to the sky. He wanted to dance a wild jig around the room. Instead, he stared and said shyly, "Hi."

"Hello there. Did you bring me here?" Ginny asked softly. There was something so desperately happy in that young face, as if he'd never been happy before and the unfamiliar feeling was almost overpowering. Ginny scolded herself for her fanciful thoughts. It was the man she had to charm, not the boy.

"Yes." Austin gently picked up her filthy hand, never taking his eyes from her face. "You were in the vineyard. I found you and came and got Matt. We carried you. I carried your legs." To his horror he felt his face go hot all over and knew it was bright red. He patted her hand a couple of times, then let it go. "You're all right, aren't you?"

"I think so. Who's Matt?"

Like a flower in the morning sun, Austin basked beneath her gaze. It took him a minute to realize she'd asked a question. "Him." He jerked his head toward the doorway and acknowledged his father as if he was an unwanted stranger. "My dad," he said sourly.

Ginny glanced over her shoulder and frowned. Was this the same person in the photos? She looked at the tall bare-chested man with his torn and stained jeans and black curly hair that brushed his shoulders. The man in the photographs reeked of spit and polish, his haircut almost military, his clothes ranging from a starched uniform to a suit and tie that defied wrinkles.

Yes, it was the same man and those were the same eyes she vaguely remembered staring down at her earlier. She'd seen eyes like that before, lifeless eyes that lacked all emotion. Ginny's eyelids fluttered shut for a second. She knew his type and the code he lived by. A strange feeling came over her that the beast that had stalked her for sport was a pussycat compared to this man. He was an experienced hunter, used to catching and devouring his prey. She'd be trussed up and turned in quicker than she could scream her innocence.

It was over. Ginny's shoulders slumped in exhaustion. She shifted her gaze and tried to smile at the young boy, who was obviously so worried about her. She was proud of herself. She'd made a good try, damned if she hadn't. But she was tired of running and hiding. She was sick to death of living a lie.

She glanced the man's way. "You a cop?"

"Ex-cop." Matt studied the woman carefully, noting the changing expressions and finally the fatalistic resignation. He straightened up from his leaning position against the wall, gently moved Austin out of the way and pulled up a chair. "I'm Matt Bolt."

He held out his hand. She shook it and quickly released it without saying anything in return, meeting his gaze directly. He admired her courage as he deliberately let the silence stretch between them, watching closely as some inner struggle seemed to be going on in her.

Enough was enough, she thought. "I'm Virginia Antonia Carney." Then she smiled sweetly and said firmly but defiantly, "You can call me Ginny."

Matt knew all the signs when a perp was ready to spill his guts and confess. Whatever she was going to tell him, he didn't want his son to hear, so he ordered Austin out of the room, reminding him on his way to shut the door.

Austin was enraged. The injustice of being sent out of the room like a child! He would have argued, but knew from experience what that stony look on his father's face meant. He wanted to cry and scream. Instead, he said on his way out, "Fine, I'll dig up some ointment for Ginny's cuts. That's if we have anything like that in this dumb house." He was at the door when he stopped, sniffed the air like a hound dog and grinned. "Coffee's boiling over." The door slammed behind him.

"I'll be right back," Matt said, cursing under his breath all the way out of the room.

Ginny was grateful for the reprieve. It gave her time to regroup, time to get her story straight— She stopped herself. No more lies, she thought. For a moment she remembered something she'd seen in his expression when she'd come to down by the river. She'd seen pain, and not the physical sort. It was as if he had recognized in her the same emotions that he'd been feeling.

Maybe she was wrong, but for some unexplainable reason, a gut feeling she had, she knew she was going to trust this ex-cop, Matt Bolt. She wasn't sure why yet, but for the past four years she'd been living on her hunches and intuition.

She must have dozed off. When she awakened he was quietly sitting beside her, waiting. "If the coffee's not burned I'd appreciate a cup," she said, playing for more time.

Matt held out the cup in his hand, the gesture intended to tell her he was all business and not about to be put off anymore. He watched her drink, trying to figure out what she'd look like cleaned up. She was small compared to his six foot four, about five-five, he guessed. He knew her eyes were brown. Her hair? He wasn't so sure. It was matted and dirty, but he could have sworn it was red. She looked thin. A few extra pounds on her bones wouldn't hurt. And there was a fragility about her as if she might shatter and break into a million pieces. Matt scowled. Just what he needed, another lame duck. Right now he wanted to know how much trouble she was going to cause him.

The silence was driving Ginny crazy. As a cop, he must have been excellent at interrogation—and intimidation. "I'm not a criminal," she blurted, and handed him the empty cup.

"That relieves my mind some." Matt set the cup down on the floor beside his chair. He leaned forward, placed his elbows on his knees, then rested his chin on the backs of his hands.

"Tell me something, Ginny Carney. Just what kind of trouble are you in? Who are you running from?"

CHAPTER TWO

GINNY STUDIED Matt's face for a long moment as she struggled with her own sense of self-preservation, trying to decide just how much she should reveal.

"I'm not a thief or a murderer," she said at last, "and I haven't done anything illegal."

"Convince me." Matt's expression was stony, his dark gaze probing.

"I guess it's obvious I've been running and hiding from something?"

"Or someone?" Matt asked.

"Actually, a lot of someones," she replied with a wry grin, trying to lighten the atmosphere.

"Name a couple," Matt said.

He wasn't going to cut her any slack. She attempted to settle into a more comfortable position, but the slightest movement made the pain worse. She sucked in a breath, closed her eyes and gritted her teeth as she drew herself up a little more.

Matt watched sympathetically, but he refused to offer any help.

Ginny took a breath, then slowly released it. "The government for one. The FBI for another."

Matt nodded, the brief tightening around the corners of his eyes the only suggestion of interest.

"I didn't do anything wrong. I just wasn't satisfied with their interference, their games, and decided to drop out of the picture." She anticipated his next question, but when he didn't ask it, just continued to look at her with those piercing eyes, she said, "Listen, all I need is a few days' rest, some decent food and clean clothes, then I'll be on my way."

Somewhere in the house a clock chimed the hour. Matt's gaze never wavered. "If you can't put me up for a few days," she went on, "if it compromises your sense of justice or ethics or something, I'll understand and leave now."

Matt blinked and his lips twisted in a cynical smile directed at himself. He couldn't believe how quickly his mind had kicked into high gear at this woman's request for a temporary haven.

In mere seconds, visions of an orderly household, of hot homemade food, clean clothes and a house that didn't smell like the inside of his tennis shoes danced through his head. To have some peace and quiet... But he was a cop—ex-cop—and old habits died hard. He wanted to know where he stood. "I think you better tell me everything."

"I'm not a criminal," she said again.

Matt nodded as his mind raced with questions. Why, he wondered, did he unconditionally believe this woman? Why had that little warning voice he'd listened to for years, the one that had saved his butt on more than a few occasions, suddenly gone mute?

He scowled. "You want to start off by telling me just how you got in the condition you're in?"

The fierceness of his expression, the hard edge to his voice, almost made Ginny flinch. But she held her ground and stared straight into his midnight gaze, which seemed to probe the deepest recesses of her mind.

"I was in a car accident..." she began, and could say no more. This was harder than she'd imagined. For four years she'd lived a secret life, lied to everyone about everything.

Ginny could tell by the way his gaze sharpened and his whole body straightened that he wasn't a man to be put off with only half-truths. He wanted the whole story, and she was just too tired to fight any longer. "Have you ever heard of the Witness Protection Program?"

Matt's surprise was genuine. He'd suspected she was running from an abusive husband or lover—hell, he didn't know what he'd expected, but it wasn't this. "You're really tangled up with the FBI?"

"Tangled up is rather an understatement. But the proper term is *was*—I *was* tangled up with the FBI. I guess you could say I jumped ship, or more appropriately, I jumped from a car accident."

Matt sat back, letting his breath out slowly. He was amazed to realize that he believed her. Then he remembered something. "There was a car crash over on the interstate a couple of days ago. Two people were killed."

Ginny looked down at herself and said almost in a whisper, "There was a third person, a little luckier, who got away with only cuts, bruises and a guilty conscience for leaving."

Matt kept talking as if she hadn't spoken. "I heard through our local sheriff that the investigating state troopers were more than a little miffed when some federal boys stepped in and took over their case, then disappeared with the two bodies...."

Matt's voice trailed away as what Ginny had just said about the car wreck sank in. He was confused and didn't like it one bit. "Who were the two other people in that car? And why did you bolt?" Matt leaned forward and asked softly, "Just who the hell are you and what're you involved in?"

Wearily Ginny closed her eyes. Her bruised body ached and throbbed. She was hungry, exhausted and soul weary. "I didn't lie about my name. I am Virginia Carney, though for the past four years I've had four different names and lived in four different states. I've worked as a waitress and typist. I've lost everyone I love...." Tears trickled down her cheeks but she refused to acknowledge them.

"I've lived a lie and lied to anyone who tried to get close to me or be my friend. I'm scared all the time, always looking over my shoulder. And I learned early on that I couldn't trust anyone, not even the government and their incompetent agents. I can't live like this anymore."

She took a shaky breath and continued, "The two killed in the car were FBI agents. They were transporting me to Austin to start a new life with yet another new identity. I was asleep in the back seat and didn't even realize we'd been in a crash until I woke up a few feet from the burning car. When I finally came to my senses and saw there wasn't anything I could do for them, it hit me there was nothing to stop me, either."

Ginny paused, waiting for Matt to say something, but when he was silent, she shrugged and went on. "I saw the accident as my chance to take my life back and I headed out on my own."

Matt had been watching and listening intently. "What are you running from, Ginny?" he asked now. "Who's after you and why?"

The pain of her loss consumed her for the first time in a long while. She felt defeated. Allowing herself a rare indulgence of self-pity, she placed her face in her hands and wept.

Tears. Matt's scowl deepened and his mouth puckered as if he'd just bitten into a lemon.

He hated women's tears. They always wormed their way into that soft place inside him that he hated and tried so desperately to conceal. He wasn't going to let this woman get to him. He wanted, no, needed answers and her sobs weren't going to coerce him into giving up.

"Listen," he began, then stopped when she lowered her hands long enough for him to see the anguish and torment there.

Matt swallowed hard, then cleared his throat. He was about to give it another try when the door was shoved wide open and he found himself staring into the outraged face of his son.

"You made her cry!" Austin growled. "You bullied her and made her cry. How could you?"

"I didn't do anything," Matt snapped. "She just—" He broke off abruptly when he realized he was explaining his actions to a ten-year-old who was glaring at him as if he'd just slithered out from under a rock. His gaze turned thoughtful as he watched his son sprint to Ginny's side and begin patting her shoulder, consoling her as best he knew how.

Matt couldn't think what to do. Ginny was still sobbing, though it was more a hiccuping sound now, as if she was struggling to control her emotions when she saw how upset Austin was. Frustrated that he'd lost control of the situation—if he'd ever really had it—he directed his anger at Austin.

"You were listening at the door, Austin, weren't you?" Matt demanded.

"Yeah. So?"

Ginny captured the boy's hand and squeezed it in warning. This was not the time to challenge his father.

"I told you—" Matt began.

"Better go check dinner," Austin interrupted. "I thought I smelled something burning."

She wanted to say something before these two males became locked in mortal combat. Austin's mouth, a miniature of his father's, had twisted into a mocking smile—an expression entirely too mature, she thought, for someone his age.

Austin lost the battle of glares with his father and mumbled, "I couldn't hear what was being said, but I heard her crying. You made her cry."

"I didn't— Oh, hell." Matt shoved back his chair and stomped out of the room, relieved for a number of reasons to leave. Once in the kitchen, he added some water around his pot roast, then leaned against the refrigerator, closing his eyes. He was a stubborn man— he admitted that. He'd never asked anyone for help, but he had to concede that he needed it now.

Austin's attitude was a growing pain in the butt and a problem he hadn't the faintest idea how to handle. The house was a wreck, the business in ruins and his life a shambles. Then, as if he didn't have enough troubles on his plate, he had to deal with a strange woman running from something in her past and more than likely the federal government to boot. He'd dealt with the feds enough in his career to know they didn't like to lose, and they were going to wonder where their protected witness was.

There was one answer he needed to have though, and the thought alone sent the blood singing through him. Surprised, Matt realized the emotion he was experiencing was excitement. Like a hunter on the chase. He hadn't had that feeling since before he'd been shot, and it felt damn good, made him realize he was still alive.

The question he needed to ask was simple—could Ginny Carney's presence in his home become dangerous?

GINNY WATCHED as Austin crossed hurriedly to the big desk, opened a drawer and pulled out a box of tissues. When he handed it to her, she smiled her thanks, wiped her eyes, then blew her nose. "You shouldn't listen at closed doors, you know." She had to find out if he had heard anything or not. If he had, even the tiniest bit, and he repeated it to anyone, she was doomed.

"Sure, I know," he said in a very adult voice. "But he shouldn't have sent me out like that. I found you, you know. And I have a right to know what's going on." Austin's lower lip puffed out, and once more he looked like the little boy he was. "He's a bully and thinks he knows it all."

"What did you hear, Austin?"

He studied her for a moment, his dark eyes sharp and probing like his father's. "Why? Is there something I'm not supposed to know, or is it just because I'm a kid?"

Ginny bit back a smile. "I was about to tell your father why I'm in this situation, and it's not something a person your age should know."

"Did your boyfriend beat you up?"

"No. Listen, Austin, please don't ask me any questions and I won't lie to you. Okay? I don't want to hurt your feelings, but I just don't think your knowing all the details will help, and in the long run it might hurt me. Can you understand that?''

At first Austin simply glared. Then, because she was smiling so sweetly at him, he shrugged. ''I'm not a kid, you know, and I'm not dumb.''

''No. I can see that, and I'm sure you're very bright for your age.''

''Austin's ten going on forty,'' Matt said. ''He's a certified genius with a 180-plus IQ.''

Ginny jumped, surprised at how quietly the big man moved.

Austin whipped around to face his father, but before he could think of a suitable retort, Matt said, ''I wonder what she'd look like cleaned up, don't you?''

The boy's gaze bounced from Ginny to Matt as he tried to figure out what trap his father was laying for him. He nodded. ''Her cuts need to be cleaned,'' he said.

''A bath and some clean clothes wouldn't hurt, either, would they? Then maybe some food and we'll have those answers to all our questions.''

Austin's eyes narrowed, wondering what his father was up to. There was a look about him he hadn't seen before. As if his father had just been given something that pleased him. Matt's happiness made Austin nervous, and his nod of agreement was tentative, unsure.

A bath! The word was like an electrical shock. Ginny struggled to get up. Her muscles protested, making her wince and suck in her breath with every move, but she managed to stand upright. It was her ankle that was the undoing of her valiant efforts. While she'd rested, her ankle had puffed up and doubled in size. She must have sprained it, after all.

Both Matt and Austin made a move to her side when she moaned in pain and started to fall. "Get on her other side, Austin, and take her arm. We're going to have to help her up the stairs together."

Ginny hadn't realized until they started up the wide staircase that Matt was almost as helpless as she was. He was a big man, but she guessed he had recently lost a lot of weight. His skin had the pallor of illness, and though his arm was fixed securely around her, she felt the tremor in his muscles. This close, with his arm around her waist, she had a good view of the damage that had been done to his body. For the first time she noticed his limp, and as he struggled with most of her weight it grew more pronounced. There was a dime-size, fiery red scar on his chest, and a larger exit wound on his back that made her shiver.

Ginny asked Matt about his wounds as they huffed and puffed up the stairs, but he only grunted in answer. It was Austin who related the history of his father's wounds, and as hard as he tried, he couldn't keep the hint of pride from creeping into his young voice.

When they reached the landing and rested to catch their breath, Ginny had time to glance around. From the size of the wide, gently curving staircase, the house must be huge.

After they had climbed the last set of stairs, they paused on a spacious landing from which led a long wide hall with closed doors on either side. The bedroom Ginny was guided into was obviously Matt's. At any other time she would have stopped to admire the vast room with its highly polished oak floors, oversize four-poster bed and antiques, but she was too tired and sore to appreciate anything but the bed, which she now swayed toward.

"Not on my clean bed, you don't." Matt chuckled. "Not like you are now. It took me almost thirty minutes to change those sheets this morning and I won't do it again. Into the bathroom, Austin."

Ginny started to protest, but the thought of a bath made her easily relent. The bathroom was large and modern, all shiny with white tiles and an old-fashioned claw-footed tub of hunter green. She leaned her weight toward the bath, but Matt pulled her back. She glanced up questioningly.

"I think not," he said. "If you got stuck in that thing, I couldn't possibly get you out." He steered her toward the shower stall, but when he let go and she tried to stand on her own, she almost fell over. Matt frowned and glanced at Austin, then back at Ginny. "Close the door on the way out, Austin."

Austin stared at his father as Matt started to unbutton Ginny's shirt. "Stop that!" he shouted. "You can't undress her."

Ginny was as shocked as Austin but was struck speechless.

Matt sighed. "Austin, your wounded lady needs a bath—bad—if not for hygienic reasons then for medical ones. I won't chance putting her in the tub, she can't stand up in the shower on her own, so I'm going to undress her and help her bathe."

"But she'll be naked." Austin's face was bright red, his eyes round and wide.

Matt glanced at Ginny and was startled to see the same heightened color and wide-eyed shock. "Do you have any better ideas, either of you?"

Ginny looked longingly at the yawning shower door, then back at Matt, and shook her head. He looked pretty harmless to her.

As if reading her thoughts, Matt said. "Don't worry. You're not very appealing right now, lady." He looked at Austin. "Out."

"But...but..."

Matt had finished unbuttoning Ginny's shirt and was pulling it from the waistband of her jeans. "Out," he ordered again, and watched with amusement as Austin took one glimpse of the lacy bra before he fled from the bathroom, slamming the door behind him.

"Shame on you," Ginny said, but she couldn't help smiling. Austin might be ten going on forty, but he was still a young boy at heart. Then her amusement turned to apprehension as Matt threw her shirt across the room and grasped the tab of her jeans zipper.

"You want to try this on your own?" he asked, noting her hesitation.

He was giving her an out, she knew, but her desire to be clean overrode any reservations she might have. "No." The sound of the zipper being drawn down was like a roar in her ears. Then Matt squatted down and eased her jeans over her hips while she gripped his shoulders. He removed her filthy running shoes, taking special care not to jar her swollen foot, then stripped the jeans off completely.

Ginny's hands tightened on Matt's shoulders, and she glanced down at his bent head. His jet black hair was long and curly, the ends brushing the backs of her hands. Odd, she thought. You would have expected with his thick dark hair and the faint shadow of a beard along his jaw that he would have had more chest hair....

Ginny slammed on the mental brakes at the path her thoughts were taking. She wasn't interested in men or sex, she told herself. That was all in the past.

Matt wasn't unaware of the long smooth legs only inches from his face or the small waist and silky mounds of pale flesh above her bra. Though it had been a long time, his body didn't respond with any outward signs of desire. He just wasn't the least bit interested, he told himself.

As he struggled to his feet, Ginny's hands slid from his shoulders to his arms and they found themselves in close contact. "I think I can make it from here," she said, her voice surprisingly low. She let go of Matt and tried to do a little hop-turn, but she lost her balance and would have tumbled into the shower stall if Matt hadn't grabbed her and gently turned her around.

Matt forced his gaze to stay on her face. "There's nothing in there to hold on to. You're going to have to let me help you." He felt her tense and knew her thoughts were running a mile a minute.

"Look," he said, "I don't have designs on your body. As a matter of fact you're not the least appealing to me—in the state you're in, that is." Oh, Lord. He could tell by the way the corners of her pretty mouth tightened and her eyes narrowed a fraction that he'd blundered. "Listen, I've been sick for almost a year, and you don't interest me—I mean, sex is the farthest thing from my mind." She was still staring. "The body's too weak. Oh, hell. Do you want to take a goddamn shower or not?"

"Yes, please." Ginny worked hard to keep from laughing. This man might profess a lack of interest, but she could tell from the colossal effort it was taking him to keep his eyes focused on her face that he was as eager as any healthy man to take a good look at her.

Matt struggled to ignore all that soft female flesh pressed against him as he reached behind Ginny and turned on the shower, quickly adjusting the temperature. Then he slid his arm around her bare waist and helped her hobble into the stall.

Hot soothing water beat down on them and they both stood silent, savoring the feeling on their sore muscles.

It was Matt who moved first. His jeans were soaked and because of his recent weight loss they were loose. The water made them heavy and they began to slide down over his hips. "Reach up and grab hold of the shower head," he told Ginny. Once satisfied that she wasn't going to fall, he let go and quickly peeled off his jeans.

Ginny couldn't figure out what he was doing and glanced around at the wrong, or right, moment to get an eyeful. Her gaze lingered a moment, then in fear of being caught, she was about to turn around when she noticed the long jagged scar that wrapped around his thigh.

"My God, what happened to your leg?"

Matt looked at his wound, then at Ginny. She was holding on to the shower head with one hand, half turned toward him, and he felt a familiar and welcome tightening in his groin. Her dark red hair was plastered to her head like a cap. Rivulets of water were running over her shoulders and down her smoothly rounded breasts. The water poured across her flat stomach, down between her thighs, then swirled around her legs. It was only when she repeated the question that he hurriedly directed his gaze back to her face.

"I was shot in the leg, too, but instead of going clean through like the others, this one smashed the thigh bone and continued on a rather destructive path. Hand me the shampoo."

She absently did as ordered, thinking how much pain he must have been in, yet male pride had made him hide his limp from her. Then she remembered that he and Austin had carried her unconscious from the vineyard and she felt even worse. He could have really hurt himself.

Lost in thought as she was, it took a moment for Ginny to realize that he was shampooing her hair. With a gentle nudge, her head was pushed under the shower head. Hot water streamed over her, rinsing away both suds and dirt. She tilted her head back, allowing the water to pour over her face. With a squeal she jumped. "Hey, wait a minute!" she protested as soapy hands grazed her breasts. But instead of stopping, Matt lowered his hands to her waist, then up her back.

"I'm not copping a feel," he snapped. "If you let go you'll fall flat on your face, so be still. This is no big deal for me."

Matt swallowed. What a lie that was. If he didn't get his mind off the silky skin and gently yielding flesh beneath his hands, his body was going to make a mockery of his words.

He was right, of course, Ginny told herself, and there was nothing she could do but stand there and let his soapy hands run over her body. But oh, my, she thought, closing her eyes, it felt so good. When Matt spoke it took a moment for her to realize that his voice was real and not part of some erotic dream. It was only when the question he was asking penetrated her hazy mind that she sobered and opened her eyes.

"What did you say?" she asked.

"I said, now that we're alone and there's no chance of Mr. Big Ears listening at the door, you want to answer a few questions?'' He massaged her shoulders, taking all the tension away.

"Sure," Ginny answered, her breath catching in her throat. But in the back of her mind her own question began to form. She was wondering what kind of lover he was.

"Tell me," he whispered. "If I was to let you stay for a while, what are the chances that someone, and I don't mean a fed, is going to come looking for you?"

"A year ago I wouldn't have even asked to stay. Not even two days ago. But when I was in that car with those two agents and they thought I was asleep in the back seat, they talked. From what I heard, the FBI kept moving me around because there was a leak in the agency, a computer glitch. Can you believe it?" she asked. "My name kept popping up in some cross-checking program of theirs. They thought the program had been breached and I was in danger so they kept moving me until they solved the problems."

Matt felt the muscles in her shoulders tighten, and he increased the pressure of his massage.

Ginny relaxed again and let her head drop forward. As she watched the water swirl down the drain, she let the world and all her problems wash away, too. She forgot she was in a stranger's shower, with a stranger's hands all over her. For the first time in a long while she felt safe, and some of the pain from her past began to ease.

"That doesn't reassure me much, Ginny—no matter why you were put in the Witness Protection Program. I just need to know if someone is going to come after you. I need to know so I can protect you, myself and my son."

Ginny stood perfectly still for a moment, repeating over and over to herself what he'd said. She turned her head so she could look at him over her shoulder. "You're willing to let me stay a couple of days without knowing anything about me or what's happened? Why?"

"First of all, I have personal reasons. And secondly, believe it or not, I can take care of myself. This town is small enough that if a stranger or strangers come sneaking around or asking questions, I'll know."

Ginny blinked the water out of her eyes. "And your personal reasons?"

"Let's just say I could use some help around the house and with Austin."

"You're not talking about just a couple of days, are you?"

"No. I'll make a deal with you. I'll protect you, keep your secrets if you stay, say, at least a couple of months—or until I decide what to do with Austin when school starts."

"A couple of months?" she whispered.

"At least. And after that, if you want to stay, well, we'll see. But you have to promise me something."

She couldn't believe he was asking her to stay. "What?"

"You must never leave here without telling me. My son seems to have taken quite a liking to you, and I won't have you hurt him by just dropping out of his life with no warning. He's had enough loss to deal with lately. Promise me that and I won't ask you to make any more." He watched her closely, trying to read her thoughts, seeing the hope, the uncertainty and doubts and, finally, the acceptance.

"I promise. Thank you, Matt." Tears filled her eyes, and she quickly turned her head away, knowing he would be embarrassed by them.

Ginny might not thank him when she found out what he wanted of her, Matt realized. But that explanation would come another day.

CHAPTER THREE

MAYBE WHAT HE WAS DOING was wrong. It could even be regarded by an outsider as taking unfair advantage of the situation, of a woman down and out on her luck. But he was smart enough to know when to yell uncle, to know he couldn't go on alone any longer.

Call it karma, kismet or destiny. His life had altered drastically in the blink of an eye. First had come the gunshot wounds and his forced retirement, and just as he was beginning to adjust to those changes, that eye of destiny blinked again. His ex-wife had been killed in an airplane crash, and suddenly he was a full-time father to Austin.

Then Ginny arrived on the scene. He believed that everything happened for a reason, and he wasn't one to let opportunities slip through his fingers.

"So," he said, "what happened to you?"

He picked up the soap and lathered up his hands. His intention was to take her mind off her aches and pains, to make her warm, comfortable and above all talkative. He ran soap-slick hands up and down Ginny's side, down over her narrow hips, around her legs. When her muscles tightened in protest, he slid his hands up her back again.

Matt noticed her arms were trembling from holding on to the showerhead. He reached up and loosened her grip, then pulled her back against his chest for support. "Tell me about Ginny Carney."

For a moment she was shocked to feel the length of his body pressed firmly against her. But the warmth of the contact was like an analgesic to her frayed nerves. She should have stopped him. But when his arms wrapped around her and he held her even closer, the sense of security, of being safe for the first time in more than four years overwhelmed her. She rested her head on his shoulder, closed her eyes and savored the sudden melting sensation that drifted through her.

"I don't know where to begin," she said sadly.

"From the beginning. Start by telling me about yourself." He waited for a long time, figuring his ploy hadn't worked or else maybe she hadn't heard him. He was about to repeat his question when she started to talk.

"I was a lawyer, you know. Graduated from Harvard Law School and worked for a prestigious old law firm. I was married, with a three-year-old daughter, Elizabeth—Beth. I risked everything for my damn self-righteousness and sense of justice. I killed my husband and daughter as surely as if I'd put a gun to their heads."

Matt turned her around, holding her tightly against his chest. When she gazed up at him, he couldn't tell if tears or hot water were streaming from her eyes. That damnable soft spot of his turned to mush. He threaded his fingers through her wet hair and pulled her head against his chest. "Go on, get it out, all of it," he said, and braced himself for the outburst of tears. But the tears didn't come, and he strained to listen to the quiet, steady voice.

"I'm from Boston, was born there in fact, and had never even left the state of Massachusetts, except on my honeymoon. My family are the industrialist Bradsworths of Massachusetts, and my father was the youngest—the black sheep. He refused to go into the family business. Instead, he opened a small bank in the suburbs of the city. It was a good life and the bank made us rich. I was sent to a boarding school, and when I was about thirteen my father died of a heart attack. I never realized until Dad had died that my mother was one of those women who have to have the admiration of men to feel any self-worth. She remarried about six months after Dad died.

"I didn't particularly like my stepfather, Anthony Coldwell, or his son, but I was at school and didn't have to deal with them much. He took over the bank for Mother, and for years everything seemed okay. I met my husband, William Carney, a Harvard graduate, and we married very quickly. It was one of those love-at-first-sight things."

Ginny glanced at Matt. "Have you ever fallen head over heels in love with someone?"

"No."

"That's a shame. It's the most magical, marvelous feeling." She sighed.

"I guess if my mother hadn't become ill and ended up in the hospital," she went on, "none of the rest would have occurred. After her cancer treatment, she was released from the hospital and I went to stay with her for a couple of weeks. I guess I felt guilty. After she married Tony I stayed away as much as I could, and after I married I had even more excuses to keep from going home.

"Anyway, after I'd been there a couple of days I went to the bank. You have to realize, Matt, that most of the employees had been with my father and the bank for years and were close to retirement. And I had to admire Tony—he didn't fire anyone, but took care of them like Dad did. But unlike Dad, who genuinely cared, Tony used his position to keep them in line in case they discovered what he was doing. The threat of losing your retirement pension is a great inducement to keep you blind and dumb.

"It was Sally Harris, Dad's secretary, who told me what was going on at the bank. Tony was running huge sums of cash through the bank, mostly after hours."

"Laundering money?" Matt asked.

"Yes. Drug money. I started my own investigation, with the help of Sally and a few other long time employees who were willing to help once Sally had convinced them I was going to put Tony in jail. That's what I promised them, and that's what I did. After months of investigation, collecting copies of records and sneaking around town, having secret meetings with the employees, I had what I thought was enough to turn my stepfather in." She smiled sourly. "Tony was so arrogant, thinking he'd never get caught. He made the fatal mistake of keeping a ledger of amounts, delivery dates and account numbers—with names to be tied to them! He kept that ledger at home in the safe—my father's safe. He was so sure of himself he didn't even bother to change the combination."

"And you knew the combination," Matt said, grinning.

"Yes. I made a copy of the ledger, then with all the information I had I went to the banking commission. Of course they immediately called in the FBI, the Drug

Enforcement Agency and a couple of other agencies I'd never heard of."

"Who else knew what you were doing?" Matt asked. "Didn't anyone warn you about what you were getting into?"

"William was the only one who knew. I didn't even consult anyone at my law firm, though I'd planned to once I handed everything over to the banking commission. I was naive enough to think they'd handle everything from that point."

"Come on, Ginny, you were an attorney. Surely you were aware of the consequences—the dangers."

"I swear I had no idea what a can of worms I was opening. I specialized in corporate law—I'm a corporate attorney, not a criminal one. Oh, everyone knows about drugs and money laundering. But I had no idea about the finer points of criminal behavior or the laws concerning them. And William was an architect, Matt. He believed like I did that the laws of our country were to be respected—and were there to protect us. He believed the criminal-justice system, though flawed, would prevail. We were babes in the woods," she said, her voice hoarse with bitterness. "We were used by everyone."

"You mean the government used you?"

"Yes. And after they used us, they leaked the story to the press so they could insure that the trial would be a media event. That bit of information came from a friend at the local newspaper, who, by the way, was the only one to finally warn me of the dangerous waters I was treading in."

Matt knew how the feds worked from his own experience. They were like a huge juggernaut that rolled over anyone or anything to achieve their goals.

"The worst came after the story was made public. My law firm decided I should disassociate myself by taking a leave of absence to keep their good name from being tarnished. Then I started getting threats."

"What happened to your stepfather?"

"He was arrested. Of course, my mother was devastated and blamed me. She refused to speak to me or see me when she found out I was going to testify against Tony. And I agreed to do that only after the feds told me they couldn't guarantee a conviction on their evidence alone. They needed my testimony.

"But I was scared. The threatening telephone calls were becoming more frequent and nastier. But the FBI agents assured me they could protect me. Tony's partners, those he'd been foolish enough to keep records on, were rounded up and arrested. But there were others at the top of his crooked business and the feds couldn't make the charges stick."

Ginny fell silent, remembering. She shivered violently and wondered if she could go on. Could she put into words what had happened next?

Matt waited, and when the only sound was the drumming of the water against their bodies, he had a gut feeling what was coming. "Grab hold of the shower head for a moment." After a second she did what he asked, but he knew she was in another world.

He quickly stepped out of the shower, grabbed a couple of towels from a nearby cabinet. He wrapped one securely around his waist and returned to the shower. Reaching around Ginny, he turned off the water and swathed her in the big bath towel. It was a tricky maneuver to perform from behind, but he even managed to tuck the ends in neatly above her breasts.

"You can let go," he said, and when she obeyed, then wobbled on her one good leg, he grabbed her around the waist and led her across the bathroom to a stool. She seemed to be in a daze, unaware of what was happening around her. "Sit," he said, then, because the stool was low, squatted beside her. "Now, finish your story. Tell me what happened to you."

"Not to me." Ginny's gaze focused on Matt. "God, I wish it *had* been me." She couldn't look at him anymore, couldn't face the horror or the condemnation that was sure to be reflected in his eyes. "Before the trial, the menacing phone calls took on a more sinister note. Instead of just trying to scare me into not testifying against Tony, they started to threaten William and Beth."

A chill ran through Matt's body. "I guess the federal boys assured you they could protect you and your family?"

"Yes." Her voice was devoid of emotion, she felt dead once again and was grateful for the numbness. "The FBI proposed the Witness Protection Program, and after William and I discussed it at length, we decided I was doing the right thing."

Matt shook his head. He could imagine what Ginny and her family had gone through. "I bet they set everything up for you after the trial. They promised to protect you and your family, and you believed them."

"Of course I did. I was so naive. So damn stupid. All they really cared about was prosecuting and convicting Tony and his partners." She looked at Matt, her eyes unseeing, her mind focused on the past. "They said they were more concerned with my safety—my family's safety. But they failed. They neglected to guard William and Beth closely enough."

Ginny fell silent for a long moment, then took a deep breath and continued, "Beth had a bad cold. She was running a high fever and William was going to take her to the doctor because I had an early meeting with some federal attorneys. Except, they never made it. I watched William buckle Beth in her car seat...watched as he buckled himself in and started the car."

Ginny's gaze cleared and she was seeing Matt again. "There was a bomb in the car." It was all she could say. There were no words to explain the horror of what she'd seen, the bottomless depth of her loss.

"Oh, my God, Ginny. I'm sorry."

She struggled to suppress the flashes of memory that threatened to overwhelm her. "Me, too," she managed. "But what Tony's friends hoped to accomplish didn't work. I was devastated, but I was also in a numbing, mindless rage. And determined to make him pay for what he'd done, or had initiated."

"You testified?"

"You bet. And all Tony's high-priced, high-profile attorneys couldn't break my story or even find a crack to put the slightest bit of doubt in the jury's mind. They convicted him and six others on so many federal charges I can't even remember them all."

"So your stepfather and his partners went to prison and you were adrift in the Witness Protection Program. Tell me something—did they ever catch the man or men at the top, the men who controlled Tony and his partners?"

"No. After the trial, I thought it was going to be over, that I'd try to pick up the pieces of my life. After all, I had nothing else to lose, did I? I wasn't going to go into the program, but they convinced me it was necessary. If something happened to me—say, like what happened to my family—it would leave an opening for Tony's slick attorney to start the legal ball rolling for an appeal for a new trial. I would never let that happen. I wanted him to rot in hell.''

Matt had a hundred questions of his own to ask when he noticed she was shivering. His leg was killing him and he placed his hands on his thighs and quickly, without thinking, pushed himself to a standing position. For a second he thought he was going to keel over from the excruciating pain, then it eased and he limped to the bathroom door, opened it and yelled for Austin.

Austin appeared so quickly that Matt's pained expression turned to suspicion, but he lacked the energy or the inclination to admonish his son for eavesdropping. He gritted his teeth and said, ''Austin, run downstairs to the laundry room and get one of my clean shirts out of the basket and bring it up here.''

''You sure it's clean?''

Matt stared at this young version of himself and scowled. ''This is not the time to play games. Now get moving.'' For a second he watched as the boy scurried away, then limped to a nearby chair stacked haphazardly with a wide assortment of clean clothes. He dug through the pile and pulled out a pair of cutoffs, slipped them on as quickly as possible and grabbed two more towels.

Ginny hadn't moved, but sat with her knees pulled to her chest, shivering with both memories and cold. When she sensed Matt standing over her she threw her head back and looked up. ''Do you know the irony of the past four years? I don't think I needed to run away and hide. When the two agents who were transporting me to Austin thought I was asleep, they talked a lot. One of the things they said was that the FBI had made a mistake, that there was no sinister crime boss Tony answered to. My stepfather was the brains of the operation.''

Matt wrapped a towel around her head and began rubbing her hair dry. ''You mean they put you into the program unnecessarily?''

''No. Maybe. I believe at the time they didn't think Tony was smart enough to plan such a sophisticated white-collar crime.'' His vigorous rubbing was beginning to pull her hair out by the roots and she grabbed his hands to still them. ''I tried repeatedly to tell them that Tony was a lot sharper than he portrayed himself to be.''

''But they wouldn't listen to you?'' Matt said. ''They were the professionals and you the amateur, right?''

''Yes.''

''So, if your stepfather was the brains and your testimony put him and most, if not all, of his partners away, you should have been safe to continue your life without fear?''

''Right,'' she said as she slipped the damp towel from his hands and began drying her own hair. ''What I don't understand is why in God's name the FBI didn't take me out of the program once they realized their mistake?''

Matt gave a snort of disbelief. ''And leave themselves wide open for a lawsuit.''

''Lawsuit?'' she asked.

''What's keeping that kid?'' he said softly, almost to himself. Then he heard the sound of Austin's feet echoing on the stairs. ''Sure. They botched the protection of your husband and daughter and ultimately caused their deaths. They browbeat you on false assumptions into a program you didn't really want to enter. Then when they realized they were wrong, I'll bet they tried to bury you. But luck, faith—whatever—wouldn't let you be lost. One of their programs malfunctioned and your name kept coming up, indicating you'd been exposed or found. If they hadn't kept moving you, someone, somewhere, would have started asking questions or making inquiries, digging into your case file, unearthing monstrous mistakes."

Matt had just finished speaking when Austin skidded to a stop at the open bathroom door. He held out his hand to the boy, then impatiently wiggled his fingers. "Either bring me the shirt or throw it to me."

Austin averted his eyes from Ginny's bare shoulders and walked toward his father's outstretched hand. "Are you okay, Ginny? Feel better?" Daring a closer look, he could see she'd been crying. "You made her cry again," he accused Matt. "You're always hurting people's feelings."

Matt wondered where that statement had come from. But he was too tired to ask. He shook the light blue cotton shirt out and gave it to Ginny. "You'd better get out, Austin, and give Ginny her privacy."

Austin whirled and fled from the bathroom, his cheeks flaming and his temper simmering.

Ginny slipped on the shirt, buttoned it and rolled up the sleeves, before she tugged the towel loose. Then she grabbed Matt's arm and pulled herself up to balance on one leg. "What's going on with you two?"

"I'll tell you later. But that's part of the problem you can help me with."

As she talked, she experimented with her injured foot, placing it flat on the cold tile floor. When she shifted a little of her weight on it she winced, but it wasn't as bad as she'd feared.

Austin poked his head in the doorway and said, "I read the first-aid book and brought a bag of crushed ice for your ankle. Matt'll carry you down to my room."

Matt's mouth twitched with amusement and one dark eyebrow arched higher than the other. "Your room?"

Austin refused to let his father make him appear foolish again. "It's the only room with twin beds. And the bed in the guest room isn't made up yet."

"I see. Well, son, I'm just too damn tired to get her down the hall to your room, so I guess it's my bed for Goldilocks."

"But..." Austin's mouth curled shut so tightly that he looked lipless.

Ginny watched with dismay. These two might look like father and son, but they were acting like opponents in a tug-of-war.

Soon she was tucked in the oversize bed, sleepily inhaling the scent of freshly washed sheets. The throbbing in her foot had eased because of the ice Austin had applied, and her eyes were so heavy she could hardly keep them open.

She must have dozed off, and when she awoke, she turned her head in confusion, at first glance unable to identify the man stretched out on the opposite side of the bed. She'd imagined herself back in time, to a Sunday morning with William lightly snoring beside her and Beth cuddled between them. But it wasn't William and Beth. It was Matt lying beside her—though why on earth he was there was a question she didn't care to ponder—and Austin propped up at the foot of the bed, his nose buried in a thick medical book.

Someone ought to do something about the boy's choice of reading material. She sighed softly, warning herself not to get too close to these two. Matt was going to allow her to stay for a while, but it would only be a short stay. She'd give herself a chance to rest, regroup and study her options, then she'd move on.

She'd make a new life for herself, Ginny thought, and she didn't need any additional emotional baggage to carry along. With her resolve more firmly etched in her mind, she turned her attention to her surroundings. She couldn't get over the size of the room. Everything was built on such a large scale. The four-poster mahogany bed with the massive carved headboard was beautifully proportioned. She figured it had to be ages old and was at least one and a half times as big as a king-size bed in width and length.

My God, she thought, the sheets and bedspread would all have to be custom-made. She didn't want to think about the effort it would take to launder the sheets and remake the damn thing. Her gaze wandered over the rest of the furniture in the room, which had obviously been made to match the bed. She wasn't an expert on antiques, but William had been and some of his enthusiasm had worn off on her. She knew quality when she saw it.

Her gaze lingered on the intricately carved floral design on an oval mirror above the fireplace. It wasn't until she caught sight of the stark reflection of a strange woman lounging against white sheets that she realized the bruised and battered person was herself. For one horrified moment she stared at the puffy black eye, the fiery scratches on forehead and cheeks. She gulped. Her bottom lip was split and swollen and her hair—what in heaven's name had happened to her hair? It was sticking out in all directions. Ginny screamed with a mixture of terror and outrage. She looked like an ugly crone.

Matt shot bold upright, his hand reaching automatically beneath his pillow for the revolver that wasn't there. "What the hell's the matter?" he demanded.

Austin sat up straight at the foot of the bed, rubbing his chin where the heavy book had clipped him at Matt's sudden movement. "Ginny, are you all right?"

But she was speechless as she stared across the room at her reflection. She wasn't a beauty and she wasn't vain, but this woman staring back at her had to be someone else. All she could do was point in shock. At first she was perplexed at the strange sound, a rumbling noise, that was coming from the opposite side of the bed. She glanced at Austin, but he was looking at his father. She turned and looked at Matt, and was surprised as she recognized the noise.

Her mouth tightened in disgust.

Matt's rumble changed to a deep chuckle, then suddenly he erupted into laughter. The sound was rich and mellow, and damn contagious. Before she could stop herself, Ginny burst out laughing, too, and Austin quickly joined in.

When she finally caught her breath, she said, "I look like a witch!"

"Red," Matt said, "a witch could win a beauty contest beside you."

Ginny's smile faded. "Let's get something straight— I'm not, by any stretch of your imagination, going to answer to *Red*."

Austin didn't understand such hostility over a nickname and made the situation worse by saying, "But your hair is red, Ginny."

"No. It's auburn," she snapped, then saw the boy's smile fade. "I'm sorry, Austin. But all my life people, boys especially, have teased me about my hair color and called me names. Red was the most polite commonly used, but I still hated it." The sparkle hadn't yet returned to the boy's eyes. "Did the kids in school ever tease you and call you names?"

"Yeah." Austin frowned, then a smile began to creep around the corners of his mouth. "Mighty Mo, Brainy Buttface, Weirdo, Nerd and Computer Brain." He'd made Ginny laugh and he tucked his chin to his chest to keep from grinning hugely. The only dark spot was that he'd made his father laugh, too.

Matt saw the way his son's eyes shifted in his direction and turned stormy. He sighed inwardly in defeat. Hell, he couldn't even enjoy a good laugh. Carefully he swung his legs over the edge of the bed and eased to a standing position.

"Austin, I think the pot roast's probably done and I bet Ginny's hungry. Why don't we go see what needs to be done and you can help me?"

Austin stiffened at the suggestion, then picked up the medical book he'd been studying. "It says here that scratches and cuts, after they're washed with soap and water, might require a topical antibiotic."

Ginny made a face. "I think you'll need a bucket of the stuff. I seem to be cut and scratched from head to toe."

Matt could tell she was exhausted, and he placed his hand on Austin's shoulder. "Come on." The boy instantly jerked away. "I'm not in the mood for any lip."

Ginny watched them glare at each other. "I haven't eaten in a couple of days, Austin, and I'm starving," she said. "Besides, I think your doctoring is going to hurt and I'm going to need my strength, don't you think?"

Austin nodded and quickly disappeared from the bedroom.

"Thanks," Matt said. "That could have turned ugly."

Ginny rearranged the sheet and comforter more securely around her. "You're too old to argue with a ten-year-old boy."

Matt snorted with a mixture of amusement and self-disgust.

"I know what you said about him being ten going on forty, but at heart he's still a little boy with problems to work out. You should try to figure out what's wrong, instead of fighting with him."

"I know what's wrong. He hates my guts."

Ginny gave Matt one of those infuriating smug smiles typical of women. The type of smile filled with secret wisdom and designed to make a man feel like an idiot. Adding insult to injury, she refused to explain—as though the answer would suddenly dawn on him if he'd just think about it long enough. Well, he damn well didn't feel like deciphering it at the moment. He wanted her to untangle the problem for him but was too proud to ask.

Matt followed Austin out of the bedroom with as little dignity and as much anger as his young son. Women! he thought. Why the bloody hell did they have to be so complicated? Why couldn't they just come out and say what they thought?

Ginny watched him go, confused by the abruptness of his departure. She repeated the conversation in her mind, trying to figure out what she'd said. After all, a little voice warned, it wasn't going to do her any good to get kicked out for making her benefactor angry. But she wasn't one to sugarcoat the truth, either.

She was so tired and sore she couldn't think anymore. Even the contents of the room didn't interest her any longer. She closed her eyes. Tantalizing smells came wafting up from the kitchen, and Ginny realized she was starving. She told herself she was only going to rest for a moment, and hoped that Matt would soon reappear with some of that pot roast....

THE DREAM WAS about William and Beth. Ginny knew they were a figment of her imagination, but seeing them again, happy and laughing, was a comfort. A faint whisper, the tickle of warm breath close to her ear and a light tap on her shoulder spoiled her dream, forcing her to open her eyes.

Ginny smelled the heavenly aroma before she saw the tray Matt was holding. Eagerly she sat up and waited while Austin added a couple of big pillows behind her and handed her a neatly folded napkin. Matt set the tray on her lap and she looked down. Large hunks of meat surrounded by even larger chunks of potatoes, onions and carrots, all swimming in a plate of greasy gravy, met her hungry gaze. It wasn't her normal fare, but she couldn't afford to be finicky.

She picked up her knife and fork and began to eat, surprised at how flavorful the food was, even if everything tasted the same. It was the silence that forced her to lift her head and look at the two males standing beside the bed, staring.

"It's delicious," She said, then saw the other trays and was embarrassed. Where were her manners? "I'm so sorry. I should have waited." She was about to lay her utensils on her plate when Matt grinned and shook his head.

"It's good to see someone enjoying my cooking."

Austin felt he had to explain. "I'm used to lots of vegetables, fruits and things," he said as he struggled to drag a heavy chair across the floor, closer to the bed. "I don't get that here."

Ginny gave Matt a look, then shifted her gaze to Austin. She shook her head. She wanted to lighten the mood and searched her mind and the room for a safe topic.

A wave of relief washed over her when she spotted a silver-framed picture of a woman beside the bed. The photograph was obviously old and there was no doubt from the family resemblance that this was Matt's mother, Austin's grandmother. What was also apparent was that the woman, with her long beautiful hair, her high cheekbones, dark laughing eyes, high-bridged nose and full mouth was an American Indian. She was wearing ceremonial attire, an intricate beaded buckskin dress and turquoise jewelry.

Eager to end the hostile tension in the room, Ginny asked, "Is this your grandmother, Austin? You and your father look just like her."

Austin stopped picking at his food and glanced at the photograph. "I guess. No one ever told me much about her. Besides, she's dead."

Ginny gulped down a swallow of her iced tea and glanced at Matt. "This is your mother, right? I mean, you look just like her."

"Yes."

Ginny waited, and when nothing else was said, she tried again. "How old was she in the picture, and what tribe was she from?"

Instead of answering, Matt put down his knife and fork, folded his napkin and tucked it beside the plate. Stiffly he struggled to his feet and gathered up Ginny's tray and his own. "If you're through, Austin, take your dishes to the dumbwaiter."

Once again, Ginny watched the two males leave the room. This time she was relieved to see them go. She guessed she'd stepped—more like stomped—on some tender toes by opening a dark closet full of skeletons. She glanced at the photograph.

"I don't know what's wrong here," she said. "But if I stay, I'm liable to be more trouble than those two are ready for, because I know how important it is to have a family full of love. I know what it costs to lose them, too."

CHAPTER FOUR

GINNY COULDN'T BELIEVE three days had passed since she'd stumbled into the lives of the Bolt males.

It seemed like two years.

She was already battle-scarred, a veteran in the emotional war between father and son. But she felt safer than she had in more than four years.

Maybe she should have been ashamed for putting Matt out of his bed, but he'd taken up temporary residence in the bedroom adjoining the master suite. Once when Austin had deserted her for a few minutes, she'd taken a hurried peek at Matt's quarters. Any guilt she felt had quickly vanished. The room was spacious, bright and cheery. A little on the feminine side, but with a comfortable-looking full-size bed.

The feminine decor of that room brought up several mysteries to ponder. Where were the women in this house? They'd obviously been here, as evidenced by the triple-mirror vanity in the bathroom, the decor of the extra bedroom and the decidedly feminine choice of bed and bath linens and lacy curtains. She wanted to ask about the lack of any female presence but was hesitant. She would probably receive the same response she had when she'd asked about Matt's mother.

Actually, Ginny thought, she was looking forward to getting up, inspecting the house. Her natural sense of curiosity and just plain nosiness were working overtime. But a major overhaul was needed before she faced the world again. Pushing aside the candy wrappers—Austin had been bringing her little treats—Ginny picked up a hand mirror from the bedside table and thoughtfully inspected her face.

She had been amused to see her first shiner ever change from black to a revolting pea green and now it was in the last stages of a rather sickly yellowish color. She'd have to check the contents of the vanity to see if there was any makeup and hope it wasn't as ancient as the furnishings. Her cuts and scratches were healing nicely. As for her ankle, well, it had never been so bad that she couldn't have limped around on it after the ice pack and couple of hours' rest.

The problem was, she enjoyed being waited on, being taken care of for a change. The only real fly in the ointment was that, like Austin, she craved vegetables and fresh fruit. And some exercise would help.

Matt had done his best. His cooking skills left a lot to be desired. Three days added up to a lot of meals, and other than the leftover pot roast, they'd eaten entirely too many fast-food-style hamburgers, fried chicken and pizza.

She felt bottom heavy, as if she'd put on ten pounds of pure fat, all lodged firmly on her hips. She glanced at her clean jeans and shirt neatly folded on a chair and thought she really ought to get dressed, get up and rejoin the world. But being pampered was such a new and pleasant experience, she decided she'd wait a little longer before ending it.

The sound of quiet footfalls in the hall warned her of Austin's arrival. She sighed and set the mirror back on the table. The boy worried her. He seemed content to spend his time with her, if not talking, then stretched out across the foot of the bed reading a book. He'd even taken to picking out reading material for her, and though she appreciated the thought and wouldn't have hurt his feelings for anything, stories about the fall of Rome or the history of modern medicine just weren't her idea of entertainment. She would have liked a good romance or a mystery novel.

"Good morning, Ginny." Austin pitched his book on the bed, then hopped up on the edge.

"'Morning, Austin." This morning the boy had combed his hair straight up. He'd liberally applied some type of setting gel and was sporting the wet spiky look. Where, she wondered, was that young boy who had found her? The one with the silky clean hair that flopped over his forehead? Every morning since she'd been here he'd shown up with a different do, each a little more outrageous than the last. It wasn't until Matt had joined them and she'd seen his quiet anger and Austin's pleased expression that she realized the boy was doing everything he could to needle his father.

"How are you feeling?"

Ginny continued to stare at Austin's hair. She had to hand it to Matt. His self-restraint was more than she could manage. "Austin, that's probably the ugliest hairstyle yet."

Austin raised his hand and gingerly touched the stiff spikes. "Is it?"

"You know your father isn't going to say anything. He's wise to your tricks."

"Yeah, but he wants to." Austin smiled, a glint of temper in his dark eyes and something else, a certainty that he would eventually goad his father into losing his cool.

"Well, Matt might be able to keep quiet, but I don't have to. It's horrible."

"I know."

"It looks dirty."

"I know that, too."

This kid was just a little too smart for his britches, but she wasn't going to play into his hands. "Do me a favor. Please go wash it out," she said casually, and picked up her book, determined to ignore him all day if he didn't do as she asked. After a long silent moment, Austin scooted off the bed and left the room. Whether he'd do what she asked remained to be seen.

"You handled that better than I could," Matt said as he strolled through the bathroom door, his arms full of laundry. "I can't figure him out."

"Can't you?" She watched as he stacked the clean towels, sheets and clothes on a chair. He was a limited cook but a superb launderer. The clothes were clean and neatly folded. Puzzled, she wondered why the laundry only got as far as the nearest chair or tabletop.

"He wants your attention."

"Well, he's going about it the wrong way."

She'd already asked one personal question and been rebuffed, but she figured if she was going to stay, she had to know something about the background of these two. "Matt, where's Austin's mother?"

Matt set the stack of folded towels on the end of the bed, then sat down himself. "She's dead—killed in an airplane crash two months ago."

"I'm sorry," she said. "That explains a lot about his attitude. But I thought tragedy usually brings a family closer together."

"Not necessarily. Did tragedy bring you and your mother closer?" He looked at Ginny for the first time the first time since he'd sat down, then he smiled, try-ing to take the sting out of his words. But he didn't like being questioned, especially when he was in the wrong and knew she was about to make him face his mis-takes.

Matt shook his head at his stupidity. For far too long he'd been the man always in control, whether in his personal life or his career. Now he felt like a stranger, standing on the outside, watching the once intelligent, self-possessed man make a fool of himself, because for the first time in his life he didn't have all the answers.

"Shelly—Austin's mother—and I were divorced when Austin was only a few months old. She was a flight attendant."

"How long were you married?"

"Too long for Shelly. Five years. I was a beat cop in Houston finishing college at night school with the in-tentions of entering law school. She hated my job but was willing to put up with it all—the long hours on the job, the even longer hours at law school—knowing that as soon as I got my degree I was going with either the district attorney's office or a local law firm. I have to hand it to her—she worked her butt off to help me and keep us financially afloat. Law school was expensive and a cop's salary isn't much to start off with. But it didn't work out the way she or I thought it would.

"I got my degree, but by that time I was a first grade detective. I loved my work and wasn't about to give it up. Not for her or the baby. So we split, and she moved to California for career advancement with her job and took Austin with her. Despite our differences, she was a great mother to Austin."

"When your wife moved to California, did you get to see Austin much?"

Matt stared off into space, seeing his past actions now for what they were—pure selfishness. "Did I see Austin? Twice in ten years. God, that sounds as bad spoken out loud as it does thinking about it, doesn't it?"

Ginny wasn't about to help him out. "Yes, it does. Why only twice?"

"Oh, hell, I don't know. He was miles away. I worked long hours. My vacations never coincided with Shelly's plans or Austin's school. Those are all lame excuses now. The truth is I never wanted kids. Shelly knew how strongly I felt, and when she told me she was pregnant everything changed. We were already having problems, but the tension of the pregnancy only made things worse. So, a couple of months after Austin was born, we split.

"I flew out to California when Austin was almost a year old. Believe me when I say I was not welcomed with open arms. And rightly so, but I was willing to take Shelly and Austin back to Houston and start over again. That went over like a lead balloon. Shelly was in a relationship with a man who not only loved her dearly but wanted Austin, too. Peter is a fine man and I couldn't find fault with him or their relationship."

Ginny was a little confused. "If Peter and Shelly loved each other, why is Austin here with you and not with his stepfather?"

Matt slumped back on the bed and stared dejectedly up at the ceiling. "Peter and Shelly never married. He was already married to a woman who wouldn't give him a divorce. By law Austin is mine. I knew that. So did Peter. Austin wanted to stay with Peter—hell, he begged me to let him.

"But Peter, for whatever reason, figured it was time that father and son got to know each other. I think letting Austin go, giving him over to me, almost killed that man. I'll never understand why he did it."

Ginny could guess but refused to say anything. She didn't know Matt or Austin well, but what she'd observed so far was that they needed each other more than they knew. Smart man, Peter, she thought. One day she'd like to meet him.

One day. Ginny realized she was thinking in terms of the future, and suddenly she felt well and eager to be up and about. It was time for her to resume her life—and at the moment that included Matt and Austin. But what a trio they made!

Well, Ginny figured, things had to improve. Yet for that to happen she needed a better success rate than she'd had up till now with the two males. "If you'll move," she said, eager to get started, "I'll be up and dressed."

Matt rolled over, dragged his hands through his hair to get it out of his face and smiled. "Your ankle's well enough?"

"I think so." She had a feeling he knew she'd been able to walk without any pain. "Thanks for letting me just loaf around."

Matt shrugged and eased himself into a sitting position. "You needed it." He got off the bed and handed her her clean clothes. "Do you think you're up to cooking dinner tonight? I like vegetables and fruit, too, you know."

Ginny grinned at the eager, pleading expression. The grin grew when she saw he was smiling. Matt had a beautiful smile, one that did strange things to her insides. For the first time, she realized what a handsome man he was. He'd be even better-looking when he put on the twenty or so pounds he'd lost. She was even beginning to like his long hair. There was something sensual about the way it waved and curled around his shoulders. It certainly didn't take away from his masculinity.

God, she was in bad shape. Embarrassed that he might be reading her thoughts, she quickly glanced down at the pitiful pile of clothes. On top were her running shoes, clean and neatly relaced. Her eyes suddenly swam with tears. William used to lace her shoes for her because she could never get them to come out even.

She swallowed hard and blinked away the moisture before she looked up. "Tell me something. How is it you can do laundry like a demon and you can't cook? And since you're so good with the washing and folding, why don't you put the clothes away?"

Matt chuckled. "I'm good at the laundry because I've always done my own. As for the cooking—" he shrugged again as if embarrassed "—I almost always ate out. And if I put the laundry away, I'd have to remember where I put it and take the time to dig it out again." He motioned at the neat piles. "It's a lot easier this way especially if you're in a hurry, and I usually am." He paused. "Old habits die hard—I was almost always in a rush. Nowadays I have time to spare."

Male logic, she thought. Who said females were complicated? She threw back the covers and got out of bed, ignoring the way the shirt she'd borrowed left so much of her legs exposed. After all, he'd seen her naked as a jaybird. The thought brought a sudden heat and high color to her cheeks and she quickly said, "Tell me something. Where did this enormous bed—" she waved her hand around the room "—and all the rest of this come from?"

Matt frowned as he glanced around. The furniture had always been in this room. "I haven't the slightest idea. I know my father inherited it from Grandfather and I believe Gramps inherited it from his father." Matt had never given the house or the contents much thought and told Ginny as much. "I was always more interested in the land, the vines. But I know part of this house was built by my ancestors in the early years of Texas, before it was a republic and when it was still under the thumb of Mexico."

Austin skidded to a stop when he saw his father in the bedroom, but he quickly forgot his animosity on seeing Ginny standing with her clothes in her hands. "You getting up?"

"Yep. Out of fear that your father would feed us more of his pot roast or another high-fat meal. I'm going to cook." She was pleased to see he'd washed the goop out of his hair and parted it neatly on one side. He'd even taken the time to blow-dry it, and now the dark hair was soft and shiny.

"He—" Austin used his shoulder to point in Matt's direction so he wouldn't have to look at his father "—is going to have to go to the store. The only thing green in the fridge is mold."

Matt muttered something under his breath and Ginny laughed.

"Austin, go get a pad and pencil. We're going to make a list." In his eagerness Austin was almost out of the bedroom when Ginny said his name again. "You're going to have to go to the store with your father."

"No way. Not me," the boy snapped.

Ginny ignored his retort and headed for the bathroom to get dressed. "Yes, you are. We can't trust your father to get the right things. He's not good at this,

Austin—he admitted it to me. So, for both our sakes, he needs your help. Meet me in the kitchen in five minutes so we can take inventory." Ginny shut the bathroom door firmly, noting with amusement that both males were left gaping after her.

When she made her way down to the kitchen less than five minutes later, Matt and Austin were seated at opposite ends of a long wood-plank table, silently waiting. She was surprised to see that they were quick-change artists, as well. They were both now dressed in jeans and clean shirts.

But it was the kitchen that captured her attention. It was spacious and bright, with sparkling white tiles, shining wood floors, a big double sink and Italian hand-painted tiles of fruits cleverly placed around the walls. The antique china cabinet was full of old bone china and crystal.

She figured she could explore when they left for the store. "Ready, Austin? Now, tell me if I go too fast or you need me to spell anything."

Matt leaned back, balancing the chair on two legs, and watched as Austin sat poised over the pad. If he had made a remark like that, Austin would have had a sarcastic retort. Ginny was treating him like a kid, instead of a child prodigy. What surprised him was that Austin didn't seem to mind in the least. For the first time since his son had come to live with him, Austin seemed genuinely happy. He was interested in something besides making everyone around him miserable, or locking himself in his room with his computers or burying his nose in a book.

Matt was so pleased with himself he placed his hands behind his head and smiled. Maybe this situation was going to work out better than he'd anticipated. He'd be relieved of the day-to-day responsibility of Austin, the daily drudge of trying to think of what to prepare for meals—the general household worries. Ginny's problems, her past, didn't trouble him. He could take care of himself and his family. Besides, he still had a few friends who'd do some checking for him and keep their mouths shut.

Ginny started opening cabinets. Her first find was a treasure, a pasta machine. She began her list, shooting one item after another at Austin. She moved to the pantry and shook her head. What were these men living on? The freezer in the laundry room off the kitchen yielded little but a cold blast of air, a strangely wrapped package and some bags of ice.

After almost thirty minutes, she finally ended up at the refrigerator. She opened it and gagged, quickly slammed it shut, took a deep breath, then stared hard at Matt. "That's disgusting. Shame on you."

He felt five years old with those censorious brown eyes glaring at him.

Austin's chuckle quickly dried into a cough when Ginny directed that same glare at him.

"You're both old enough to know better," she said.

"Yes, ma'am," Austin mumbled, then shot a defiant look at his father.

"Yes, ma'am," Matt said.

She would have to scrub the nasty thing before she could put anything in it. Austin started double-checking the long grocery list. "Can you think of anything I missed?" she asked.

Matt let the chair back down on all four legs with a thump. He moved down the side of the table and, over his son's shoulder studied the list as intently as Austin.

For a second Ginny wondered at the man's deep scowl, then thought of how much all those supplies were going to cost. "I'm sorry," she said. Both males glanced up. "I never thought to ask. I mean, I got carried away and went through here like a tornado, never giving finances a thought."

"Don't worry about money," Matt said, then tapped Austin on the shoulder. "Turn the page." He studied the list intently, then gave Ginny a sheepish look. "I don't see any sweets." When Ginny didn't comment, he went on as if she hadn't heard. "I'm partial to Twinkies. Austin here likes Snickers and Butterfingers."

"You like Butterfingers," Austin mumbled. "I like M&M's—peanut ones."

"Then how come you ate all my Butterfingers?" Matt started to laugh. "And come to think of it, you did a pretty good job on the Twinkie supply, too. I saw all the wrappers in your room."

Austin shrugged and ducked his head, trying to keep from laughing. "I think Ginny ate them."

"No, no. You can't blame me. I'm a Snickers fan."

Austin tried again. "I was starving to death, willing to eat anything."

"Now that is the biggest fib you've told so far." Matt gently mussed his son's hair.

As if he realized he was actually getting along with his father, Austin quickly stood up and gathered his sheets of paper. "Where are we going to get the groceries? I've seen this hick town's answer to produce, and it's cabbage and onions."

Ginny thought it was time to intervene. "Why don't you two hold off on the sweets and we'll see what I can come up with?"

Matt headed for the door. "I guess it's time to get going," he said, then stopped short, patting himself down, double-checking for his checkbook and wallet. Then he fished his car keys out of his pocket and stood shaking them as he thought of something.

"Listen, Ginny, there are a few workers on the place, but they won't come up to the big house. And I haven't told anyone I have a guest, so stay inside." He glanced at his watch. "We're going to be a while, probably have to drive to Austin. Look for us, say, in a couple of hours." He seemed reluctant to leave.

"I'll be fine." She followed Matt to the door. "I keep my promises. I'll be here when you get back." Austin was waiting on the wide porch, leaning against the railing. The Bolt males eyed each other and she sighed. "If you want to eat, try to get along long enough to get back with the groceries."

Being cooped up for three days was too much. The lure of being outdoors, of sunshine and fresh air almost made her forget her promise as she stood holding the screen door open. Instead, she watched them disappear around the corner and she smiled. It was evident from the way Austin was waving the pages of notepaper around and moving his head that he was going over the list with Matt.

She heard the sound of a car engine and paused as she was about to shut the door. In a few moments a big black Mercedes sedan glided by and she thought that for an ex-cop Matt lived well. Then she noticed that, though the car was in top condition, it was an older model.

Ginny pulled the screen door shut and frowned. The latch was a hook-and-eye type, but the eye was loose and wobbled in the wood. She thought about closing the door but there was a good breeze coming through the kitchen so she left it open. Eagerly she whirled around. The first thing she was going to do was have a look at the house.

She sprinted from the kitchen with nary a twinge of protest from her ankle. She caught a glimpse through an open doorway of the room where Matt and Austin had first brought her, then she was up the stairs, her hands lingering on the satiny finish of the banister. She rushed down the hall in the opposite direction of the master suite, opening and closing doors as she went. There were two other bedrooms besides the one she slept in and the one Matt was using, and an adjoining bathroom between them. Each was spacious, with large windows to bring in the light, but both were empty of any furnishings and hollow sounding.

The last room at the end of the hall was Austin's. She carefully eased the door open. Not knowing what to expect, she braced herself, remembering her childhood and the mess her room was usually in. But she was surprised by the tidy room. Twin beds with bright floral coverlets. Books organized by title and, she thought, subject. She stared at the computer and all the gadgets attached to it, like an octopus stretching out its arms. This was Austin's world, a place where he could lock himself away, where he didn't have to hide his pain.

There was a row of framed photographs neatly arranged beside the computer and on the bedside table. All were of a beautiful blond woman in different poses and different settings. Austin was in a couple of the pictures with his mother, and there was one in which the two of them were joined by a bearded man. They were all laughing, and their obvious happiness brought a lump to Ginny's throat.

Austin had lost his mother, the man he probably looked on as his father, and his home and friends. Matt had lost his career and a life he loved. And she'd lost everything, too. She'd lost her identity as Virginia Antonia Bradsworth Carney, her home and family. Her career, her husband and child. All three of them were lost souls, their emotional pain weighing them down so that she wondered if they would all survive the strain.

She didn't know how long she stood there staring at the photograph, lost in her own memories, until she was jarred back to the present by a sound from downstairs. She hurriedly wiped her wet cheeks, surprised to realize she'd been crying.

It had to be the latch on the screen door rattling with the breeze. Ginny stood still, listening. There was no way she could ignore the sound. After all, this was a big old house and she was totally unfamiliar with its creaks and rattles. She'd have to go see for herself.

At the landing she hesitated, closed her eyes for a second and listened. Was that a voice she heard? Or was it just the wind playing tricks on her overactive imagination?

Ginny eased down the remaining steps. When she reached the bottom, she leaned back and slid quietly along the wall to the kitchen doorway. Taking a quick peek around the corner, she saw nothing and sighed with relief. She was just about to step into the kitchen when she heard another noise, one she recognized as a cabinet closing. Bouncing back, she pressed herself into the wall again. Someone was in the kitchen, and Matt had made it plain that no one should be around the house today. Her heart felt ready to jump out of her chest, and she could barely breathe.

Could she have been wrong about the FBI making a mistake? Maybe one of Tony's friends had found her, after all. She inhaled deeply, quietly. She'd never find out, she told herself, by standing frozen to the spot like a scared rabbit. But she needed a weapon, and from the sounds in the kitchen she'd better hurry up. Then she remembered seeing a broom propped against the kitchen wall just inside the doorway.

For a fraction of a second her body wouldn't work, refused to move. Then her fear subsided. She eased partly around the door, spotted the broom and snatched it up. She flattened herself against the wall once more, the broom clutched against her chest as she listened to the sound of the cabinets opening and closing.

She got a good grip on the broom, twisting the solid wood in her hands. The footsteps were coming closer now, almost to the doorway. Her palms were sweating. She held her breath, silently ordering herself to move her butt. Suddenly she screamed at the top of her voice and leapt forward, the broom raised like a club. She swung her weapon down, catching the back of a man's head with a satisfying thud. She was in the process of readying herself for another whack when she saw the man crumple to the floor.

He was moving, struggling to get up, but Ginny felt as if she'd been turned to ice. Her eyes were locked with the pale gaze of a mad animal. The screen door separated them, but the animal was bouncing against it, snarling and snapping, trying desperately to rip the mesh away and tear her throat open. And when she thought he was about to succeed, she started to scream again and turned toward the hall, intending to race upstairs and lock herself in the bathroom.

Ginny heard the man yelling at the animal, and at her, to shut up. She followed his orders, but only because she suddenly found herself flat on her bottom on the hard floor. The man had grasped her ankle, and the wild animal raged on.

"Well, well. Look here, Dog. A new bone for you to chew on." He let go of Ginny's ankle and rubbed the egg-size lump on the back of his head. "Who the hell are you?" He winced. "And why'd you hit me?"

Released from his grip, Ginny scooted on her backside as far away from the man as she could. She had a quick look at the wildly barking animal and was surprised to see it was indeed a dog. Ugly, dirty, but a dog and not a savage beast. Her gaze narrowed on the animal. She had a feeling the two of them had met in the vineyard a few days ago. Her gaze shifted to the man she was sharing the floor with.

"Who are you?" she demanded.

My, my, she wondered, what had she stepped into? Was she just lonely, or was every male she ran into good-looking and sexy? Her intruder was tall, tanned and blond, with a pair of the most beautiful sea green eyes she'd ever seen. He was fashionably dressed in expensive slacks and shirt. She spotted a sports coat thrown over the back of the kitchen chair.

Giving herself a firm scolding, she realized her interest was mirrored in his eyes. But before she could ask another question, he shouted at the dog again to shut up—with no results. Then he turned on her.

"I'm Jason, Matt's brother. And you are? Dammit, Dog. Shut the hell up."

"I'm a friend of Matt's. Funny he never mentioned a brother to me. Is his name really Dog? And can't you make him go away?"

"I guess we're even. Matt never mentioned you, either. And, yes, that sorry mutt is named Dog and obviously he doesn't listen to anyone."

She studied Jason. There wasn't a hint of family resemblance except maybe for the height and build, but nothing else. "How do I know you're Matt's brother and not a thief?"

"How do I know you're his friend and not a burglar?" Jason smiled. A smile that never failed to work on women, no matter what their age.

Ginny scowled. A charmer. The dog's barking had become a little hoarser but gave no sign of letting up. "Quiet, Dog," she shouted, and they were both shocked when the animal fell silent, flopped down and fixed his pale eyes on her. "Why does he keep staring at me like that?"

"I've never seen him do that before. Maybe he likes you."

Ginny shivered, noticing the dog's teeth still showed. "I don't think so."

Jason chuckled. "That's Dog's way of smiling. Now, can we get back to you?" He hadn't missed the healing cuts and scratches or the fading bruises on her face. "Who'd you tangle with? My brother? No, he's not a woman beater. How long have you known Matt and how long have you been here?"

She'd promised herself she was through telling lies, but until she and Matt had time to decide exactly what they were going to tell people about her presence in his house, she had to have a cover. "I tangled with a flight of stairs and I knew Matt in Houston and I've been here three days."

Jason had a way of stretching the truth himself and could spot a comrade when he met one. He decided to let it slide for the moment.

"You don't look like Matt," she said.

He smiled at her again, and Ginny detected a resemblance, after all. Matt and Jason had the same charming smile, Matt just wasn't as free with his as Jason.

"Or maybe *he* doesn't look like *me?*" He rubbed the back of his head again and climbed rather shakily to his feet. He grabbed hold of the back of a chair until the spots cleared from his vision and the room stopped spinning. He held out his hand to Ginny. "Remind me never to play baseball with you. I have a feeling you have one hell of a swing."

Ginny hesitated, then accepted the outstretched hand. "Actually I'm better at golf and—"

She never finished her sentence. Jason grabbed her by the shoulders and firmly set her down in the nearest chair. He shouted for the dog, who had immediately started howling again, to shut up, then turned his attention to his captive. "What are you doing in my home? Who are you? And don't try that story about being Matt's friend and being here three days. I was here yesterday and the day before. Neither Matt nor Austin said a word about having a guest." He reached over to the wall phone and picked up the receiver. "Start talking or I call the sheriff."

CHAPTER FIVE

HER NATURAL REACTION when forced into a corner was to keep cool and lie, and she didn't see any reason to change tactics now. "Put down the phone and stop acting like a jerk. Of course I know Matt. Why else would I have the run of the place?"

Jason didn't like being called a jerk. He lowered the phone but didn't return it to its cradle. "Listen, if you'd been here, Matt could've kept it a secret, but Austin would've told me."

"But he didn't, did he? And I'm here."

"You're from Houston?" he asked. "And that's where you knew Matt and Austin?"

She had him now and almost smiled. "Yes, I know Matt from Houston, but Austin's been living in Los Angeles with Shelly and Peter. I came as soon as I could after hearing about Shelly's death."

Jason gave her one of his most charming smiles and hung up the telephone. Without saying a word he walked to the opposite side of the table, pulled out a chair and sat down. "So you're one of Matt's women. If I'm a little startled, it's because my big brother doesn't usually bring his lady friends home. I'm also not used to having the back of my head bashed in." He gingerly touched the area, winced, then looked at his fingers. "That's surprising. I'd have thought you hit me hard enough to break the skin, but you didn't."

"Maybe you have an incredibly hard head." His clothes had to be designer, Ginny noted, and his shoes Italian. His hair was fashionably styled, his nails manicured, and on his wrist was a Rolex. He was no farmer, no lover of the land. This man obviously liked his creature comforts, and from the wicked sparkle in his eyes and the sexy smile, she concluded that women were at the top of his list. She remembered something he'd said earlier. "If this is your home, where have you been for three days?"

"This was my home until the prodigal son returned."

What surprised Ginny was that there was no bitterness in his words. She returned his smile. "Well, Jason Bolt, I haven't made up my mind about you. You don't look at all like Matt."

"Van der Bollen."

"What?" she asked.

"The last name's Van der Bollen. So's Matt's. He changed it to piss the old man off. We have the same father, different mothers."

She remembered the photo of the Indian woman in Matt's bedroom. Matt must have inherited his mother's coloring. Ginny got up and opened a couple of cabinets before she found what she was looking for. She pulled out the pasta machine and started taking it apart to clean it. "I never knew Matt changed his name."

"It's not surprising. He and Father never got along. Always fighting about the grapes and the wine. Hell, they hated each other. I was around eight when Matt ran off to Houston, and it wasn't until three years ago, when Father died, that he came back. And that was only for the reading of the will. He wanted nothing to do with his inheritance."

Ginny scrubbed harder at the grime on the pasta rollers. When Dog started growling, she glanced around to see Jason walking toward her. "Why'd they hate each other?"

Jason shrugged, picked up a dish towel and started drying the clean parts of the machine. "Maybe they were too much alike, I don't know."

But he did, Ginny thought, he just wasn't willing to tell her.

Jason flipped the damp cloth over his shoulder and lounged against the refrigerator door. "And speaking of my brother, just where is he?"

"He and Austin went to buy groceries."

"Together?" Jason jerked upright as if he'd been jabbed with a knife. "You're joking?" When she didn't answer, he hesitated a moment. "You *aren't* joking, are you?"

She couldn't help laughing at the look of shock on his face. "No. I made a list, and Austin didn't trust his father to get everything right."

"That's Austin. But you mean they actually left together? Locked in the same confined space for longer than five minutes?" Jason burst out laughing. "I don't believe it."

Ginny reassembled the pasta machine. "They were even talking to each other as they left, too."

"*No.* You must be a witch." He gazed at Ginny as if she'd suddenly lost her mind. She was tying a clean dish towel around the lower half of her face, covering her mouth and nose. He watched, fascinated and puzzled, as she retrieved a small bucket from under the sink and started pouring a hefty amount of ammonia into it. He waited until she added water, then asked, "What are you going to do?"

"If you'll move your carcass, I plan to wash out the refrigerator."

"Oh, Lord. Let me out of here." He backed toward the door.

"Chicken." She positioned a plastic trash bag between her feet, took a deep breath and opened the refrigerator.

The screen door slammed shut.

Dog growled, sniffed the air, then whined, but he didn't leave his post outside the door. Ginny noticed that the animal kept a keen eye on her. The damn thing made her nervous.

She began emptying everything out of the refrigerator and in no time had it clean and fresh-smelling. She emptied the freezer and the automatic ice maker, as well, afraid the gross fumes might have permeated even the frozen food.

She was standing back inspecting her handiwork when Dog started that crazy barking of his. Frowning, she walked to the screen door and saw Jason coming up the walk. He was carrying a large basket and almost tripped over Dog as the animal planted himself directly in his path.

"Get out of the way." Jason tried to push the mutt aside with his foot and was snapped at for his trouble. He lowered the heavy basket and glared at the dog. "What the hell is the matter with you?" He glanced at Ginny. "Suddenly he doesn't trust me. Maybe if you told him to move his mangy hide, I could give you this."

Ginny couldn't think of one reason why the vicious animal would mind her, but he obviously wasn't going to let Jason come any closer. "I might if you tell me what's in the basket."

"Oh, you're that type, are you?" He chuckled. "Don't like surprises?"

"No."

Jason tried once more to move around the dog, but Dog wasn't having any of it. "Peaches. Fresh tree-ripe peaches. Van der Bollen peaches. Juicy. Sweet."

"Dog, move," Ginny ordered.

Jason and Ginny watched as the animal quickly moved aside.

Once in the kitchen, Jason set the bushel basket down, looked at Ginny, then at Dog. "You are a witch, aren't you?"

"Maybe." But her attention had wandered from the flirtatious Jason to the peaches. The room suddenly smelled of fruit and sunshine. She quickly picked a plump ripe peach, washed it off under the sink faucet and took a large bite. Sweet, sticky juice ran down the corners of her mouth. She closed her eyes and pictured a peach cobbler, all brown and bubbly with butter and cinnamon and sugar.

Ignoring Jason's grin, she finished the peach as she searched for the ingredients. "Don't just stand there," she said. "See if you can find some cinnamon in the pantry."

She absently thanked him when he handed her the small bottle, then began peeling the peaches. It had been years since she'd felt like baking, and she became so lost in the pleasure of the task that she forgot Jason was even there.

Jason made himself comfortable at the big table, watching the attractive woman work. He didn't know what to make of her. His father had always told him Matt liked whores and sluts. But this woman was neither. She was pretty and funny and bright. But there was an underlying sadness about her that tugged at him—and also made him curious. Maybe Matt had put that look of longing in her eyes. Maybe Matt had put the bruises on her face. Hell, he realized, he didn't even know his own brother well enough to make such judgments. And whose fault was that? he asked himself.

MATT STOPPED DEAD in his tracks on the walk, almost tripping over Austin, who'd also come to an abrupt halt. Even the sight of Jason's car, annoying as it was, couldn't distract his attention. The tantalizing blend of aromas wafting from the kitchen nearly overpowered him, short-circuiting his brain and filling his head with childhood memories.

"If you don't recognize that lovely scent, Austin, it's peach cobbler." Matt breathed in again. "And if I'm not mistaken, fresh bread." Matt readjusted the grocery bags that were slipping from his grip and nudged his son in the backside with his knee.

Like a dog, Austin sniffed the air and sighed. "Dessert."

He sprinted toward the back door, almost tripping over Dog. Boy and animal eyed each other. It was only when the animal spotted Matt that he slunk off the back porch and disappeared around the corner of the house.

Austin started shouting Ginny's name until Matt hurriedly silenced him. "Remember our talk," he said. "We've got to be careful."

Austin glared at Matt and charged into the kitchen. "Ginny, what smells so good? Look." He held up two shopping bags. "Look what I got..." In his excitement, he'd forgotten about Jason's being there and looked at his father for help, wondering if he'd said too much already.

Matt jostled the three grocery bags he was carrying. "Grab one of these things, Jason, before I drop it on the floor."

In the commotion Austin dashed across the room, dumping his bags in a corner and all the while talking a mile a minute. "We got everything, Ginny. Even that Reggiano Parmesan cheese you wanted. We went to this special cheese shop."

Jason knew immediately that something weird was going on. Austin and Matt never got along, but at the moment they seemed like bosom buddies. "Hey, runt. Where you been?"

"Hi, Uncle Jason." Austin ducked his head into one of the bags Matt had carried in and held up the cheese, showing Ginny. "Matt and I went shopping for food. Ginny's going to stay with us. She's going to cook dinner, too."

As smart as his son was, he wasn't any good at subterfuge. Matt hoped that was all he would tell Jason. He glanced at the counter where a large baking dish was cooling on a rack. "You see, Austin, I was right. Peach cobbler." Then he eyed the two loaves of French bread, still hot from the oven. He wrapped his arm around Ginny's shoulder, holding her firmly to his side and sending a clear message to his brother. "Thanks for bringing the peaches up."

"Hey, what are brothers for. And I'd invite myself to stay for dinner and dessert, but I have a date." Jason leaned against the wall and watched the two of them. Something about the scene didn't set right in his mind. He touched the back of his head. "You want to be real careful around her, brother. She swings a mean broom. But then you probably already know that, don't you?"

Ginny gave a quick laugh and looked at Matt. "You'll never guess what happened. I was upstairs and heard something. When I came down, I spotted a stranger in the kitchen." She placed her arm around Matt's waist and squeezed to warn him. "You did tell me that no one was around and I thought he might be a thief, so I clobbered him with the broom."

"Dropped me like a lead balloon. Almost knocked me out cold."

Matt worked at hiding his pleasure. His brother was a pain in the butt, and it was good to see him knocked down a peg. The only problem was that Jason didn't seem to mind. He thought it was all a joke.

Austin's mouth dropped open in shock and pleasure. "She coldcocked you?"

"As deadly a right-hand swing as I've ever seen. Don't under any circumstances play baseball with her. She'll beat your pants off."

"Actually," Ginny said, "it was more an over-the-head-with-both-hands slice."

"What I can't understand is, why didn't someone tell me there was a beautiful woman staying here?"

"Maybe because I know your reputation with women," Matt snapped.

Jason wasn't in the least put off. "Oh, I don't think that's the reason." He shifted his gaze to his nervous nephew. "Is it, Austin?"

Matt was fidgeting beside her, and Ginny figured it was time to put an end to the questions. It was as plain as the antique clock on the wall that Matt and Jason didn't get along, and she had a feeling Jason wasn't above grilling a child to satisfy his curiosity.

Glancing at the three brown grocery bags, she said, "Surely this isn't all?"

Matt grinned at her ploy. "The car's so packed with food and bags that I thought Austin was going to have to sit on my lap and drive." He dropped his arm from Ginny's shoulder and started toward the door. "How about giving us a hand, Jason, before you shove off?"

Jason took in the three bland expressions and shrugged. "Lead the way, big brother." Something was going on, he thought, something they didn't want him to know about. A mystery. He didn't like secrets, but he loved mysteries and intended to get to the bottom of this one.

Ginny and Austin silently watched as the two men left the kitchen. Then Austin put his finger to his lips and led her to the opposite end of the kitchen, where he pointed at the two large shopping bags he'd carried on his lap the whole way home.

"These," he whispered as if the very house had ears, "are for you. I'm going to hide them before Uncle Jason comes back."

"For me?" Curiosity got the better of her and she pulled one of the bags closer to see what was in it, but the paper slid through her fingers as Austin whisked it away and disappeared from the kitchen with both bags. She waited for him to come back, then asked, "What's in them?"

Austin laughed. "Special things." His eyes were sparkling with mischief, and he was almost dancing with the pleasure of the game. Then he glanced out the back door. "They're coming back."

Ginny didn't get a chance to question Austin further. Matt commandeered him to help, too. Suddenly she was surrounded with overflowing bags of groceries and fresh fruits and vegetables. She decided it was time to get busy herself, and she started putting things away.

For a while she lost herself in the activity, enjoying being in a kitchen again, surrounded by friendly voices and laughter. Though it wasn't William and Beth's voices, the warm feeling persisted. And even when she admitted she was playing make-believe, it soothed the pain in her heart.

She was so busy telling Matt and Austin where she wanted things placed, washing vegetables, repackaging meat and finally making fettuccine noodles that she didn't notice Jason was still there until he touched her on the shoulder.

Matt was filling the gallon glass jars with flour and sugar, but he kept a close ear tuned to their conversation. Austin made no attempt to appear disinterested. He stopped his chore of catching the pasta as it squiggled out of the machine and placing it on the drying rack.

Jason gently wiped a smear of flour off Ginny's cheek. "I have to leave. I hope our next meeting isn't a repeat of this one."

Ginny remained cool beneath his searching look. "Then you'd better remember not to sneak up on me," she said.

"Yes, ma'am." He turned to leave, then paused at the door. "It'll be nice to have a woman around the place. You're staying for a while?"

"Possibly" was all Ginny said.

Jason's alert gaze danced from Ginny to Matt. "Is Ginny going to take over the afternoon meals?"

"Possibly," Matt said.

Jason's grin was easygoing. They were playing games with him, but he didn't care. He had his own methods of getting to the truth. "By the way, Ginny, I don't believe I got your full name."

For a second she panicked. For four years she'd had four different names and suddenly she couldn't remember who she was. Then she remembered. She didn't have to lie about her name anymore. "Ginny Carney."

Jason gave a wave and left. Halfway down the walk leading from the kitchen, his steps faltered. He stopped, slowly turned and looked back at the house. He hadn't missed the way she'd hesitated when he asked her name, or the way Matt had suddenly stilled and Austin refused to look at him. He smiled and started back down the sidewalk, whistling a tune. Oh, he dearly loved a mystery—and Ginny Carney was just that.

After the screen door closed behind Jason, the three in the kitchen worked silently with a kind of nervous energy. It wasn't until the sound of a departing car reached them that they paused in their tasks, lifted their heads and gazed at one another. Matt started laughing first, followed by Austin's giggle, then Ginny joined in.

"Did you see the look on his face?" Matt asked. "He doesn't know what to think."

Ginny remembered what had happened earlier and started laughing again. "If you think that was funny, you should have seen his expression after I clobbered him. He couldn't believe a female got the better of him."

Austin finished hanging the last of the long strings of fettuccine on the rack and dusted the flour off his hands. "Uncle Jason's smarter than you think. He knows something's up." The boy hopped down from the stool he'd been standing on and disappeared from the kitchen. When he returned he deposited the two shopping bags he'd hidden earlier on the closest chair. "Come sit down, Ginny, and open your surprise."

Ginny eyed the two smug males, wondering what shared secret had forged such camaraderie between them. Like Austin, she dusted the flour off her hands, then wiped them clean on a towel before walking over to the beckoning bags. By the time she was seated, she was as excited as Austin.

Pulling the covering tissue from the first bag, she gasped. She yanked out the denim dress and held it up in front of her. It was sleeveless and scooped-necked, so if she wanted to she could wear a T-shirt under it, and had brass buttons that ran all the way up the front. She held it against her and found that it came to midcalf.

Ginny glanced at Austin and smiled. "I love it."

"Matt picked it out," he said grudgingly. "But that's not all. Keep looking."

His excitement was contagious, and she began pulling the rest of the items out of the bag. A pair of jeans, two T-shirts in pale yellow and blue, and at the bottom of the bag a pair of running shoes, the same brand and size as the ones she had on. She'd noticed that everything was her size and gave Matt a long look. He was the most observant man she'd ever met. "I don't..." Her throat closed up.

"Wait, wait." Austin held up a hand and wouldn't let her finish. "There's one more bag. And I picked these out."

The first thing she touched was satiny smooth, and she drew out a short silky nightgown, followed by five pairs of panties and a lacy bra. Ginny glanced at Austin in shock. His face was bright red and he was glaring at his father.

"You put those in there," he growled at Matt like an angry young bear. Then he gave Ginny a pleading look.

"I swear—I didn't pick them out—I never touched them."

Not wanting to embarrass him further, Ginny set the lingerie aside and removed the remaining packages from the shopping bag. When she had unwrapped them and spread them out on the table, she was speechless. Makeup. Eye shadow in a soft brown, mascara, an eyeliner pencil, translucent powder, peach-colored blush and a peach shade of lipstick. The child had bought her makeup and a gardenia-scented perfume. What shocked her was that they were just right for her. Her surprise must have shown because Austin was laughing.

"Didn't I tell you, Matt?" he said gleefully. "Girls love their makeup better than clothes."

"But, Austin," Ginny began, "how did you know what to buy?"

Matt leaned back in the chair, watching the two. He'd made a good decision, he told himself. They genuinely liked each other. And he had to admit that Austin was right. Ginny did seem more excited over the makeup than the pretty underwear. There was just no telling about women, he thought.

"Austin, how?" Ginny asked again.

Austin dragged a chair over beside her and sat down. "Mom used to do color charts for other flight attendants. You know, for clothes and makeup—things like that. They worked up a chart and matched colors. Then they'd go shopping. Sometimes, if I didn't have anything to do and wanted to go to the mall, I'd go with them. I just picked up the knack, I guess." The more he talked about his mother, the harder it was for him to continue. He swallowed, wanting to cry and yet refusing to in front of Matt.

Ginny saw the overbright eyes and the struggle to hold the tears back and knew the reason. Austin might seem ten going on forty, but he was still a child. She couldn't help herself. She grabbed him and hugged him, and for a second he clung to her, then his body language told her it was time to release him.

Ginny turned her attention to Matt. "I don't know what to say. How can I repay you?"

"Thank-you is sufficient, and what's a little money between friends?" His throat felt sore and he cleared it. Must be the dry air, he thought.

"Thank you," she said, then gave them both a sweet smile and stood up. "I better finish putting this stuff away and get dinner started."

Matt thought it was a good time to discuss other matters. "Ginny, I told Austin about your problems."

She spun around and stared at him. "You what?"

"Please don't be mad," Austin said. "I knew everything, anyway." Bright color stained his cheeks. "I listened at the bathroom door when you were telling him about what had happened to you. I'm sorry about Beth and your husband, and I wouldn't tell anyone even if they pulled my teeth out."

Ginny collapsed in the nearest chair and glared at Matt. "You told a child."

"I'm ten," Austin said huffily, then added, "But I'm smart. Besides, I can keep a secret."

She wasn't sure what to say and continued to stare at Matt. "Are you just going to sit there and say nothing after dropping such a bomb?"

"Secrets are dangerous," Matt said. "Living a lie is dangerous. Both have a way of coming back and biting you on the butt when you least expect it. My advice is to tell the truth—just stretch it until it fits your needs.

You want our help, and I need yours. You can't possibly think that we could've kept the truth from Austin, do you? He's smart and he'd already figured out you were running from something. Besides, we need him to reinforce whatever story you decide to come up with.''

Ginny shook her head and shifted her gaze to Austin. ''I don't know. For four years I've had only myself to protect. What if I'm wrong and someone does come after me? I could be placing you both in danger.''

Austin moved close to Ginny and put his hand on her shoulder. ''Matt said he could protect you, and I can take care of myself. And I can help, really I can.'' He started talking faster. ''I'm useful. An encyclopedia of information, and . . . and . . . and I have the world at my touch with my computer. I can tap into any mainframe, even the government's, without anyone being aware.''

It was Matt's turn to shake his head. ''Oh, no, you don't, mister. There will be no illegal hacking in this house. Understand?''

''Yeah, yeah. Sure.'' He dismissed his father's order with a wave, as if he was swatting at a pesky fly. ''Ginny,'' Austin pleaded, ''stay. We'll protect you. Matt said he'd find a way to get you clear of your problems. He was a cop, you know? He knows how to do these things.''

She still didn't like a ten-year-old child knowing the details of her life, but apart from leaving there was nothing she could do. And the thought of being on the run again, of hiding and lying, held about as much appeal as being boiled in hot oil. She'd been looking over her shoulder for the past four years and hadn't trusted anyone. Now, as she looked at the sadness and longing in Austin's dark eyes, any resistance she might have felt caved in.

Ginny touched Austin's smooth cheek with her fingers and smiled. "You're very persuasive." She stood and said, "If we're to have any dinner, I'd better get busy."

Matt retrieved his wine ledgers from the study, and Austin went in search of a book, both returning to settle down at the kitchen table. A comfortable silence fell over the room, broken occasionally by Ginny's humming or the noise of a spoon clanking against the side of a pot.

Matt wondered why he suddenly felt so at peace. He hadn't been this relaxed since before he was injured—if then—and the kitchen had never seemed such a welcoming, warm place. He closed his ledger and looked over at Ginny. "I know Jason must have asked you a dozen questions about what you were doing here. What did you tell him?"

The primavera sauce was almost ready. Ginny had been concentrating so hard on remembering William's special recipe that she was startled by the sound of another voice. She had to ask Matt to repeat his question, and when he did, she said, "I lied my way out of his questions. Of course he was more concerned at that particular time with the bump on his head."

Matt smiled. "But he did question you? Don't let his pretty-boy looks fool you. He's no dummy, just easily distracted by anything in skirts."

Austin sat in wide-eyed silence. He had a feeling he was about to hear something important and didn't want to miss it. He'd never heard his father say more than a few words at a time and so was afraid to move and make his presence known for fear he'd be told to leave the room.

Ginny set the large saucepan aside. It wasn't going to take more that a few minutes to stir the vegetables and garlic into the hot olive oil and then add the cheese and pasta. "I told him I knew you in Houston. He didn't believe me at first until I mentioned Austin, his mother and Peter. Of course he wanted to know about my bruises and I told him I fell down some stairs. But I think he suspects I was one of your girlfriends. He seems to think you have a lot of them."

Matt glanced out the screen door, where Dog had quietly stationed himself once again. "We're going to have to come up with a better story, one as close to the truth as we can get. The cover story about your clumsy fall on the stairs will do. Even if he thinks someone beat you up, he won't be suspicious when you don't want to discuss it. I'm going to tell him you lost your husband and child in a car accident and are down on your luck... need some help. All true." He leaned back in the chair and stared at the ceiling, his eyes narrowed in thought.

"I've hired you to help around here."

"Doing what?" Ginny asked.

"Taking care of the house, helping Austin, cooking the noon meal for the men—things like that. And, of course, I'll pay you a salary."

"What men? What noon meals?" She couldn't figure out if the tiny twitch of his lips was a smile or not, but he ignored her question.

"Have you ever been to Houston?"

"No. I've never been in Texas before."

"Where were you coming from when the accident happened?"

"Nashville, Tennessee."

Matt shook his head. "That could be a problem. I've never been there, so we can't say we met there. I guess we're going to have to stick with you knowing me in Houston. That means you'd better learn something about the town."

"And about you," Ginny added.

"Right."

He didn't continue and she waited. When he remained silent she said, "I'm not a mind reader. You're going to have to tell me something about yourself besides the fact that you're an ex-cop. Was Jason right? Do you—did you—have a lot of women?"

Matt disliked being questioned and he especially hated talking about himself. He glanced over at Austin and frowned.

Ginny knew what he was going to say. "Austin has a right to know, too. He's going to have to help me keep everything straight." She received a crooked grin of thanks from the boy and knew he didn't want to show any interest in his father at all.

"So," she said, "speak."

Dog barked loudly from his position on the porch, and they all glanced around in surprise, then laughed. It was the tension breaker they needed. But Ginny soon found that getting Matt to talk about himself was not easy.

"What can I tell you?" Matt asked. "I was a cop, a good one, and I'm not anymore. I lived in an apartment alone. I did my own laundry, ate most of my meals out and dated a few women."

Ginny glanced at Austin and grimaced, then she looked at Matt. "For a man of... How old are you?"

"Thirty-six," Matt replied. "How old are you?"

"Thirty-two, but we're not talking about me. Let's see..." Ginny mused as she set the pan on the burner and started to assemble the primavera. "Thirty-six and the sum total of your life could be expressed in two or three sentences? I don't think so. Where were you born, why did you move to Houston, and what made you become a cop?"

Matt rubbed his face and scowled. "All right. I give up. You're not going to let it go, are you?"

"No, we're not," Ginny said, including Austin.

"I was born in this house, in Austin's room, actually. My mother ran away when I was around nine or ten leaving me with my father and grandfather. They both despised me, I think."

"Why?" Austin asked, the first sign of interest he'd ever shown in his father's past.

"Because I looked like my mother, who was an Indian, but unlike my mother I wasn't a pushover. I never cried when I got whipped, and I got whipped more times than I care to remember. When Grandfather finally managed to make Mother run away, I stopped talking to him. Never said another word to him until the day he died."

Ginny was as wide-eyed with shock at the revelation as Austin was. "Why did your grandfather hate your mother so? And where was your father when all this took place?"

Matt glanced at Ginny, then at his son. Maybe it was time—time Austin knew he wasn't the only one to have had a hard time. "Grandfather hated my mother for a couple of reasons and never let her or my father forget them. First, she was an Indian, and not the woman the old buzzard had picked for Dad to marry. Second, she and her family were migrant workers, picking the grapes and moving with the seasons. She wasn't educated, but she was beautiful and sweet and everyone loved her, including my father. He knew damn well Grandfather would never in a million years approve. So he and Mother ran off and got married. About ten months later I was born.

"Dad thought my arrival would soothe the old man, but he was wrong. Grandfather's hatred for my mother seemed to increase year by year. He was a mean, vengeful old man, and Dad was just like him. I think he picked mother because he knew he could rule her life. Hell—" Matt yanked the rubber band from his hair and combed it out with his fingers "—between the two of them they almost killed her with their meanness. Even as young as I was, I couldn't blame her for leaving. I was just angry with her for leaving me behind."

"Why didn't she take you with her?" Austin ventured to ask. He was just curious, he told himself, but he wouldn't feel sorry for his father.

"Because, Austin, as much as they detested me and no matter how many times you sliced the pie, I was Matthew Van der Bollen. I was the firstborn son. To my grandfather, a man raised in the beliefs of the Old World, I was the rightful heir and the one destined to carry on the Van der Bollen lineage."

Ginny set the table, placing the plates and silverware in front of them. "What I don't understand," she couldn't help but ask as she filled their glasses with iced tea, "if your father loved your mother enough to defy the old devil in the first place, then why'd he let her leave?"

Matt straightened his dinnerware. "I wondered that myself. Then I heard Grandfather tell my dad that if he went after my mother, he would cut him out of his will.

Above all things, my father loved the vineyard. He loved making the wine and wasn't about to give it up." Matt was silent for a moment, his thoughts deep in the past.

"I guess only two things saved me from going bad, and I mean probably bad enough to do jail time. Two things my father did, unknowingly of course, that ultimately proved to be my salvation. When I was around ten or eleven, he started sending me away for the summer to an old friend in Épernay, France." He explained to Austin, "That's in Champagne, a province of France where champagne was first made. I worked in the vineyard and learned all about making wine and champagne. And I never let my father know how much I loved it."

"What was the second thing he did for you?" Austin asked.

"Dad remarried. Not that I was very fond of Barbara. She was a vain, selfish woman, but, kid, I got to tell you, when she said jump, my old man asked how high. It was almost worth putting up with her whining and temper tantrums just to see that happen. Then Jason came along, and from then on I came and went pretty much as I wanted."

"Why did you leave and go to Houston?" Ginny asked.

They'd talked—or rather Matt had—through dinner. It was as if once he started he couldn't stop. Ginny served the fettuccine primavera and watched Austin and his father devour it as if they hadn't eaten in months. She'd never seen a child pack away so much food and didn't think either of them would be able to find any room for dessert. She should've known better.

Matt wiped his mouth, surprised to realize he'd finished dinner. He glanced at Austin's clean plate, amazed
to see that the mound of food he'd thought his picky
son wouldn't eat was all gone. He waited until Ginny set
the heaping bowl of peach cobbler, crowned with a
nicely rounded scoop of vanilla ice cream, in front of
him before he answered her question.

"When I was almost eighteen, I told Dad I wanted
part of the grapes to make champagne. The wine business was changing. More people were drinking wine,
and there was going to be a demand for champagne. He
thought I was crazy. We argued constantly until it finally dawned on me that I was never going to be anything more to him than a worker. And it wasn't just
because of me. He would never have turned over one
grape to anyone other than himself. The land, the win-
ery, the vineyard were his, and he meant to keep them
in his grasp until the day he died. If I couldn't have a
hand in the business, be somewhat of a partner, I certainly wasn't going to stick around and be his slave. So
I hitchhiked to Houston and applied for the police
force. End of story."

CHAPTER SIX

THE TRUCE between father and son vanished with the sunrise. Austin showed up at the breakfast table with a bright neon green strip on one side of his hair. He had earphones glued to his head, and from them came an irritating thump, thump, thump of the bass.

Ginny looked in dismay at his clothes. What had happened to the sweet child of yesterday? His shirt was so big it looked as if it belonged to Matt. His jeans hung in folds and bagged at the seat. With no hips to support them, the only thing holding them up was a belt, pulled in tightly at the waist. He grinned at her, then did a couple of strange moves, or maybe, she thought, they were dance steps.

"I'm hip-hop cool," he said, then began to rap, "I'm hip-hop cool. No bod-ies fool. Don't go to school. Don't live by no rule."

She tried to look as stern and disapproving as Matt, but she couldn't stop the giggle that burst like a bubble from her lips. Suddenly she picked up the beat and rapped on her own. "Yo young man. Look's like a load in yo pants—so I won't get too close. Yo—yo. The rule be cool. So don't be no fool."

Austin glared at her and fled from the kitchen, but she thought she heard laughter as he raced up the stairs to his room.

"Where did you learn that?" Matt asked when he could speak again.

"I haven't the foggiest idea." She was as surprised as he was. "We'll wait awhile and see if he comes back down. You know, he acted as if he really wanted to go on a tour of the place last night. I can't believe you haven't shown him around."

"He's never seemed interested before." Matt rinsed out his coffee cup and added it to the already full dishwasher. Ginny switched on the machine and they stood looking at each other.

Matt didn't seem as pale and tired as he had yesterday. He was standing straighter and limping less. Maybe a nutritious home-cooked dinner and a good night's sleep had helped. She let her gaze linger on his face, trying to detect any other changes, then realized it was his hair that held her fascinated. Silken waves, shiny and thick, that just brushed his shoulders.

She'd never found men with long hair particularly attractive, but with his jet eyes, high cheekbones and square jaw, he had a kind of savage, rugged appeal. Who was she kidding? she asked herself. He was damn sexy. She turned away and busily began wiping the countertop.

What intrigued her about his hair, though, was the fact that for so many years he'd been staunchly establishment and proud of it. The long hair seemed like a complete contradiction of his past beliefs and accomplishments. She couldn't help asking, "When did you decide to grow your hair long?"

He shrugged. "I wore it like this for a couple of years when I was on the vice squad. I liked it, that's all." Matt grinned and pulled a rubber band from his shirt pocket to put his hair in a ponytail. "Besides, it always irritated me to have to take the time to get a haircut. If you didn't want to look like a peeled onion after the barber got through with you, you had to endure some hairstylist chattering away at you all the time she snipped and clipped. I thought I'd go crazy.''

He watched Ginny closely, picking up on the nervousness in her movements, and wondered what had set her off. The cuts and scratches on her face were healing nicely, and the bruises, with the help of the makeup, were only visible on close inspection. He liked her hair, the way it hung straight and smooth until just below her ear, where it curled under. Whenever she moved her head, her hair shifted in a sinuous swish and sway. He grinned. She might protest that the color was auburn, but he likened it more to red....

Matt caught the trail of his thoughts and slammed on the mental brakes. One thing he didn't need or want was to get involved with Ginny. Keep it friendly but keep his distance—that was his resolve.

Matt's intense scrutiny was making Ginny clumsy. She scuffed the toe of her shoe on the floor and stumbled. Angry with herself for acting like a silly teenager, she whirled around at him. "What are you staring at me for?"

"Don't be so touchy, Red." He thought a good dose of anger would do them both good and ease the sexual tension that had mysteriously manifested itself in the room.

"Do not call me that—ever."

"As much as you like everyone to be color-blind, I'm not. Your hair's not auburn, auburn has brown in it—and yours is red, Red. Admit it."

She took a couple steps closer, knowing full well he was deliberately teasing her to get her riled, but she couldn't stop the quick flush of temper either. "It's auburn."

Matt grinned and held up his hands in surrender. "If you say so . . . Ginny."

"I say so." She was relieved to hear Austin stomping down the stairs. Matt made her feel funny, and though it had been a long time—in her college days—since she'd felt that way, she didn't welcome the long-forgotten sensations. She wanted no emotional involvement with Matt or any man. William would always be the love of her life. No other man could take his place in her heart, and anything less than what she felt for William wouldn't be fair to anyone else.

Ginny welcomed Austin's appearance and was happy to see he'd changed clothes. She was as willing as Matt appeared to ignore the remaining green stripe in his hair.

She walked over to the screen door and stepped out into the morning brightness. For a second she just stood there taking in deep breaths of air, sweet with the scents of honeysuckle and roses. This was her new beginning, she thought. She glanced back into the kitchen.

"Come on, Matt, Austin," she called. "I need a tour of the place!"

The three of them set off down the path to the gate in the stone fence. It was a long walk, when they got there Ginny turned to gaze back at the house.

A large two-story building, it was constructed of pale pink granite blocks that glistened in the sunlight. The windows were arched and wide, and a porch ran the length of the front. From a distance, the house seemed to snuggle down in a stand of old oak trees, the huge limbs sheltering the green lawn from the intense summer heat.

Ginny was surprised to feel Austin's hand on her shoulder and turned to see that he'd climbed up on the high stone fence.

"There's nothing for miles and miles but vines," he said. "The only place to play is in the yard. But there's some neat things to see." He glanced at his father and said defiantly, "Uncle Jason showed me."

Matt nodded, realizing for the first time how much he'd neglected his son. But he hadn't exactly been feeling up to par. He pointed off to his right. "Around back is the garage, and beyond that is the cookhouse and barn."

After an hour in the morning sun, Ginny was hot. She'd seen endless rows of vines, and though Matt explained the differences between the varieties of grapes, she was completely confused. A red grape didn't necessarily produce a red wine, and the green grapes with careful blending could be turned into a red wine. Then of course there were the grapes he was most proud of— the Pinot Chardonnay, the base for the champagne he intended to produce.

Matt noted his audience's flagging interest and moved on, pointing out the empty shell of a building he wanted to turn into a wine-tasting center for visitors. He paused at the wine cellar, then decided that the cool darkness would be a welcome break. He grasped the handles of the wide double doors and pulled hard, grunting a little when they resisted his efforts, then slowly gave way and opened.

Ginny marveled at the thickness of the wood, the iron hinges and hardware. When the doors opened, the cool, fragrant air caused goose bumps to rise on her damp skin. Matt stepped through the dark hole, and Ginny looked at Austin, found him gazing up at her and asked, "Have you been in there?"

"No" came his whispered reply.

"Kind of spooky, that first step into the dark unknown."

"Thanks, Ginny."

"Will you hold my hand?" she asked.

"Oh, sure, if you're that scared." He grasped her hand and squeezed it hard as they stepped inside.

"Don't move." Matt's voice floated to them from a distance. "Let your eyes adjust, then look over to the right."

She could just make him out and another set of double doors. "What is this place—Fort Knox?"

A high-pitched laugh tinged with madness drifted their way. Austin clenched her fingers until they were numb. "Come on, Matt. That's not funny."

"Sissies, both of you. My father used to scare the pants off me in this place." Then he thought about what he'd just said and struck a match on the nearby table.

A golden glow lit their way, and they soon stood before the doors. "They're very old, aren't they?" Ginny asked.

"About two hundred years old," Matt told her. "Solid oak and almost as hard as petrified wood. Grandfather bought them in France from the Benedictine abbey of Hautvillers. It almost bankrupted him shipping them over, that and the oak casks for aging."

He glanced over the circle of light from the candle he'd lit, his dark eyes shining like polished jet. "Ever since that first summer in France, I've been fascinated by the method of making champagne. Father wouldn't hear of it—too expensive and time-consuming, too tricky." He paused. "You know, I almost believe in destiny, though. The Benedictine abbey of Hautvillers, where Grandfather bought the doors, is the place where the monk Dom Pérignon changed the methods of wine-making by producing a sparkling wine—champagne—back in the seventeenth century.''

Matt rubbed his hand lovingly over the satin finish of the oak door, and when he spoke his voice was low, as though he was speaking to himself. ''I'm going to make champagne, Texas champagne, from the cuttings of the original vines Dom Pérignon pruned and cared for. Wine from grapes with a pedigree as royal as any dynasty in Europe.''

Matt grabbed the crude iron handles and gave the doors a yank. They glided open with a bare whisper of sound.

The cold was more intense, yet not uncomfortable, and a wonderful smell wafted over them, one Ginny couldn't identify. She inhaled again as did Austin. It was an exciting fragrance, yet she still couldn't put her finger on it. But she did know one thing—once inhaled, it was a scent she would never forget. And whenever she smelled it, this fragrance would bring back memories of the cool darkness and a deep, soothing voice full of hope and dreams.

Matt flicked on a main switch, and the pale illumination of low-wattage electrical lights guided their steps down a gentle, descending slope. After a long walk the ground leveled out. He could use any of the flashlights that were hanging along the path, but Matt thought this was a treat for the first visit. Suddenly he sensed Austin's uneasiness and explained, ''The light won't damage the wine that's aging in those oak casks, but it might damage the wine that's stored in those bottles.'' He pointed to an area lined from floor to ceiling with dark glass bottles.

Ginny and Austin gazed around in awe.

The place was huge, cavernous. Dark, dry and cold. Ginny turned around in awe, unable to speak she was so stunned by the place. On one side stood a long line of huge oak casks, each about the size of a car, dark and shiny with age. Farther down she could see rows of smaller oak casks, stacked one on top of the other, four casks high. On the other side was rack after rack of bottles lying on their sides in neat pockets.

"We're in a cave, Ginny." Austin whispered reverently. "We walked down into a cavern."

"You're right, son, a limestone cave older than man."

"Uncle Jason told me there were ancient cave drawings somewhere on the property, that you knew where they were but had never told anyone. Are they in here, Da— Matt?"

"No," Matt lied, and turned back. "Come on, you two. Without a jacket you shouldn't stay in here very long. The cold can get to you."

After the cool darkness, the heat and dazzling sunlight came as a shock. It took a moment for them to get oriented and catch their breath. Ginny watched Matt walk away and glanced at Austin. For a moment she caught the hurt look in his eyes before he replaced it with anger.

"Uncle Jason wouldn't lie to me."

"Maybe the cave's dangerous, and your father doesn't want you to go exploring by yourself." They were far enough away from Matt that he couldn't hear.

"I have to see it," Austin said stubbornly.

She noticed Matt had stopped walking and was watching them. "Well, talk to him, Austin. Nicely, for heaven's sake."

"You mean butter him up? No thanks."

Matt pointed out a stone building not far from the entrance to the cellar. "That's where we bring in the grapes from the fields, extract their juices and begin the process of fermentation, blending, bottling and corking. The first draw of the wine, what I consider the finest, is syphoned off into the oak casks, then transferred and stored in the cellar to age. The rest of the wine is bottled and stored until it's labeled and shipped out."

Ginny would have commented, but another building caught her eye. A long narrow building built of the same stone as the house, which she now realized was native to the area. One side was screened in, and she could barely distinguish through the screen the long trestle tables, benches and fans on tall stands.

"What's that building for, Matt?"

He shrugged and wouldn't look at her or the building, as if he wanted nothing more than to ignore it. "There's the barn over there. Let's go have a look. If old Jericho's there, I'll introduce you. Do you like horses, Austin?"

"No."

"Matt," she said, "what's that building over there used for?" She gave him a sharp glance. If she hadn't known better she'd have thought he was embarrassed.

"It's the cookhouse," he said quickly, then stopped and looked at her. "Where you'll be cooking the noon meals for the hands."

She thought she'd misunderstood him at first. "What?"

"I'm paying for the men to take their meals in town. Since you need a job and can cook..." He left the rest of the sentence hanging on the morning breeze.

The blood drained from her head. She wanted to laugh and protest at the same time. She was no chef. Oh, she had several dinner specialties, William's recipes, and she knew her way around a kitchen, but she wasn't used to cooking for a crowd.

She felt compelled to ask, "How many men?" then wished she hadn't when she watched the slow smile form on his lips.

"Including Austin and myself—seven, maybe eight."

She staggered and grabbed Austin's shoulder. "Did he say eight?"

Austin was laughing at her antics, sure she was joking. "Or maybe just seven."

"Oh, Lord help us. You're teasing me, aren't you, Matt?"

He shook his head, afraid to speak lest he start to laugh. Her look of panic was priceless. But he knew one thing—Ginny Carney was not a quitter. He was waiting to see how she'd handle the situation.

"Is there a problem?" he asked. "You're a great cook. Besides, the men aren't picky. They just want a good wholesome meal once a day."

She straightened her shoulders and told herself she'd faced worse. "Once a day? Just the noon meal?"

"Right."

Ginny gave him a weak smile. "When do I start?"

"How does tomorrow sound? Why don't you go take a look around and familiarize yourself with the place while I check on something in the barn. I think you'll find it pretty well stocked. Take an inventory of anything you need and I'll send one of the men with the truck to pick it up."

"Truck?" She stood still long after he asked Austin if he wanted to come to the barn and long after the child refused. She watched Matt disappear around the corner of the cookhouse.

"Ginny." Austin pulled on her arm to get her attention. "Is something wrong?"

"Yes," she breathed. "I've never cooked for that many people. The most I've ever cooked for was five, and William actually did the cooking. I just helped."

"But it couldn't be difficult, could it?" he asked. "It's just bigger quantities—right?"

The child was beginning to sound like his father, and it was damn irritating. "Let's go take a look."

She almost fainted when she entered the narrow kitchen. Everything looked so institutional—all gleaming stainless steel and white tile. A set of double steel doors was the first thing she opened, and was immediately engulfed in an icy cloud from the walk-in freezer.

She quickly slammed the door, stunned by the racks of packaged meat and other frozen foods. Then she glanced down the long counter. There were two sets of double sinks separated by a wide chopping block, obviously meant to allow room for two people to work. The thought of help was a relief.

Everything was so big—the blender, food processor, can opener. The overhead cabinets with glass fronts revealed plain white plates, saucers, bowls, cups and large glasses. The cabinets below held oversize pots and pans and baking dishes.

On the opposite side of the room was a double refrigerator with glass doors, a dishwasher, a commercial stove with eight burners, a microwave oven and an additional built-in oven in an alcove with two deep fryers. This kitchen was set up to feed fifty.

Ginny leaned against the counter and closed her eyes. She couldn't picture herself cooking for a bunch of men. Then she laughed aloud. She was an attorney, a damn good one, and in the past four years she'd been a typist and a waitress and a store clerk. She could do any damn thing she set her mind to. Feeding eight men would be a piece of cake.

Austin was staring at her, trying to figure out why she was acting so strangely. He was afraid she was going to leave. "I'll help."

Wrapped in her own misery, she'd forgotten about the child. "And I accept your offer." He seemed so pleased with her answer that she forced herself to smile. "I hope you know how to peel potatoes?"

"Yep."

Ginny only half listened to Austin's chatter as she made a more thorough search of the kitchen, noting the big plastic containers of sugar, flour and cornmeal. When she came across what looked like a three-ring binder, she almost set it aside, then absently opened it.

"Austin," she shouted, "we're saved! Look, recipes. Large-quantity recipes." She hugged the book to her chest, then set it on the counter as Austin pulled a step stool over to stand on.

Ginny thumbed through it, then found a notepad to make a list. "Talk about fat city. Just about everything's fried and swimming in grease or butter. People shouldn't eat like this. We need vegetables and fruit, Austin."

"Probably lots of onions, too." Suddenly Austin wasn't so sure. "You know, Ginny, these men are laborers. They sweat. Maybe they need all that heavy food, the fat and protein, as well as the carbohy-drates."

"Absolutely not," she said.

As they talked and laughed, neither noticed the pale eyes that watched them from the porch steps of the cookhouse. It wasn't until Austin gave Ginny a high five that Dog growled, surprising both of them.

"God, where did he come from?" She motioned for Austin to stay still and eased toward the screen door, making sure it was latched. The animal showed all its sharp wet teeth, its weird eyes gleaming with strange lights as he stared at her.

"It's you, Ginny. He's after you."

"Thank you, Austin. That makes me feel so se-cure."

Austin laughed. "You know, the more I think of it... He was close to you when you were knocked out down by the river. Maybe he was the first to find you and thinks we robbed him of his meal."

"You're so reassuring, Austin, alleviating all my fears."

In a flash, Dog disappeared, and few seconds later Matt came through the door. He seemed to be the only person Dog was scared of. Or maybe, Ginny thought, it was the presence of the older man behind Matt that had frightened Dog.

"Ginny, this is Jericho Jones." Matt stepped aside so she could get a good look at the tall, thin old man. "Jericho stays pretty close to the place. So if you need anything and I'm not around, give the bell out on the porch three pulls, and Jericho will show up. That goes for the bell at the house, too, but give it two pulls."

Jericho Jones doffed his beat-up and sweat-stained Stetson, then held it to his chest. "Mornin', ma'am."

Ginny returned the smile, wondering why the man's wide row of gleaming white teeth beneath the thick gray moustache reminded her of Dog. His voice was polite, gentle, but there was a sharp glint in his rheumy blue eyes that belied his age and gentlemanly tone. She doubted that he was a man who missed much.

GINNY LAY in bed, her arms behind her head, listening to Matt's light snoring from the master suite. She'd insisted on changing rooms, even though to use the bathroom she'd have to travel through his domain.

Soon after the inspection of the cookhouse, Matt had disappeared and she'd spent the day with Austin. He was an exhausting child, so intelligent and full of emotions he hadn't yet got a handle on. She was worried about him. He didn't play except at his computer, and even then he didn't play games but rode the Internet wave, as he called it.

Matt worried her, too. He seemed to have a perverse sense of humor and took entirely too much pleasure in getting her to lose her cool. For the past four years she'd managed to hold all her emotions in check. Deep-sixed them till she was numb. But now she was starting to feel again, her responses instinctive, instead of calculated, and she wasn't sure whether or not that was a good thing.

In the past few days, her thoughts had turned more and more to William and Beth, bittersweet memories lingering in her mind. At night she would awaken with a jolt and sit straight up in bed, still hearing the sound of the explosion.

She sat up now and reached for the glass of water on the night table, only to find it empty. She would have to slip through Matt's room to refill it in the bathroom.

Ginny eased the adjoining door open and tiptoed around the foot of his bed.

"Having problems sleeping, Red?"

His voice nailed her to the spot. At the use of the nickname her muscles tightened, but she'd made up her mind that he wasn't going to rile her with it again. "Just thirsty." She felt her way around in the darkness, aimed for the bathroom doorway and fumbled for the light switch.

Matt waited until she was on her way back across the room before he turned on the lamp beside the bed. "What's the matter? Worried about starting your job tomorrow?"

"No, and you can stop needling me about it. I'll make out."

"Yeah, but what about my men?" Matt grinned and rubbed at his sandpaper-rough chin.

Ginny had her own way to get back at him, and she moved to his bed and sat on the edge of the mattress. "What're you going to do about Austin, Matt? About his schooling? He's worried that you're going to send him to the local school, and he's far too advanced for that."

She'd ruined his mood and he frowned. "Listen, he's ten years old, and in California he was going to be a senior in high school. Hell, here he'll be in college. How am I going to cope with that? The only thing I'd even consider is the University of Texas, and I haven't heard from them yet."

Her surprise at his answer must have shown. "You mean you've checked it out? And you haven't talked with Austin about it yet?"

"Red, what if they take him—and they most likely will—he can't commute from here. It's too far. There are no buses. Where's he going to live? Who's he going to live with? I can't just dump him on anyone."

"That'll work itself out some way, but not to tell him you're even trying? Really, Matt, don't you know how worried he is?" The more she thought about it the angrier she became. "It's eating him up."

Matt didn't like being made to feel like a heel. "Hell, I thought I was doing the right thing by keeping it from the kid. I didn't want to get his hopes up."

"Well, maybe. But if the university doesn't take him, what are you going to do?"

It was too late, or too early, for those kinds of decisions. Matt noticed that she was still wearing his shirt to sleep in. Something in his mind clicked, and he acted on pure hormonal instinct. Reaching out, he grasped her shoulders and pulled her toward him. The scent of gardenias clung to her warm skin, and before his mouth covered hers he inhaled deeply of her sweetness.

She saw it coming but was too surprised to react and could only watch his face drawing closer, his lips parted. She knew what to expect and braced herself for his anger at being rebuffed. Over the past four years she'd fended off many advances, and she'd learned never to struggle or fight. Instead, she knew to go cold, lips squeezed tightly together, eyes wide open. Passion cooled very quickly on unresponsive lips.

But something was horribly wrong here. Her lips were suddenly on fire, her mouth soft, accepting and responding, taking his kiss with a hunger that seemed bottomless.

They jerked away from each other, alarmed and astonished. "I can't..." Her head was reeling. How could she be unfaithful to William? What was the matter with her?

"God, I'm sorry," Matt said. "I don't know where that came from. Some knee-jerk reaction to having a sexy half-naked woman in my bed so early in the morning. I didn't mean a damn thing by it."

After a moment, his words sank in. Ginny was relieved. It was just one of those silly things that happen. "Maybe I should move to one of the rooms across the hall. Just so this sort of thing won't ever, ever happen again."

"First thing tomorrow," he promised. "I'll get some of the men to help move the bed."

"Good." She got up and straightened the covers where she'd been sitting. "It didn't mean anything, right?"

"No. No, of course not."

She was at the door when she looked back at him over her shoulder. "I'd like to start running again. Is there a smooth surface around here, somewhere besides the highway?"

Matt reached for the lamp. "Sure. The drive. It's two miles to the front gate and two miles back. All nice and even." He turned out the light.

Ginny crawled into her bed, feeling empty and alone—and guilty.

CHAPTER SEVEN

GINNY SAT on the stone fence, finishing her coffee,
hypnotized by the way the dawn sky lightened to lilac,
then segued from a brilliant red into orange and finally
yellow.

Hopping off the fence, she started her stretching ex-
ercises, absently working the stiff muscles. It was a
beautiful, clear, cool morning. So perfect it should have
made her feel wonderful, but there were nagging darts
of guilt pricking at her conscience, heating her cheeks
whenever she thought of what had happened. How
could she have kissed Matt like that? she wondered. She
yelped in pain as she pulled too hard on her foot and
overextended her thigh muscles.

She had seen it coming, recognized the stillness in his
expression, the way his lips parted and the look in his
eyes. She'd known he was going to kiss her before he'd
ever touched her shoulders, so why hadn't she pulled
away? God, she'd been an open invitation, sitting down
on the edge of the bed dressed as she was. Why had she
allowed it to happen?

No great voice of wisdom answered her question.
Disgusted with herself, Ginny set off down the long
driveway. Maybe she could outrun her guilt and anger.
She started off slowly, walking, then increased her pace
until she'd worked up to a moderate jog. But as much
as she tried not to think about Matt's kiss, the more it

persisted in replaying itself in her mind, and she found herself running faster.

Her wild spurt of energy played out quickly, and she was forced to slow down to catch her breath. There just was no answer, she concluded, or at least not one she was willing to face. As she picked up the pace again, a movement off the side of the driveway caught her eye. For a moment she lost her rhythm and stumbled, then slowed. Dog, running along the edge of the vineyard, slowed his pace, also.

She didn't know what to do. Stop? Walk slower? Turn around and go back to the house for help? She eyed him, realizing he was matching her step for step again. Ginny ran a little faster. Dog did the same.

She laughed.

The damn animal was enjoying himself. His tongue hung out one side of his mouth, his shaggy tail was pointing to the sky. His gate was smooth and long, punctuated occasionally with a happy bounce. She'd never been around animals, never had pets, and reminded herself not to lose sight of the fact that this animal was vicious looking. Ah, poor Dog. She'd condemned him on looks and smell alone.

Ginny decided to continue her run but kept a watchful eye on her jogging companion. She was surprised when she reached the front gate and turned for the return trip. Dog barked a couple of times at the closed iron gate, then headed back with her. The damn animal had managed to take her mind off her problems. She was actually enjoying the morning.

It was Dog who alerted her to the fact that she was almost to the house and that Matt and the old man, Jericho, were waiting. Her pace slowed until she was walking toward them. Dog had disappeared and she suddenly wished she'd gone with him.

It wasn't going to be easy to face Matt, and she braced herself for the expected humiliation and formulated an apology in her mind. But it was the old man who diverted her attention as she approached. Something was different about him. As she continued to look at him, he turned his back to her, then quickly turned around again.

Ginny had to bite hard on her lip to keep a straight face. He'd looked peculiar because he didn't have any teeth, but when he swung back around to face her, he gave her a big white-toothed smile.

"I see you've made a friend out of that fleabag. He don't take to most."

"Does he have fleas?" The mere suggestion made her scratch her head.

"Naw, too mean for fleas to bite him. He'd bite back." That struck him as funny and he started to laugh.

"I was just telling Jericho to keep the front gate locked," Matt said.

"Ain't never been locked before," the old man responded as he pulled a plug of tobacco out of his pocket and with a tiny pocket knife cut off a sliver and slipped it between his lip and gum.

Ginny had never in her life seen anyone chew tobacco.

Matt watched the two of them. The old man knew he was the center of attention and played it to the hilt, exaggerating each move. When he slipped the tobacco in his mouth and her eyes widened, his lips twitched in amusement. "The gate stays locked," Matt said. "I'll give keys to the men."

Jericho eyed Ginny. "Ain't never been any locked doors around here."

"There's a woman and child on the place," Matt explained. "Times change, Jericho. The world's changed and it's not safe anymore. Locked doors are just a precaution."

"Ain't nothin' changed round here, 'cept your pa's six feet under and you're back."

Matt knew from long experience that the old man would only do as he wanted to, and he didn't like the way Ginny was grinning and enjoying herself. "Keep the gate locked, Jericho. That's an order."

"Only one to watch out for is that boy of yours with his crazy hair and them spikes sproutin' out of his head." He made a sound of disgust and walked away, slipping his false teeth into his shirt pocket once more. "Damn things," he mumbled. "More trouble'n they're worth."

Ginny chuckled. "Did he just take out his teeth?" Her smile faded when she realized Matt was staring at her. "Listen," she began, then stopped. To hell with it. Let him make of their kiss whatever he wanted.

Matt leaned against the fence. "You going to have a meal ready for the men around noon?"

Leaning down, she picked her coffee cup off the ground where she'd left it. "I hope so. Is Austin up?"

Matt laughed. "Are you kidding? I finally made him go to bed around two this morning. He was reading for entertainment—about Alexander the Great." Matt shook his head. "When I was ten, I thought comics were the only things kids read."

Since he seemed in a talkative mood, she decided to ask a few questions that had been bothering her. "Tell me something. What happened to all the furniture in the house? Most of the rooms are empty."

"Dad left most of it to Delta in his will. But that was just the stuff she'd bought since they married. All the old furniture is stashed in the attic."

"I take it Delta is your stepmother?"

Matt's laugh was self-mocking. "Right."

"Dammit, Matt. Getting information out of you is like pulling teeth." She didn't like the way he was looking at her. "It's for Austin's sake that I'm asking."

He shrugged. "If Austin wants to know, why doesn't he ask me?"

"You're joking! Just look at yourself. The minute you even think about the past you get that thunderous scowl on your face and snap at anyone around."

"What do you want to know?" he growled, then grinned and said it again.

"I don't understand the setup with Jason, and where is his mother? Why isn't she here? If this was Jason's home, where does he stay now? And—"

Matt held up his hands in surrender. "Stop. I give up."

She was so serious and earnest he wanted to laugh. One thing that being shot and nearly dying had taught him was that life was too short to dwell on problems from the past, but she seemed determined to drag out the whole sorry mess. He had to admit he liked the way she expressed herself, standing there in her cutoffs and one of the T-shirts he'd given her. Her fists were jammed on her hips, forcing the shirt to stretch provocatively across her chest, and her long legs glistened with a sheen of perspiration in the morning sun. He cocked his head to one side, enjoying the way the breeze played with her hair and the movement of her full lips as she talked.

It took the sound of his name to draw him out of his thoughts. "Jason has an expensive house in Austin. He has his own business, several businesses, in fact, and is quite wealthy. You don't have to worry about him, even though he likes to say he was kicked out of his own home. The land, the house, the vineyard and some other interests were left to me. Jason has a share in the profits from the wine, but no hold on the land or anything else."

"But I thought you and your father hated each other? Why...?"

Matt finished for her. "Why would he leave it all to me? Old World tradition—the firstborn son receives everything. Neither Grandfather nor Father would've gone against anything in the will of old Joseph Van der Bollen, my great-great-grandfather, who came to Texas in 1834. Of course, I didn't know that until the lawyer explained it all to me."

Ginny could tell she'd gotten as much information as she was going to get for a while, but she found it all fascinating and wanted to know more about these Van der Bollens.

"Does that satisfy some of *your* curiosity?"

She was going to correct him, then thought better of it. After all, she didn't know if Austin cared about his past or not. "Yes. No. One more question," she said. "Why'd you change your name?"

Matt pushed away from the fence and worked his sore leg, rubbing his thigh as he moved. "Because I hate it."

Well, she thought, that was a definite end to her questions. "I guess I'll get some breakfast and a shower, then go over to the cookhouse and get started."

Matt watched as she started up the walk to the house and couldn't resist calling, "Hey, Red, you ever get back to sleep this morning?"

The question seemed sincerely asked, and before she knew what she was doing, she said, "No. Did you?"

"Slept like a baby."

She was at a total loss as to what to say and raised her voice in exasperation. "Don't call me Red."

"Sure. Let me ask you something else, though." She stopped again, turned and glared at him. "If I were a frog, would you kiss me like you did this morning and turn me into a prince?"

"Not likely!" she snapped, then spun around and headed toward the house.

"Didn't think so, Red," he said barely loud enough for her to hear, then grinned when he saw the way her back straightened. He strolled away singing a snip of an old song his mother used to sing to him: "A frog he would a wooing go, heigh-ho, heigh-ho..." He couldn't think of any more, but as he glanced over his shoulder and saw Ginny standing at the kitchen door, her stance vibrating with anger, he realized it was enough.

GINNY WAS PERCHED on a stool in the cookhouse kitchen, flipping through a two-year-old *Field and Stream* magazine, a smug smile on her lips. This wasn't going to be as hard as she'd imagined. Ten-thirty and she had everything just about ready. All that was left was cooking the meat and preparing the fresh vegetables. She couldn't wait until she saw the look on Matt's face.

"Hey, Ginny." Austin peered in through the screen at the back porch. "Need some help?"

Ginny motioned him in, pulled up another stool and patted the seat. She tried to ignore his new hairstyle—his spiked hair stuck out in all directions in stiff points, the tips sprayed bright orange. She bit her lip to keep from saying anything, but it didn't help.

"That's interesting," she murmured.

"You think so?" He touched the tips of the spikes. "I wore normal clothes today."

She shook her head. He went from one extreme to another. This morning his attire was normal enough for a nerd. His jeans were pulled up high and held in place with a belt. He'd tucked in the plain white shirt, buttoned it to the throat and had on a bow tie. The contradiction between the hairstyle and his clothes made her wince.

"This is going to do it, Ginny. He's going to lose his cool today."

"You're playing with fire."

"You don't think it'll work?"

"No. I think it will only serve to make you look foolish."

"Aw, Ginny, you're no fun."

"Why do you do it, Austin?"

"I've analyzed my motives, you know."

"And what's your conclusion?" His clinical tone astounded her. Then she remembered he was considered a child prodigy.

"I've concluded my being here is poetic justice. Since he ignored my existence for ten years, I'll just keep reminding him of what he missed every hour of every day. He didn't want me when I was born, and he doesn't want me now. But he's stuck with me."

Austin made a show of straightening his bow tie. "Also, I figure my behavior is based on the rather childish reasoning that if I make him angry, really angry, he'll send me back to Peter or away to school. Either way, he'll be rid of me and I'll get what I want."

Ginny swallowed. How did you reason with someone whose IQ was higher than yours? She was at a loss. "Want to help clean the broccoli?"

"Sure." Then he glanced around the kitchen and frowned. "You haven't started yet?"

Ginny grinned and waved her hand like a magic wand. "Finished. Or almost."

"Really. You're good," he said. "What are you fixing?" She told him and he approved, his mouth watering. "Can I eat lunch here, too?"

"Of course." She glanced at the clock on the wall, jumped off the stool and went to gather her ingredients from the refrigerator. She put Austin to work filling the two-gallon automatic tea maker, setting the table in the other room and filling the oversize glasses with ice.

The smell of food cooking permeated the cookhouse and floated out on the breeze. Dog inched a few feet closer, his gaze fixed on Ginny through the screen. Jericho sniffed the air. His growling stomach told him it was time to eat, and he walked away from his work, leaving his tools lying where he dropped them. He wasn't going to wait for the dinner bell and let the younger men get ahead of him in line. Memories of home cooking made his stride a little longer and faster. He was halfway up the walk when Matt met him.

"Smells good," Jericho ventured, and rubbed his hands together in anticipation.

"Does at that." They were standing at the washbasins off to the side of the porch, scrubbing their hands and faces, when Austin rang the dinner bell. Matt smiled as Jericho grabbed the towel from the hook, dried his hands and face, then disappeared through the doorway. By the time Matt was ready to go in, there were five men standing at the basins cleaning up.

"Take a look and see how many plates to fix, Austin," Ginny said. When he told her seven she set to work fast. They'd found a big foldout cart at the back of the pantry and cleaned it. Now Ginny carefully arranged the food on the plates and passed them to Austin to place on the cart. All seven plates were filled, and she grasped Austin's arm before he wheeled the cart in, double-checking to make sure she hadn't forgotten anything.

"Salad plates are on the table?"

"Check." Austin said.

"Salad on the table? Iced-tea glasses full?"

"Check and check."

"Rolls are in the baskets on the table?"

"Check again. Ginny, everything's ready." He started to wheel the cart out when he stopped and cocked his head.

"What's the matter?" Ginny demanded. "What'd I forget?"

"Jason just walked in. Quick, fill another plate."

In a matter of seconds Ginny had prepared a plate for Jason. She watched as Austin and the cart disappeared through the swinging double doors. Immediately she sat down on the stool and let out a long breath. She hadn't wanted to admit it, but she was nervous.

Once again she mentally reviewed her menu. Boneless, skinless chicken breasts, pounded thin and panbrowned, were smothered with a marinara sauce to simmer, then topped with a thick slice of provolone cheese and set under the broiler to brown. William had taught her about contrasting textures and artful presentation. She had chosen a mixture of long-grain and wild rice for a nutty flavor, steamed but still crunchy broccoli and hot rolls. Then, for a refreshing finale, instead of dessert she'd made a fresh-fruit compote.

She'd cooked a healthy and nutritious meal and watched with satisfaction as Austin, who'd remained in the kitchen, cleaned his plate. Glancing around, she noticed what a mess the kitchen was. The thought of cleaning it was daunting.

"There's more broccoli," she said to the boy.

"No, thanks."

"You might need your strength when you get through helping me clean this place up." Austin glanced at her, then looked away, seemingly distracted by the talk in the other room. He'd been acting strangely since he'd returned from serving the meal. "Is something wrong, Austin? You could have eaten with the men if you'd wanted to."

The sound of raised voices and chairs scraping against the floor, signs of a mass exodus, caused Austin's head to pop up like a jumping jack. He started talking fast and a little too loudly.

Ginny frowned and waved him to be quiet. It didn't take but a moment for her to realize that the men were grumbling about her healthy food and the fact that there wasn't enough to fill a baby's stomach. Her shoulders slumped, then she angrily grabbed the pot of cold broccoli and pushed open the screen door. She intended to throw pot and all off the back porch when she realized she was losing control and sat down on the top step, the pot between her legs.

Absently she picked out a limp stalk and threw it to Dog, who was sitting at the edge of the shadow from the building. He snapped the tidbit up as if it were steak and ventured a step closer to receive another, which he neatly caught before it hit the ground.

Austin joined Ginny on the porch. "I didn't want to tell you how they turned up their noses at the food. All except Matt and Uncle Jason."

Ginny twirled a stalk of broccoli between her fingers, then pitched it to Dog, who was now only a few feet away. Failure sat heavily on her shoulders. She wanted to apologize but couldn't bring herself to do it. The barbarians just didn't have any taste, she told herself.

Bunch of field hands. Their idea of good nutrition was probably barbecue chicken instead of fried, beans swimming in pork fat instead of vegetables. What did they know about what was good for them?

Austin eyed the animal. "That dog is eating broccoli!"

"Well, what do you expect? The animal's got taste. Go get the leftover chicken and rice, Austin. That dog's going to get a healthy meal."

Austin, hesitant to approach Dog, let Ginny place the bowl on the ground. They watched in amazement as the mutt ate his fill, then sat licking his chops before he stretched out at the foot of the steps, his teeth gleaming at them in that strange smile of his.

"He smells awful," Ginny said. She stood up and held the door open for Austin. "Come on, you can help me clean up."

"Well," Austin hedged. "Actually I have something—"

"Oh, no, you don't get to weasel out of this. Come on." She stopped as she faced Matt and Jason. "I know they didn't like my cooking," she said before Matt could say a word.

"I thought it was wonderful." Jason smiled reassuringly.

Ginny didn't realize she was staring at Matt, trying to gauge his reaction. "Well," she demanded when he just stood there. All of a sudden Matt started laughing, and Ginny grumbled that she didn't think it was funny.

"I'm sorry," Matt said when he caught his breath. "But you should have seen Billy Bob and Wayne. I'll bet they're off to the nearest McDonald's about now."

Not to be outdone, Jason said, "Roberto, Gomez and Dan are more polite. They at least made a show of eating."

"You two ate it," she said, "so how bad could it have been?"

"Yeah, but we don't have any taste," Jason teased, ignoring the warning tap on his shoulder from Matt. "Besides, I don't know of anyone who likes broccoli. And what was that fruit thing called, anyway?" His voice trailed off when he noticed that Ginny was eyeing a broom standing in the corner.

She didn't think either of them was in the least amusing, and she pushed by them, heading for the dining room. She stood at the foot of the table, a lump in her throat, looking at her ruined meal, and wanted nothing more than to sit down and cry. But it was stupid to be so upset over a meal. There was only one bright spot—one clean plate. Ginny pointed to it, not trusting her voice to speak. Stupid, she admonished herself again. She wasn't a cook, never claimed to be. She was an attorney, for heaven's sake.

Matt shot a look at Jason to silence him, but it was too late. "The clean plate is Jericho's," Jason said. "He's kinda like Dog—he'll eat anything. I've even seen him eat live worms."

That did it. Foolish tears filled her eyes and she stomped out of the cookhouse and headed for the main house. She passed Jericho on the sidewalk without a glance in his direction. She didn't know what it was that made her look up, but over the sound of Austin shouting at Jason and Matt, she thought she heard a car approaching. Blinking away the tears from her eyes, she stared, all thoughts of food and men fleeing her mind. Coming slowly up the road, directly toward her, was a police car.

Ginny stood as if rooted to the spot. She felt cold with fear, even as the sun beat down on her. She didn't see Matt or Austin move to stand beside her, but watched the car, noticing by the marking on the side that it was a sheriff's vehicle. She didn't feel Matt's steadying arm around her shoulders. She didn't hear his whispered words or realize that Austin had slipped his hand into hers and was squeezing it tightly.

She was too numb to notice the way Jason and Jericho watched, puzzled and curious by her strange behavior and the even stranger behavior of Matt and Austin. She was unaware of the gleam in Jason's eyes and the thoughtful narrowing of Jericho's gaze.

As she watched, the car came to a stop. A tall man struggled to get out, then reached back in the open door, fetched his Stetson and placed it firmly on his head. Suddenly he was moving with a long easy stride toward them. Ginny felt her heart drop to her toes. Even beneath the brim of his hat she could see the assessing look he gave her. Just as quickly his attention turned to Matt.

Matt stuck out his hand and smiled. "What brings you out this way, Argus?"

"Got some trouble with the federal boys, Matt. Seems they lost two of their agents in that accident over on the interstate, and they've managed to misplace some woman they were transporting to boot." He laughed and Matt grinned. "Can you beat it? They're looking for some gal named Patricia Bright. Mad as wet hens that she's up and run off on them." He looked at Ginny. "Excuse me, ma'am, I've forgotten my manners." He stuck out his hand. "I'm Sheriff Argus Gillespie."

The congenial, easygoing, good-old-boy facade didn't wash. This man was as sharp as they come. His hazel eyes hadn't missed a thing. She figured he was forty-five, maybe fifty. It was hard to tell. He was a big man, easily six foot five inches. And every inch was muscle. She didn't hesitate to return his handshake. "Ginny Carney. Nice to meet you."

"Ginny's an old friend from Houston, Argus. Ginny, Argus is our local sheriff." He could feel Ginny trembling slightly and admired her nerve. "You still haven't told me what brings you out this way, Argus."

"Well, you know these federal boys, Matt—you worked with them. They haven't bothered me much— yet. Just questions and interruptions. But I don't like the way they do things. A little too big for their boots— kind of sticks in your craw. Anyway, word's around town that all of a sudden you have a strange woman on the place, so I had to check it out." He tipped his hat to Ginny. "Can't be too careful, ma'am, you understand?"

"Yes." Ginny thought she was going to faint.

"But since Matt here says you're an old friend from Houston, that's the end of it, I guess. Right, ma'am?"

Ginny realized he'd asked her a question and quickly nodded in agreement. She gazed directly and unflinchingly into those shadowy hazel eyes and knew he didn't quite believe her, even with Matt lying to protect her. For the first time in days, all her fears came crashing down on her.

"If you'll excuse me," she said. "I have things to do. Austin, so do you. Goodbye, Sheriff."

She didn't give the boy time to answer her, but took a firmer hold on his hand and half dragged him to the house. When the door was firmly closed behind them, she collapsed into the nearest chair. "I think I'm going to faint."

But she didn't. Her brain was too busy. What was there for her to do? Run? She couldn't face that prospect again. Besides, she'd never find another setup like this one, and just the thought of leaving caused a stab of pain.

The realization struck her then. She'd done the unthinkable.

She'd allowed herself to care again.

CHAPTER EIGHT

"DO YOU THINK he's suspicious, Ginny?" Austin asked.

She looked pale, and he was scared she might indeed faint. In desperation he picked up a magazine and began furiously fanning her. "Are you going to do something gross, like throw up?"

"No," she mumbled. But she did feel sick. Sick at heart. The realization that she'd somehow dropped her guard, broken her vow to herself, that she cared about Matt and Austin, came as a horrible shock. When had this happened? Why hadn't she seen it coming? Dear God, hadn't she been through enough?

There were no answers, and Ginny knew she could wrestle with the problem all day and still draw a blank. However, she did know she could remedy the situation. She could put a stop to it.

Ginny pushed the hair from her eyes and smiled weakly at Austin. "I'm okay."

But Austin wasn't paying attention. He'd moved to her side, blocking her view of the door. After a moment she realized why. The old man, Jericho Jones, was standing there watching them. She got quickly to her feet and crossed to the door. "What can I do for you, Mr. Jones?"

"Jericho, please, ma'am."

"And please call me Ginny. Ma'am makes me feel so old." She watched in fascination as he smiled, the glare of his false teeth almost blinding. Surely someone had told him they didn't look real?

"Yes'm. But I just dropped by to let you know that those boys don't have no taste. It was a fine meal. Look forward to tomorrow." He touched the brim of his Stetson and started to leave, then stopped. "I'm real partial to fried chicken and mashed potatoes, though." He turned to leave once more, then changed his mind. "Young Argus is a good man to know."

Ginny and Austin watched him walk down the sidewalk in silence, then they turned and gazed at each other.

"What was the cryptic remark about the sheriff for?" Austin asked.

"I haven't the foggiest idea. Do you think he noticed I was about to drop dead with fright?"

"No telling about Jericho. He doesn't like me much, and I think he's as strange as that dog of his." Austin eyed Dog as the animal made himself comfortable on the porch, and wondered why he hadn't followed the old man. He directed a smile the animal's way and received a flash of sharp teeth in return. Austin couldn't suppress the shiver that slithered up his spine.

"He gives me the creeps, Ginny."

She was still mulling over Jericho's departing statement and didn't hear him. "I can't believe I lost my cool like that in front of the sheriff," she said.

Matt heard her as he opened the door. "I thought you did all right, and once I filled Argus in on the noon meal fiasco and how upset you were with the men hardly eating anything, it explained a lot about the way you were acting. But you're going to have to get used to seeing him, Ginny. Two of the hands, Billy Bob and Wayne, are his sons. He likes to drop by unexpectedly and check up on them. He also has a key to the gate, so keep your guard up.''

"Then you don't think he suspects anything?"

"Oh, he's curious—that's his nature." He didn't tell her that Argus had asked him to keep his eyes open for anything unusual, that the escapee might be hiding out somewhere nearby. "The problem is the FBI hasn't told Argus or anyone else that the woman they're searching for is not a criminal. The very fact that they're being so closemouthed has placed you in a rather dangerous position."

Ginny gave him a wry grin. "Maybe they just want to be rid of me."

"That's not funny." The idea had crossed his mind, too. If the FBI had screwed up as badly as he thought, her statement might not be too far from the truth. He knew from experience how great officials were at covering their butts. In Ginny's case, the government agency seemed to have bungled the job from the beginning.

Two innocent people had died, then they'd placed their prime witness in a program full of problems. Now their witness was loose and just might talk. If the truth became known, there'd be a full-scale investigation, and he suspected heads would roll.

Matt decided Ginny had a right to know what was bothering him, but he didn't want his son to hear. "Austin, have you done that research I asked for?"

"No." The boy suddenly turned sullen.

"Why?" Matt asked. "I thought you could find anything about anything on that computer of yours."

"Not the computer—that's just the hardware. It's the Internet. And I *can* find out anything you want to know."

"Well, obviously not, because you haven't yet."

Austin left the room in a snit and stomped up the stairs. Matt waited until he was sure Mr. Big Ears hadn't crept back down. "I wanted to tell you—"

"What was that all about? He didn't fall for that trick. He knows very well you just wanted him out of the room."

"Look, I have enough problems right now without worrying what he thinks. I'm trying to—"

"Well, you should."

He could see she wasn't going to let the matter go without an explanation. "When we went to pick up the groceries the other day, I made an offhand remark that I was going to have to trade my old Mercedes in for a truck if I had to continue to haul stuff around, but I said I couldn't make up my mind what I wanted. Hell, we were actually getting along, and he offered to do some research and find the best model and price. You know, I have this strange quirk—when someone tells me they'll do something, I expect them to do it."

Matt pulled out a chair, turned it around and straddled it. Crossing his arms over the back, he gazed at Ginny. "Besides, I wanted him gone so I could talk to you."

"If it's about the meal, I'm sorry. I'll do better tomorrow." She started to get up. "And I have to go clean up the mess."

Matt waved her to be seated. "Lupe, Roberto's wife, will be cleaning everything up. You don't have to worry about that. Personally I thought the meal was great, but it's not the sort of food men who do manual labor in the hot sun need. Take a look at the recipe notebook that's there and come up with something better." He'd been sidetracked again.

"Be careful," he warned, getting straight to the point. "Your disappearance has put a lot of people on alert. We don't know how far up in the FBI your file has gone or who's privy to the circumstances of your case. If it's only known on a low level to a few people, you might be in real trouble."

"I don't understand."

"There are always rogue agents willing to cover their mistakes by eliminating the problem."

"Do you mean to sit there and tell me I could be in danger from my own government? Well, isn't this a pretty mess I've gotten myself into."

Matt couldn't help it. She looked so outraged he laughed. "It's not that bad, but I'll tell you this. If Argus says he's having more trouble with those agents, then I'm going to fill him in and tell him your story." He wanted to laugh again, but didn't, as that look of outrage was directed at him. "No, listen to me before you fly off the handle.

"Argus is a good man and this is a small town. I don't think in the years I've been away that things have changed much. People kinda take care of each other here. Argus's father used to be sheriff, and he pulled my butt out of the fire so many times I can't even remember them all. Argus became a good friend until I ran away, and we've managed to keep in contact over the years.

"What I'm trying to tell you is that once I've told him about you, I can persuade him to help."

Ginny shook her head. She'd been on her own far too long and she didn't trust anyone. She was only now learning to trust Matt.

"Ginny, I swear I can protect you. We'll figure out something to get you free of the FBI and make sure you're not at risk from your stepfather."

The mention of her stepfather was like a dash of icy water in the face. "He destroyed me, Matt. Took everything I hold dear—my husband and daughter, my home, my life, my career. He turned my mother against me, and I was never able to talk to her again. She died last year."

"Don't let him take anything else from you, Ginny. Start taking back. If you have to, fight. You have a right."

"Do you understand the hell my life has been? I've had four different identities, lived in four different states and worked at jobs I wasn't trained for. I was always looking over my shoulder, waiting for death to catch up with me." She paused to take a deep breath. "And do you know where Tony is, what he's doing?"

"Prison."

"Oh, yes," she said sarcastically. "I did some research and found out he was sent to sunny California. Get this. He's in one of those federal country-club prisons for white-collar criminals. He plays tennis and basketball, for god's sake. He works in the library. He reads, watches television, and the government feeds him three good meals a day. That's his punishment, Matt, for laundering money. No matter that he had my family killed—they couldn't prove that. It's not fair."

She didn't remember standing up, nor did she know how she wound up in his arms, but the strength of them around her suddenly made her feel better. "I want my life back," she whispered against his chest. She would have said more, but she felt a change in his body and followed the direction of his gaze. The old man was standing outside the screen door, his hand raised as if he was about to knock.

"What is it, Jericho?" Matt asked, and set her aside.

"I just wanted to fetch Dog. Didn't want him bothering the lady or the boy. But he seems to have a mind of his own. Taken with the lady, I think. Wants to stick around here. That okay with you, Matt?"

"Sure, but he could use a bath when you get a chance."

Jericho laughed, showing his toothless gums this time before he covered his mouth with his hand. "Ain't likely he'd stand still for that."

They watched him leave and Ginny's eyes narrowed. She wondered how long he'd been standing there. She asked Matt the same question.

"Doesn't matter. You don't have to worry about Jericho. He's been a fixture here practically forever, of course, from time to time he gets the itch to wander. But that doesn't happen often, and when it does, everyone knows that he's gone."

She still didn't know what to think or believe. What she did know was that she missed Matt's embrace, and the realization worried her. She wiped her hands on her thighs and looked around. "I guess I need to..." She struggled to think of something to do. "Dust."

"You're not a maid, for heaven's sake. I can hire a maid."

"Then why haven't you?" She raised her voice. "The place could use a good cleaning."

"Because I didn't want some nosy female tiptoeing around all day."

"Well, what am I, then?" She knew it was a ridiculous argument, but she had to vent her frustration somehow.

Matt shot her an exasperated glance, then called out, "Austin, come down here."

Austin showed up much too soon to have been in his room the entire time. She had to hand it to the boy. If Matt had directed that angry glare at her, any resolve she felt might well have weakened a little. Eavesdropping was wrong, and she didn't like the idea that Austin knew so much about what was going on, but she realized he did it mostly to irritate his father.

Austin gave his father a fleeting glance as he dropped a stack of papers on the kitchen table. "My research shows the best truck you should buy, if that's what you want. There's the breakdown on cost and add-ons. Red's a popular color, too."

Matt's interest was kindled, and all thoughts of punishment were forgotten. "Prices include extended cab and full-size cargo bed?"

Ginny was fascinated. All the animosity between father and son was forgotten. The anger had vanished as if it had never existed. They were talking civilly to each other, and even their expressions had taken on a kind of silly rapture.

Austin looked offended. "Of course. There's also leather interior, air bags, power everything, but..."

"But what?" Matt looked up from the report he was scanning.

"There's already a truck on the place, isn't there?" Matt nodded. "Unless you plan to do a lot of hauling, you really need a four-wheel drive. Personally, for the money, I like the Jeep Cherokee."

Matt was astounded and impressed, but he shouldn't have been, knowing that Austin didn't do anything by halves. What did surprise him was his son's interest in cars, and he wondered what else they might have in common. "A Jeep, you say?"

"Yeah."

"I think there's a dealership in Fredericksburg, want to take a look with me when I go?"

Austin was trapped. He wanted desperately to go look at trucks but didn't want his father to know how excited he was. He eased into a chair and thought about it for a moment. "I think you'll get a better price in Austin. I checked some of them out."

"Fine," Matt said, realizing he was walking on quicksand with his son. "You tell me which ones have the best deals, and we'll go there and have a look."

The anticipation was too much even for Austin. He couldn't stand it any longer. "When can we go?"

"How about tomorrow morning? We'll get an early start and try to be back for the afternoon meal."

"Early start for what?" Jason asked. He'd entered the house without anyone noticing.

"Matt and I are going to look for a new truck," Austin said. "Want to come?"

"Hey, great. I know a dealership in Austin."

Ginny didn't want anything to interfere with Matt and his son, and she immediately stepped in. "More than likely they'll be gone most of the day. I might need some help. Please don't desert me, too, Jason. Say you'll be around?" Her appeal to the male ego worked like a charm—though she noticed that Matt was looking at her with a strange expression. But then all of a sudden he realized what she was doing, and his dark eyes gleamed.

Jason gave Austin a shrug and a charming smile as part of his apology. "Sorry, Buddha, maybe another time."

"Buddha?" Ginny asked.

"Sure, Buddha—the bearer of enlightenment and wisdom, all knowing, all seeing, wise beyond time— that's Austin. Right, kid?"

Oh, he was a real charmer, Ginny thought, but she couldn't decide if Jason was deliberately trying to interfere with Matt and Austin, or if he had truly wanted to be included in the outing. It was something to ponder.

SWEAT RAN DOWN the sides of her face and trickled down her neck, soaking her T-shirt. The early-morning sun was already blistering, the air almost suffocating in its stillness. She'd pushed herself too hard, pounding down the driveway as if the hounds of hell were snapping at her heels. How long had she lain awake and listened to Matt's light snoring? Had she really counted the number of times he'd turned over? The sooner she changed rooms, the better.

When she finally reached the stone fence at the house, she stopped, leaned over and grabbed her thighs. Panting like Dog, she thought, then noticed her jogging companion was in better shape then she was. But Dog had found a puddle of water, lapped it almost dry, then rolled in the cool mud. She looked at him with envy.

She'd figured out why she was having so much trouble wrestling with her attraction for Matt. She was a healthy adult. The fact that for the past four years she'd never met anyone she was the least bit interested in only made the temptation more appealing. And forbidden. She still loved William and the thought of being with another man intimately appalled her. The logical side of her argued that William was dead and that he, above all people, would want her to get on with her life. But the emotional side of her refused to listen. She would never have been unfaithful to William when he was living, and she couldn't contemplate being unfaithful to him in his death.

Ginny moaned and sat down hard on the ground, her hands gripping her bent knees. She closed her eyes and dropped her head. How could she be attracted to any man, especially Matt? He was nothing like her gentle, funny, easygoing William. It was the feel of something rough, warm and wet on her leg that forced her attention away from her misery.

She opened her eyes and became perfectly still upon finding herself almost nose to nose with Dog. She stared into his steady pale gaze, terrified, then a tongue darted out and touched her tear-damp cheek. Ginny gazed into that ugly face, those mesmerizing eyes and could have sworn he understood her torment and unhappiness. Without thinking, she grabbed his scruffy neck, buried her face in his dirty, shaggy coat and wept.

She couldn't afford to let herself be overwhelmed by her misery. Then she would have to grieve for William and Beth, and she wasn't ready to do that yet. She struggled to suppress her feelings once more.

Ginny didn't know how long she held Dog, but it was the smell of him that finally jarred her back to reality. She lifted her head to stare him in the eye. Two brown dots over his eyes twitched, his tongue hung out one side of his mouth, and his shaggy tail thumped against the ground. Ginny wrinkled her nose at him.

"You need a bath." Both ears drooped and the pink tongue disappeared. "Be at the cookhouse after lunch and we'll discuss it."

She patted Dog on the head and stood up. Her hands were dirty and she knew her face had to look worse.

Surprisingly, though, she felt much better and she jogged to the house.

Matt could tell she'd been crying and felt a tightening in his gut. "Mornin'," he said, then immediately backed away with a look of distaste at the offensive smell. "What happened to you?"

"Dog and I had a close encounter. I hugged him."

"Lucky Dog." He followed her but stopped at the bottom of the stairs. "If I go roll in something dead and rotten, would you hug me?"

"Not likely," she yelled from the top step, and quickly turned away to keep Matt from seeing her smile. That, she thought, was one of her biggest problems— Matt's teasing. She started off down the hall only to be stopped again by his voice.

"Hey, Red. Go drag Austin out of bed. Tell him if he wants to go with me, he'd better get moving."

She smiled again. There was a difference in Matt's voice lately. The gruff growl was gradually fading to a more normal pitch. And she was happy to see that he was looking forward to taking Austin with him.

Ginny changed direction, heading for the boy's room. Now her only concern was Austin. He had a way of throwing a wrench in the works. She was just about to knock on his door when it opened.

"I heard him," Austin said, "and I'm ready."

Ginny squeezed her eyes shut, making a show of her reluctance to look at him. She only opened them when Austin laughed. Then her eyes widened. He'd taken extra care to look like a normal boy. His jeans and shirt were clean and neat. Even his sneakers were clean. Ginny clasped his shoulders and turned him around, not trusting him not to have painted something on the back of his head.

When she saw only his shining hair, she sighed dramatically. "It's a good thing. I didn't want to have to strip you naked as a jaybird and stick you under the shower."

"Ginny!" His cheeks burned. "You wouldn't have!"

"Well, we don't know that, now do we?" She touched the silky hair, brushed it off his forehead. She wondered how many times she'd used that same gesture on Beth, and felt the lump in her throat expand.

"You miss her, don't you?"

"Very much," she said softly. "Your father's waiting."

Austin picked up a stack of papers, then looked up at her. "I miss my mom, too." He sniffed, then rushed past her and down the hall.

The sound of his footfalls echoed with his parting words in her heart. He was, after all, just a little boy who missed his mother. "Have fun, you two," she whispered to the emptiness around her. Then, after a moment, she turned and walked to her room.

"Ha! Let them eat fat," Ginny said as she scooped another hunk of butter up and flung it into the bowl of mashed potatoes. "Let their arteries clog up and choke the life out of them." She set the electric mixer going, added more salt and pepper, then turned to check on the last of the chicken frying in the deep fryer. She flicked off the mixer, retrieved the basket from the spitting oil and placed it on its hook to drain. Then she opened the oven and added the crispy brown pieces to the pile on the tray to keep warm.

She moved around the kitchen with ease, as if she'd been working there for years. A baking sheet the size of two large cookie sheets held buttermilk biscuits, almost golden brown. She glanced at the clock and stirred the gravy. Her movements were efficient, precise, as if she knew what she was doing, which, she assured herself, she did. But to convince herself of that, she'd had to give herself a strong talking-to. How hard could it be? She had the recipes. She wasn't a novice in the kitchen. She could manage. And it was a good thing, too, because Jason's promise of help hadn't materialized.

All too soon, it was lunchtime. She was just carrying out the last of the food, the heavy tray of hot fried chicken, when the door opened and the first person to test her new menu came in.

Jericho had been tantalized all morning by the aromas coming from the kitchen. He knew chicken when he smelled it, and he was sure there'd be mashed potatoes, but he'd only dreamed of the hot biscuits and gravy. He stopped, his eyes on the pile of fried chicken, when he remembered his teeth. He quickly wheeled around, fumbled in his shirt pocket, slipped his teeth in and turned back around.

"I done died and gone to heaven, ma'am."

"Ginny," she corrected.

"Yes'm." He took his seat at the head of the table, tucked his napkin into his collar, then paused, his arm outstretched for the chicken. "Don't ring the bell until I got my plate filled. Once those Gillespie boys get a whiff, they'll go through this grub like a tornado, suck everything up 'fore you can bat an eye."

Ginny smiled. It was only a couple of minutes later when three more of the men appeared. Freshly washed, they ducked their heads in greeting before introducing themselves as Roberto, Gomez and Dan.

Roberto and Gomez, she concluded, had to be brothers. They were Mexican Americans, with dark hair and flashing eyes. They were in their early forties and very handsome. Dan was sandy-haired, tall and lanky, and looked to be closer to fifty.

The hands were all polite and a little shy—and definitely in a hurry to get at the food. She watched the men good-naturedly tease Jericho about his table manners, telling him he should have waited until they were all there before he started eating.

"Like one hog waits for another?" Jericho mumbled around a mouthful of mashed potatoes.

She'd just about given up on the young Gillespie boys, deciding they'd gone into town for hamburgers, when she heard their deep voices over the sound of running water. She waited by the door, holding it open. When the boys vaulted up the steps, she introduced herself, taking her time, talking to each of them, but their attention was glued to the table heaped with quickly disappearing food.

They were tall like their father. Billy Bob, the oldest, she concluded, was blond and had his father's hazel eyes. She smiled broadly at Wayne. He was freckled, with carrot red hair and a smile that lit up his face.

Billy Bob had had enough of manners and gentlemanly ways. "'Scuse me, Miss Ginny." He squeezed past her and headed for the table. With an apologetic but embarrassed grin, Wayne followed.

Ginny retired to the kitchen, but she could hear the sounds of the men enjoying her cooking and wondered why it made her feel so good. Lupe, Roberto's wife, showed up while she was eating her own healthy green salad. She immediately fixed a plate of food for herself, set it aside, then began to clean up the kitchen. Ginny thought it would be nice to have another woman to talk to but soon leaned that Lupe was deaf. When she finished her salad, she felt she was just in the way, so she motioned to Lupe with a smile that she was going out to sit on the back steps.

The rear of the cookhouse was shaded by a large oak tree, and the breeze felt refreshing against her hot skin. Dog, she noticed, was lying beside the tree. He was stretched out on his back, his legs pointing upward, his belly round and full of mashed potatoes, biscuits and gravy.

Ginny leaned against the door and closed her eyes. There was a certain peace, a quiet feeling of fulfillment she hadn't known in a long time, and she savored it. She didn't know how long she stayed that way, but when she heard chairs scraping against the floor, her peace was shattered. She listened to the sound of the voices, unable to hear what was being said. But it didn't matter. She knew there wouldn't be any food left. She'd accomplished what she'd set out to do, and it felt damn good.

She was still sitting there when the Gillespie boys rounded the corner, their Stetsons stuck at cocky angles on their heads, toothpicks sticking from the corners of their mouths. She nodded, expecting them to pass her by on their way back to work, but they stopped, and it was Wayne who spoke for both of them.

"Best home-cooked meal we've had in a long time, Miss Ginny. Thank you."

"You're welcome, Wayne, Billy Bob."

They nodded and moved on, and in a second the three older men appeared. As they expressed their thanks, they eyed Dog, who had stationed himself at her feet and was showing the men his teeth. She absently rubbed his head.

"You're welcome. See you tomorrow," she said, then got a good whiff of Dog. "Pee-you. I think it's time to see just how much you like me, Dog." Ginny spotted the faucet and hose and slipped back into the kitchen for a bar of soap.

She'd never bathed a dog before, but she had bathed a squirming baby. How hard could it be? Halfway through the bath, she didn't know who was wetter, herself or Dog. After she scolded him a couple of times, he stood in one place, and she didn't have to chase him all over the yard. But once she got him wet and soapy he took it into his head to shake every few minutes. After she gave him the final rinse, she jumped back, but not far enough. Dog shook his long shaggy coat until it was almost dry, then set off running around the yard, around the tree and her feet.

For a second she thought he'd gone crazy. "Why, you old faker. You enjoyed it."

"He done gone and made a liar outta me, ain't he?"

Ginny had been so engrossed in what she was doing she hadn't noticed that Jericho had taken her position on the porch steps. He was about to say something when Dog stopped in front of him, his ears and head held high.

"'Scuse me." He stood up stiffly and walked away.

The old man was probably getting senile, she thought, and started washing the soap and dog hair off herself. She'd just finished rolling up the hose when Jericho rounded the corner as fast as his old legs would carry him. He slowed only when he was in front on her.

"Get in the barn and stay there," he whispered urgently. "Take Dog with you."

"Why? What's the matter?" She wondered if he'd suddenly lost his senses.

"Sheriff's up at the house looking for anyone about. He's got a suit with him."

"A what?"

"Suit, ma'am. Government man."

CHAPTER NINE

THEY'D COME to get her!

Fear gripped her. She didn't hesitate to question Jericho's advice but took off running, heading directly for the yawning dark hole of the open barn doors. Dog stayed close to her legs, keeping pace beside her.

She didn't give herself time to think until she was deep in the shadowy interior of the barn. Then she stopped, breathless, her heart pounding. All the strength had drained from her. Her legs were shaking so badly she glanced around frantically for a place to sit. She spotted a bale of hay by a stall door, walked over and collapsed on it. Dog hopped up beside her, positioning himself as close to her as possible, giving her cheek a wet swipe with his tongue.

Ginny wrapped her arm around him, burying her fingers in the clean soft fur, and fought to calm down. "How'd Jericho know, Dog?"

Dog gave her a quizzical look and another kiss.

"And why am I sitting here talking to you?" She leaned back and stared at the animal. "When did you become my bosom buddy?" Dog's shaggy tail slapped against the hay and he flashed his canine grin. She would've asked him another question, but suddenly her hair was yanked from behind. With a painful tug and tilt of her head, she swung around, only to find herself face-to-face with a horse. She gave a throaty scream and hopped up.

Dog did the same, but he must have thought her reaction amusing. He gave her a toothy smile and danced around making low growling sounds. "You think that was funny, do you?" She eyed the horse suspiciously, watched as it leaned its big head out of the stall and nibbled at a corner of the hay.

Ginny gave a sigh. "He—she—it only wants to be fed, Dog, not make a meal of me." She touched the back of her head to see if she had any hair left and was relieved to find it all there. The horse was slowly chewing, but its gaze was fixed on her. Farm animals, she thought, were an intelligent breed. They seemed to have an almost human awareness. City girl that she was, it made her downright nervous.

Afraid to move for fear of disturbing some other creature, she stayed where she was for a while. But she found herself listening intently for the sound of approaching footsteps until every nerve in her body seemed to be in a state of alert.

To break the tension, she paced the length of the barn and back, Dog by her side. She wondered what Jericho would have to say about all this. He obviously knew she was in some sort of trouble with the law. She had to decide how much she wanted to tell him. That he'd be full of questions was a foregone conclusion.

Damn Matt for putting that niggling fear about the FBI in her head and then leaving her here to deal with it alone. "Damn, damn," she snarled, and kicked a dented rusty bucket. She paced the length of the barn once more. How long did it take for two males to look at trucks, for heaven's sake? They were as bad as women shopping.

As she passed the stall, she realized Dog had tired of the game and now sat on the bale of hay. Dog and horse alike watched her every move. When the horse gave a loud sigh, she stopped in front of him. "My sentiments exactly." Bravely she ventured a little closer to the horse, reaching to touch him, but she recoiled a step when the animal snorted, his curling lips revealing big yellow teeth. Did animals usually make a show of baring their teeth, she wondered, or was it just these two?

Then she thought of Jericho and laughed. It wasn't just the animals.

She tried again to approach the horse, even though her steps faltered. But she made herself reach out and touch the velvety nose. The horse didn't take her hand off at the wrist and actually seemed to appreciate the stroking. She remembered Dog's peculiar look of ecstasy and absently began to scratch the soft skin.

"What's keeping Jericho, horsey?" Dog whined and Ginny directed the next question at him. "What's going on, Dog?"

She'd no sooner voiced her question when Dog's ears perked up. He jumped off his perch on the bale of hay to stand beside her. Ginny began to back away, moving deeper into the shadows, when she saw Jericho stroll through the open doorway. The old man stopped, letting his eyes adjust to the gloom as he searched for her. She watched, smiling as he half turned to slip in his false teeth.

"Miss Ginny, it's safe now."

Ginny walked toward him, still undecided what to say, when he touched a finger to his lips and motioned for her to follow him. She glanced around curiously, knowing they were alone except for the animals, but she followed him. He held open a door to the back office and she stepped inside.

"Thank you, Jericho. Tell me something. How did you know I didn't want to talk to the police?"

Jericho chuckled and offered her a chair. When she shook her head, he sat down himself, relieved to be off his feet. His old heart was pounding with excitement.

"When young Argus showed up yesterday you went as white as flour." He dug in his pocket and drew out his plug of chewing tobacco, shaved off a sliver and put it in his mouth, then he remembered his manners and offered Ginny some. He laughed when she turned up her nose.

"What did the sheriff want? Was the man with him—" she remembered the term he'd used "—a suit?"

"Yep. Always able to spot 'em. He was FBI all right."

Ginny closed her eyes, feeling her world closing in on her.

Jericho watched the young woman closely. He suddenly felt sorry for her. She looked so forlorn. "I don't think you have much to worry about. Argus's a good lawman and knows when to keep his mouth shut."

Ginny decided she needed to sit down, after all, and pulled up a rickety wooden chair. "What do you mean? And why did you tell me to hide? Why didn't you just turn me in?"

"I ain't a judge. I don't know what you've done. As to turning you in...Matt trusts you. That's enough for me. Besides, Miss Ginny, you're just not the criminal type."

"Thank you. I haven't done anything wrong." She glanced around the room, realizing it was his domain. "What did the FBI want?"

"Far as I could tell, he questioned the sheriff about any strangers in the area. Female types. Young Argus told him about you and he wanted to meet you."

Ginny groaned.

"Oh, don't worry so much. Argus wouldn't have told him much."

"Well, he knows there's a stranger in the area, a female. He probably has a good description of me, and I'm sure the sheriff told him my name—that's enough right there. He'll be back for me."

"Nope."

"Nope?" she repeated.

"That's right. Argus had a run-in with the feds about three years ago. He'll be polite, helpful even, but won't tell them a dang-blasted thing. But don't sell him short, either. The whole time the fed was trying to get information, so was Argus. The suit was real evasive about why he was looking for you."

Jericho chuckled and went on, "Matter of fact, when I showed up playing the senile old geezer, Argus was telling him that the woman staying here was an old friend of Matt's from Houston. Come to take care of him and his motherless child. Then he proceeded to fill the suit in on Matt's background and career. The man didn't get much out of Argus, though he did ask your name and description. Argus told him he didn't remember much since his meeting you was only in passing. Young Argus didn't even ask me where you were. Didn't want me lying to the federal boys. He just kinda told me in a questioning way that you were out with Matt and the boy."

Ginny stared at the worn and scuffed floor between her feet, silently thinking about her options. "He'll be back. They don't give up that easily."

"Maybe. Maybe not. Matt and Argus are a lot alike, smarter than they let on, real silver-tongued devils when they want to be. So it depends on how cunningly Argus uses his silver tongue with that city boy. But one thing you can depend on, Argus will come calling again real soon. He don't like being made a fool of. Matt and you got some talking to do. And let me tell you this—don't lie to young Argus or he'll eat you for lunch."

"Thanks for the warning and your help."

"Welcome." He watched her, the way her smooth brow furrowed with worry. "You gonna run again?"

Ginny jumped, unaware she'd been so lost in thought. "No. I'm through with running."

Jericho nodded his agreement. "Only thing running ever did was get you caught."

"You still haven't asked me what I'm running from."

He shrugged. "Figured you'd tell me if you trusted me."

They smiled at each other and Ginny told him her story. He listened carefully. When she finished and fell silent, he glanced around his office. "Well, girly, you couldn't have landed in a better place. There's people here that need you more than they know, and you need them. Time to make a stand. Time to fight back. I ain't too old to pack a pistol, and I'm still a crack shot. Ain't no critter or man gonna come sniffing round here." He gave an evil chuckle. "And you keep cooking like you did today, missy, and the rest of the boys'll lay down their lives for you. Especially them Gillespie boys. They're already walking around moonstruck."

Her voice was lodged somewhere around the lump in her throat, and she could only nod. Standing up to leave, she noticed the framed pictures on the wall and moved closer for a better look. A gangly, painfully thin boy with a mop of dark hair stood stiffly beside a tall, handsome blond man. There was something about the child's face that made her take a second look.

"That's Matt," she said.

Jericho moved beside her. "Yep, and his father, Herman Van der Bollen. Ornery as a mule and mean to boot."

"Mean?" she asked.

"Used to wallop the hell out of that boy. 'Course, Matt gave him a hard time, but weren't no cause to hit the lad so hard or so much. Talked to him somethin' awful, too, telling him he was a no-account just like his mother and would never amount to anything, just like his mother."

"But he married Matt's mother. Were you here back then?"

"Off and on." Jericho took the photograph down, picked up an old rag and dusted it off. "Yeah, she was a beautiful, sweet-spirited woman no man could resist. And she was chaste and religious. Wouldn't let no man touch her, so Mr. Herman married her." He shook his head.

Studying the other photographs of the family, Ginny realized that Jericho had been around a long time, but she couldn't for the life of her determine his age. "I can see where Jason gets his blond good looks. Herman Van der Bollen was good-looking."

"Didn't hurt that boy none that his mama made a man's eyeballs drop out, either. She's gallivanting in some foreign city right now."

Ginny moved down the wall, looking at pictures of people she didn't recognize. Her attention was snagged by an old photograph of a man in his middle to late twenties, a wisdom beyond his years emanating from his

eyes. He seemed to typify the legendary image of a
Texas cowboy—tall, well built, his stance cocky, a Stetson shading his eyes. He was dressed in jeans and
leather chaps, boots and a simple white shirt. At his
waist was a wide hand-tooled belt, the holster and pistol slung low on his hip. His arms were hanging by his
sides and in one hand he held a rifle. She smiled. "Now
that is a man."

She noticed the badge on his shirt pocket and turned
to ask Jericho who it was. His face was bright red.
Alarmed, she thought he was having some kind of attack, then it hit her. She glanced at the photograph
again, then back at Jericho.

"That's you?"

He yanked off his Stetson and ran his hand through
his thick gray hair, his face redder than ever. "Yep."

She glanced back at the photograph and became
aware of the many framed commendations surrounding it. "You were a Texas Ranger?" She didn't know
much about them except that Texas Rangers were a very
special breed.

"Yep. Long time ago when things were different." He
was embarrassed and, donning his hat, walked out the
door.

Ginny took one more glance around, impressed and
confused. She wondered about his family, and why he'd
been with Matt's family for so long. She hurried after
him, Dog at her side, and found him stroking the horse.
There were a million questions she wanted to ask him,
but when he looked up, she saw his closed expression
and thought better of it.

She kept her distance from the biting horse and
asked, "What's his name?"

"Her name. Ernestine."

For some reason the name struck her as odd. They had a canine named Dog and a horse named Ernestine. She jumped back when Jericho opened the stall door and disappeared inside. After a moment of listening to Jericho's low loving voice, she ventured closer. The stall was bigger than she realized, the floor covered with fresh-smelling hay. Jericho was running his hand over the big animal, and Ginny noticed how shiny her dark red coat was.

"She's sure fat," she said.

Jericho motioned her closer, then took Ginny's hand and laid it against the warm tight belly. "She's pregnant."

Ginny froze when Ernestine's head turned to one side to see who was touching her. But after a sniff and a snort she resumed eating, and Ginny couldn't resist touching and stroking. Without a word, Jericho placed a wide brush in her hand, pulled the leather strap over her knuckles, then stepped out of the stall.

The work was hypnotizing, soothing, and Ginny lost herself in the task. It wasn't until Dog barked and Jericho popped back into the stall that she returned to the real world.

"Matt and the boy just drove up," Jericho said. "Tell him to come see me."

Ginny handed him the brush and smiled. "Thank you, Jericho. For everything, especially introducing me to Ernestine."

He touched the brim of his hat, then said, "She's a good listener when you got troubles, so come bend her ear any time you need peace and quiet. The old gal's a better listener if you brush her down, pamper her a little."

"I'll remember that, and thanks again." Ginny waved as she set out across the yard, rounded the cookhouse and headed for the main house. She spotted Matt and Austin and picked up speed. It wasn't until she was almost upon them that she realized they weren't waiting for her but were walking around and admiring a brand-new, bright red Jeep Cherokee.

"Isn't she a beauty, Ginny?" Austin yelled.

"Nice," she said breathlessly, and looked at Matt. She couldn't tell if the goofy expression was pride in the car or his son.

"Nice?" Matt mocked. "Nice? She's gorgeous. Rides like a dream, and can she move."

"We tried out the four-wheel drive over at the granite quarry, Ginny," Austin said.

"Smooth as glass, eh, Austin?" Matt said. "Ginny, come look inside."

She didn't have the heart to dampen their enthusiasm and so was subjected to a detailed inspection of the vehicle's stellar features. They were so enthralled that Matt only thought to warn Dog mildly that he wasn't allowed to jump in the front seat. Oohing and aahing in all the right places, she waited until they wound down a little before suggesting a cold drink.

Austin ran up the walk, then stopped, "Tell her, Dad—Matt, how I got more for your old car."

"It's true," Matt said to Ginny. "Austin went armed with facts and figures that were indisputable. Sat down across the desk from the salesman and quoted those prices until the guy was sweating. Bet he never forgets the Bolt men. Right, Austin?"

"Right!" Austin hollered and let the screen door slam shut in their faces.

Matt and Austin's good humor was contagious, and she found herself laughing. "Why's he in such a hurry?"

Matt grinned. "He's a city boy, Ginny. He has a lot to learn." He opened the door and stood aside to let her pass. "We were riding around the quarry, and he had to...relieve himself. When I pointed out he had the whole outdoors and just had to choose a spot, you'd have thought I'd suggested he stand in front of an audience, he was so outraged."

Something in her expression, in the stiff way she held herself, caught his attention, and all the while he was talking he watched her closely. As much as he wanted to continue telling her about his amazing son, he couldn't ignore the warning bells that were clanging in his head.

"What happened? Was the meal another disaster?" He grinned. "The way you smell, maybe you cooked one of the horses by mistake." He didn't get a wry smile or a sharp retort. Something was truly wrong.

Her legs suddenly gave out, and she collapsed in the nearest chair. She didn't know where to start, and after a couple of attempts, she did the unthinkable and burst into tears.

Matt tensed, then froze. If ever there was a time he was at a loss for words it was now. His hard shell cracked, and the soft spot in his gut ached. He couldn't move, didn't know what to do, just stood there helplessly watching.

Austin rushed in the room and skidded to a stop. "Why'd you make her cry again?"

"I didn't. She just started blubbering on her own." Matt panicked. "Do something, son."

"If you didn't do anything—" Austin snatched up a box of tissues and gave his father a scorching look "—then you must know girls do this sort of thing all the time. Hormones. PMS. Mom did it, too." He consoled Ginny by patting her on the shoulder. "Want to go lie down?"

It was too much. Austin's voice of experience. Matt's look of horror when he thought it was a female thing. Ginny buried her face in the tissue and started laughing. After struggling for control, she glanced up and started laughing again.

"Oh, my," she finally managed when she caught her breath. "You two have finished off a very upsetting day." The laughter was a miraculous antidote to her fears. She told them about the sheriff, the government man and Jericho's rescue, and both father and son sat listening intently. When she finished relating her tale, the silence that followed was unnerving.

"What're we going to do, Matt?" Austin turned to his father, his adult demeanor vanishing at the thought of Ginny leaving.

For the first time, his son had reached out to him for help, Matt realized. Something inside him ached, like when women cried, stealing his breath for a second, depriving him of the ability to speak.

When his father remained silent, Austin said again, "Dad, what're we going to do?"

Matt stood up and reached for the telephone. "First thing is to call Argus and invite him to dinner. We'll let Ginny tell him what happened to her."

Austin braced his chin on his fist. "Is that wise? What good will it do?"

"For one thing, he'll tell us what's going on. What the feds are up to."

Ginny shot Matt and Austin a hard look. They were talking about her as if she wasn't there. Making decisions without her okay. Making plans without her approval.

"Can the FBI take Ginny away or arrest her?"

It was a question she would have asked—eventually.

"Austin, Ginny hasn't broken any laws. No one's going to take her away." Matt held up a hand when the sheriff answered. "Argus. Matt here. Jericho said you dropped by."

Ginny and Austin watched Matt, each trying to figure out what the sheriff was saying. When the silence went on too long, Austin reached over and grasped Ginny's hand.

"Matt's going to take care of things. You'll see."

Ginny was amazed at how much Austin's attitude toward his father had changed. The best thing that could have happened to this estranged pair was forcing them to be together. Matt was a good man, even though he didn't think so, and Austin needed his father in his life.

Matt's voice jerked her wandering thoughts back to the present. "I understand. No, honest. Come to dinner tonight and we'll have a story to tell you." Matt grinned at Ginny. "Yes, we. I'm involved up to my neck. So's Austin." He was about to hang up, paused, then laughed. "I'll tell her."

Matt hung up the phone and returned to his chair. "He's coming by. Seems your meal this afternoon was a hit. Says he can't stay for dinner tonight, but if you'll invite him again and cook the same thing you did at noon, he'd love to come."

A deep frown settled on Ginny's brow. "What did he say about the FBI? About me?"

"Nothing that he didn't already tell us. The agent said the FBI's looking for a woman, Patricia Bright, who escaped while being transported. He wouldn't tell Argus what the woman was wanted for. Argus told him he couldn't help him. But the agent was at McDonald's yesterday and heard two boys talking about the new lady cooking meals out at the vineyard and wanted to see for himself."

"But he didn't see me," Ginny said, "and more than likely he'll be back to have another look around. Matt, is this going to get you in some sort of trouble?"

"No." Matt took out two tall, fluted crystal glasses, a bottle of champagne and a canned soft drink from the refrigerator. He handed Austin his drink. "You're too young to appreciate this."

Austin's eyes widened. "How old were you when you first tasted champagne?"

Matt grinned. "That was then. This is now. And right now, this is one subject I'm more knowledgeable about. When you know as much about wine as I did at your age, you can taste it. Mind you, though, a good vintner only tastes the wine—he doesn't swallow it. Now—" he set the glasses down and expertly opened the champagne with barely a sigh "—not only am I a superior vintner, but I'm a connoisseur of good bubbly, as well." He held up the bottle. "This is Dom Pérignon, which, I might add, is the finest champagne ever bottled."

He was in a strangely elated mood, Ginny thought, and as much as she wanted to know what else the sheriff had said, she decided to let Matt have his little game. She waited until he'd filled their glasses and returned the bottle to the refrigerator, then lifted her glass to his in a salute.

"When's the sheriff coming?" she asked.

"He's on his way now and very curious." Matt took a sip, watching her over the rim of his glass, wondering why the hell he felt so damn content. His life had been slowly falling apart ever since he'd been shot. He'd felt like crap for so long he'd forgotten there was any other way to feel. What had changed? And when? His lips twitched in a secret smile as Ginny quickly emptied her glass. He fetched the cold bottle from the refrigerator and refilled it. "Good?"

"Wonderful," she replied, raising the glass to her lips. She sighed. "Does it always get better with a second glass?"

Matt grinned.

"Matt!" Austin said. He didn't understand why Ginny and his father were smiling at each other as if they were sharing some secret joke. "The sheriff's here."

Dog's wild barking from the porch confirmed this. Matt opened the door and stared at Dog, but this time the animal wasn't intimidated and merely stared back.

"Hey, what happened to this mutt? He almost looks like a dog."

Ginny joined him at the door. "I gave him a bath."

Matt looked at her in amazement. "You're joking. How?"

Ginny shook her head, not really hearing his question. All her attention was focused on the big man moving slowly toward them. It was almost a relief to see him in jeans and shirt, instead of a uniform. He was a handsome rugged man, tall, broad-shouldered and fit. His brown hair was thick and just beginning to gray at the temples.

She waited while Matt and the sheriff went through the male ritual of shaking hands, thumping each other on the back and making cryptic jokes as if they hadn't seen each other in years, instead of a day. Even Austin was included in their tribal greetings. Miffed that she— the principal player—was being left out, she coughed, and the sheriff turned and held out his hand.

"Nice to see you again, Miss Carney."

She took his hand, mirroring his sincere smile. "I'm afraid I've caused you some problems. I'm very sorry."

Argus laughed. "Don't worry yourself over it for a minute. If Matt knows the truth and accepts it, then I will, too, once I hear it from you. But I must tell you, I've never had so much fun giving the FBI the shaft. Did my heart good." He stopped and shot an uncomfortable look in Austin's direction, then glanced at Matt.

Matt motioned for everyone to sit down. "Austin knows everything, Argus."

"I found her," Austin said proudly. "Out in the vineyard by the river."

Matt poured Argus a glass of champagne and held it out, but the sheriff shook his head.

"I wouldn't turn down a cold beer or some of your 1988 Chardonnay, though."

Matt pushed the champagne in front of him. "Come on, taste it, Argus. It's Dom, the genuine article. I promise you, you've never tasted anything like it before. Pure heaven." Then he waited.

Ginny watched the way the big man's hands gently handled the fragile champagne flute, the way he held the glass to the light and the way he sipped at the liquid and closed his eyes, his expression settling into deep concentration. It was almost feminine, and she had to fight to keep a straight face. Then she realized two things at once. Matt was doing the same thing, and it didn't take a rocket scientist to know that this ritual was part of being an expert vintner.

"You're right, Matt," Argus said. "It's like drinking the sun and stars at the same time, isn't it?"

Matt nodded and continued to talk as he took another bottle from the refrigerator and refilled everyone's glass. "Argus has one of the finest palates this side of France, Ginny. He works in the vineyard and the lab when he's not sheriffing." He tilted his glass in a salute to his friend, then waited a moment and said, "Good?"

Argus held his half-empty glass to the light again, studied the liquid and nodded. "Probably the best— and the most expensive—I've ever had. Damned if it doesn't get better the more you drink it."

Matt laughed, a rich joyous sound that came from deep within him. "Believe it or not, Argus, the first glass was the real thing, but the one you're drinking now is mine."

"What do you mean, yours?"

"The last year I was here, I made this, Argus. Right after the harvest I syphoned off enough of the finest juice for myself and made fifty bottles. Dad found out what I was doing, but instead of destroying everything outright, he just watched me like a hawk, taunting me that I couldn't do it, contemptuous of my efforts. When I'd finished, he demanded to sample it. I wouldn't let him. Hid every damn bottle down in the caves. It's about nineteen years old and still perfect. I intend to start making it again full-time.''

Argus took another sip. "This'll make you a very rich man if you price it right."

Ginny realized the vineyard was of great importance to these men, probably to the entire town. Her own problems had taken a back seat for the moment, and it felt good. She sipped her champagne, this time closing her eyes, amazed at its unique taste. She let the bubbles play over her tongue and slide down her throat. But she should have known her quiet peace wouldn't last.

Austin figured he'd been a good boy long enough. "Sheriff, are the FBI going to take Ginny away if they find out she's here?"

It took a second for Argus and Matt to rejoin the real world, and it was Argus who answered. "Well, Austin, I don't know. Why doesn't Ginny tell me why the feds are so freaked out about her disappearance?"

Ginny realized she'd been forced to think and talk about her past more in the last couple of days than she had in years. But each time she told the story, the pain in her heart eased a little. When she finished telling Argus, the ensuing silence seemed to last forever. She watched Austin wipe his eyes and wanted to cry herself.

Argus held out his glass to Matt for a refill. "That's quite a story, Ginny. I'm sorry for your loss. What I have to know is, have you definitely made up your mind to leave the Witness Protection Program?"

"Yes," she said, and no one in the room could doubt that she meant it.

"Are you comfortable, Matt, with the idea that someone, besides a lawman, might come looking for her?"

"I can take care of it, Argus."

The sheriff nodded and grinned. "With some help you can."

Austin couldn't stand being left out. He finished his drink and set the can down on the table with an attention-getting thump. "So, what about the FBI?"

Argus glanced at his watch. "Well, Austin, I think it's time to bring them in so Ginny can tell them her decision, don't you?"

"Yes," Austin said, but frowned as the sheriff reached behind him for the telephone.

Argus dialed the local hotel. "Betsy, ring the FBI agents' room for me, will you?" He smiled at Ginny, who was looking unsure. "It's the only way," he told her. "Agent Harrison—Sheriff Gillespie here. You remember how to get to the Van der Bollen place? Good. Then maybe you and your partner might want to take a drive out here and have a chat with Ginny Carney."

His grin increased with each utterance on the other line, and then he turned to Ginny and smiled hugely. "You heard right, Mrs. Carney."

Suddenly Ginny didn't feel so well. She wondered if all those wonderful bubbles were trying to come back up. She couldn't have talked if she'd wanted to.

Matt reached out and grasped her hand, and she held on to it like a lifeline. Neither noticed the way the sheriff watched them, nor his look of surprise.

Austin jumped up from the chair, noisily shoved it back so that it struck the wall, then, without explanation, sprinted from the room. In a short time he was back, a stack of papers clutched protectively to his chest.

CHAPTER TEN

GINNY'S HEART began to pound when she heard Dog's wild barking. A few moments later, there was the sound of a car coming up the drive. Doors slammed. It was dark out now, but the yard lights had come on and Ginny could see both agents standing beside the car, perfectly still, eyeing Dog's menacing stance.

Matt chuckled. "You'd better call him off, Ginny. He just looks at me with contempt now."

Ginny called Dog and the animal reluctantly moved away, letting the two men pass. She watched their approach with dread. Though they were strangers to her, she recognized them by their conservative appearance, the dark suits, the air of authority. Her heart dropped to her toes. They were going to take her back.

Argus met them at the door and quickly introduced Matt and Austin, then everyone turned their attention to Ginny.

"Miss Bright. I'm Agent Harrison and my partner here is Agent Wilson. We've been searching for you everywhere."

She'd lost her voice and could only nod.

"Are you ready to leave now?" Harrison asked.

"No." She surprised herself with her firm answer.

"Okay," Wilson said. "We'll give you a little time to thank these people for taking care of you, but we really must leave quickly and get you settled elsewhere."

Ginny looked to Matt for help, but he just sat back in his chair, his arms crossed over his chest. She glanced at Argus and found him inspecting his fingernails. As a last resort she turned to Austin, and he was thumbing through his stack of papers. She realized that Matt and Argus were allowing her to make her final decision.

"You don't understand." She glanced from one agent to the other. "I'm not leaving here. Not with you or anyone else."

They were both shocked. "You can't do that, Miss Bright."

"It's Mrs. Carney, Virginia Antonia Bradsworth Carney." It gave her a brief thrill to see their shocked expressions at the use of her real name. "And I'm staying right here."

"Miss—Mrs. Carney. You're under federal protection. You must come with us."

"I'm no longer under federal protection, Agent Harrison. And I no longer choose to be. My stepfather was sent to a country-club prison where he's treated like a king, and I was sent running for my life. I'm an attorney, for heaven's sake. You placed me in typing pools and waitressing. You forfeited your hold over me when you screwed up my records and allowed anyone who could turn on a computer to access them. But most of all, you lost me when I realized you never intended pursuing an investigation for those responsible for killing my family. When you realized Tony was the one who gave the orders, you'd already gotten your conviction and didn't want to prolong it, so to hell with my husband and daughter's murder."

"Listen to me, Mrs. Carney—Ginny," Agent Harrison said. "If you don't come with us, we're going to arrest you and anyone else connected with hiding you."

Matt slowly uncrossed his arms, rose from his chair and moved toward the agent. "Do not—" he moved closer "—come into my house—" he tapped the agent on the chest with a finger "—and make threats against my family and guest."

Ginny couldn't have spoken if she'd wanted to, she was so fascinated by Matt. She just kept shaking her head, trying to decide if she should laugh, cry or dance a jig at the unadulterated pleasure of seeing these arrogant men brought down a peg or two.

Agent Wilson stepped around his partner and approached Ginny. No one had noticed that Dog had slipped in behind the two men and slunk on all fours beneath Ginny's chair. Wilson's shoe leather was quickly scarred from the snapping of sharp teeth and he stepped back in alarm. When he found the large figure of the sheriff looming beside him, he froze. But he wasn't about to give up.

"Ginny, you can't know what you're doing," he said. "Your case is unique, the situation salvageable. We can help you solve your problems."

"Oh, I don't think so." Austin's small voice was like a dousing of cold water, and everyone whirled around to look at him. "My research shows that the Witness Protection Program has been plagued with problems for years. The locations and identities of more than twenty-five percent of your protected witnesses have been compromised. An estimated fifteen percent have left the program and gone out on their own. The program is riddled with incompetence, leaks and bad agents taking payoffs." Austin glanced down at the papers in his hand. "I see that even you, Agent Harrison, were recently reprimanded for mishandling an informant."

"Who the hell is this kid?" Harrison asked.

Matt bit his lip to keep from smiling and said proudly, "My son."

Agent Wilson wasn't going to let a kid outdo him. "Ginny, you'd never make it. You'll never be safe."

"Actually," Austin said thoughtfully, "you're wrong. Statistics show that only one percent of those who left the program on their own have died, and most of the deaths were accredited to natural causes. It's more than possible, even probable, that Ginny will live a long happy life—with us." Austin meticulously straightened his papers, pushed them aside and gave both agents the benefit of his innocent dark gaze.

Agent Harrison had had enough. "If you won't come willingly, Mrs. Carney, then I'll have to arrest you."

Matt opened his mouth to speak, but Argus silenced him. "What are the charges?" he asked.

"Fleeing the scene of an accident, Sheriff Gillespie."

Argus tucked his thumbs in the waistband of his jeans, rocked back and forth on his heels and stared at the agents, amusement playing around the corners of his mouth. "Golly gee," he said in his best imitation of the country bumpkin these men probably thought he was. "Agent Harrison, I hate to tell you this, but the accident was in my jurisdiction. You don't have any authority in this area. Besides, how can you even hint that she fled from the scene without a statement? Now, boys, I questioned the little lady. She must have gotten a real hard bump on the noggin, 'cause she don't remember a damn thing—excuse me, ma'am— about any car accident. Do you, honey?"

Ginny closed her eyes and shook her head. She waited, listening to the door slam, and a few seconds later the sound of a car starting. Then she burst out laughing. The others joined in, but after a while she had to ask, "How smart was that, treating them like idiots?"

"Not very," Argus answered, "but it was better than prying Matt off them." He rose to leave, then paused and gave Austin a hard look. "Don't ever tell me where or how you obtained your research."

"Yes, sir."

Argus thumped Matt on the shoulder. "Have a talk with the boy, Matt. What he did had to be highly illegal, and the feds aren't going to be happy about that."

"I covered my footprints," Austin said.

Argus made a show of covering his ears. "I don't want to hear it, boy."

"Yes, sir," Austin replied, then mumbled under his breath, "They're stupid, anyway."

Matt closed the door, then spotted a very quiet Dog under Ginny's chair. He opened the door again and pointed. Dog whined, glanced at Ginny, then slinked out into the dark night.

WHAT WOKE HER, Ginny couldn't say. It had been a dreamless night, peaceful, without the past rising up to disturb her. She lay still, listening to the sounds of the house, knowing something wasn't quite right. She'd become accustomed to the creaks and squeaks, recognizing the occasional moan for what it was—the wind or changing temperatures playing with the old wooden beams in the attic. Then it dawned on her what was wrong. The silence, eerie in its absoluteness. There was no snoring, no restless tossing or moaning from Matt's room.

She noticed a thin sliver of light that shone beneath the adjoining door, and she glanced at the clock. It was only two in the morning, and without thinking, she threw back the covers. The brass doorknob was cold under her palm, making her hesitate. A whispered warning echoed in her mind, but she ignored it and opened the door.

Matt was propped up in bed, a book balanced on his naked chest. He glanced up. "What's the matter?" he asked, and laid the open book across his chest.

"I was going to ask you the same thing." What the hell was she doing here?

Her hair was mussed, her eyes sleepy, and there was an endearing imprint of the sheet on her cheek. Matt swallowed. It didn't help that the thin cotton shirt of his she was wearing seemed transparent, or was that just his overactive imagination? Either way it didn't halt the sudden desire that surged through him like a tidal wave.

Ginny was close enough to see what he was reading, and she grinned. "Do you eat, drink and sleep wine?"

Matt glanced down at his chest and shrugged. "I tried to keep up with new innovations over the years, but I was pretty busy. Since I've been back I've been catching up. What are you doing awake?" He patted the side of the bed, then moved over some.

She didn't want to tell him that he'd awakened her. That she was so attuned to him that his very presence disturbed her. As she sat down on the side of the bed, the whispered warning that she shouldn't be here sounded again, but she waved it aside. "Do you think the FBI will come back?"

"They'll give it another go. If nothing else, they'll try and scare you by officially informing you that either you go with them or the government can and will legally dissolve all responsibility for your safety."

While he was talking, she was worrying at one of the shirt buttons. He eyed her movements apprehensively, sure that at any minute the shirt was going to come undone and leave a tantalizing portion of flesh exposed. Unable to bear the tension—or exception—any longer, he reached out and grabbed her hand. But instead of letting go, he continued to hold it.

"What's wrong, Ginny? Why can't you sleep?"

"I don't..." Her voice was as low as a whisper, soft, breathless. She liked the feel of his hand, the strength and warmth. "I don't know." But she did know, and the knowledge only made the emotional tug-of-war going on inside her that much worse.

Dear God, she wanted him so badly she ached inside. Her emotions were seesawing, her passion tempered with caution until she was numb with doubts. She should have known better than to come into his room. But once he touched her, she was lost.

She wanted to be held in a man's arms again, wanted to be kissed with passion, made love to. She wanted to make love with Matt, to drift on that cloud of desire and let the world fade away. If just for a short while, she needed to feel like a woman again. The promise of losing all touch with reality, of letting go for the first time in years, was as provocative and alluring as the intimacy of the act itself.

"Why'd you come in here, Ginny?" Matt asked.

"I don't know." She'd held her emotions in check too long. The memory of William was always with her. But tonight when she needed him to give her the strength to resist, when she tried to conjure up his beloved face, his image wasn't as clear as it usually was. How could she say such things to Matt? How could she admit that she wanted to make love with him? Best to be silent, she thought.

"Don't you know, Ginny?" Matt threw the book to one side, sat up and gently tugged on her hand, pulling her closer. "Maybe the real reason you can't sleep is the same reason as mine." She gazed steadily at him with those velvety brown eyes and he felt himself melt. "Maybe you keep thinking about me in here and you in there, and maybe, just maybe, we should be together. Like this."

He leaned forward slowly, giving her a chance to stop him, but instead of backing away, she leaned into his kiss, her arms slipping around his neck. God, he thought, it felt good to hold a woman again, to lose himself in the passion of the kiss.

Matt rolled over, taking Ginny with him, so that she was stretched out beneath him. The kiss grew deeper, arousing him in ways he'd forgotten. His hands wandered under the shirt, touched the silky warm flesh of her waist, then immediately roamed upward to her breasts. She was full and round. The urge to kiss those firm peaks was too great, and grabbing the fabric with his fingers he gave a yank, sending buttons flying across the bed.

Ginny closed her eyes, savoring the feel of his mouth on hers, the touch of his hands on her breasts. The longing inside her was like a rushing river, her loneliness a deep, painful ache. A voice in her head whispered warnings—she was letting down her guard, losing control—but she ignored them. It had been too long. Dammit, she was human. She had needs. She wasn't going to think about anything, she vowed, except how wonderful she felt. Then Matt's lips found her breasts, and she almost stopped breathing.

Matt had been celibate for too long, fearful that maybe his injuries had damaged more than flesh, blood and bone. No one had even aroused his interest in the past year. But now, all sensations returned and his passion soared. Ginny, with her red hair, sad eyes and soft skin, had restored his appetite. And even more than that, she'd opened his heart and made him believe in himself again. She'd breathed new life into a cynical, disheartened wretch.

Ginny shivered as his hands and mouth roamed over her. She shuddered with pleasure as one hand moved slowly downward, teasing before it slipped between her legs and found her warm, welcoming wetness.

Her hands drifted down his back, tickling his ribs, then slid over his buttocks. Matt trembled at her touch and squeezed his eyes shut. "Ginny, Ginny. It's been a long time and I'm holding on by a thread. If you continue to touch me I'm going to completely lose control." He was pleased when she laughed, a throaty sound full of passion. He planted tiny kisses along her neck. "Let me make love to you."

"Please." It was all she could say, all she could think to say.

His hand fumbled for the drawer of the night table. But he couldn't go on, not without telling her. "Ginny?"

"What?"

"Ginny, I would never hurt you, you know that, but it's been a long time for me—and I've never been a gentle lover even at my best."

"Yes . . . yes. Fine." What was he talking about?

But whatever he'd attempted to tell her was swept away by his deepening kiss and the speed with which he entered her. The most marvelous surge of feeling rushed through her—like fire and ice. He grasped her leg, pulling her closer as he filled her. She pulled him closer, demanding more with an aggressiveness she'd never experienced before. When her climax came, its intensity took her by surprise and left her breathless.

Matt struggled for control. But he was fast losing his determination to hold on. When he felt her shudder with release, he groaned out loud with a mixture of pleasure and pain as his body surged with his own climax.

They lay together, connected in body and soul, while their breathing slowed. Then Matt rolled over and got out of bed, heading toward the bathroom.

Dear God, what had she done? Ginny asked herself.

She covered her eyes with her arm, trying to shut out reality. But her body wouldn't allow her to deny what had just happened... what she'd let happen. Hot tears leaked from the corners of her eyes. How could she have done this? But even as she posed the question, she knew she felt no guilt—and that left her even more confused. She rolled over and buried her face in the pillow.

She was ashamed—but not for what she'd done. What embarrassed her was her aggressiveness, the desperateness she had displayed. God, had she really put a stranglehold on him with her legs, afraid he might try to get away? She'd been overwhelmed by her own desire, with not so much as a thought for Matt. Lifting her head, she stared at the bathroom door. Is that why he had gotten up so quickly and left the bed?

There'd been only one man in her life up to now. It had been love at first sight and such an easy, comfortable relationship. She didn't know what to make of the tumultuous emotions she experienced with Matt. A hundred questions plagued her. What should she say when he came out? Should she wait for him to come out, or should she just sneak off to her own bed? She buried her face deeper in the pillow, hoping against hope she'd smother herself and never have to face Matt again.

In the bathroom Matt splashed cold water on his face. One side of his chest, the side where the bullet had entered, was on fire and his thigh throbbed with pain. But he felt more alive than he had since he'd awakened in the hospital to find he was still among the living.

He glanced at himself in the mirror and grinned a little cockily. He still had it in him, he thought. He chuckled softly, but the laughter quickly died as he pictured Ginny in his bed, still naked and warm. He dried his face, opened the door and was about to switch off the light when he caught sight of her. That was not the posture of a wanton woman waiting for more.

"Ginny?" She lifted her head and stared at him. A sharp peculiar pain infiltrated that soft spot in his middle. He was in danger of being exposed and making an idiot of himself. He pulled up short by the side of the bed, watching as she struggled to button a shirt with no buttons.

"I'm sorry," she whispered, trying to hold the shirt together, pull it down and get out of bed all at the same time.

"Sorry about what?" He could see the tracks of tears on her cheek and braced himself.

"Everything. This…" She waved toward the bed. "I don't know what happened."

"Sure you do, Ginny. We made love."

"Yes—no. I don't love you. I love William." She hadn't meant to say that but couldn't take the words back now.

Matt felt himself go cold inside.

Ginny was afraid that if she said anything more she'd only make the situation worse, when she turned to leave, Matt grabbed her arm, stopping her.

"I'm not William, Ginny. And I never will be. You knew that when you came in here. You knew that when I touched you. It was my name you called out, not his." Tears filled her eyes as he watched her, waiting for an answer. "Do yourself a favor and accept that William is gone—and give yourself a chance to live again."

Matt let go of her arm and turned away, listening to her quiet footsteps and the closing of her bedroom door. He'd damn well have to remember to get those men up here tomorrow and move her across the hall.

GINNY STOOD under the shower, letting the hot water beat down on her. Sleep had never come. Her run had been ruined because she couldn't focus, and as hard as she tried to put what had happened out of her mind, her body wouldn't let her. Every move was a reminder of the pleasure she had experienced. When she closed her eyes she could still see his face and body. Her mind would turn traitor, making her relive every touch, every kiss, in the most haunting detail. And most of all she knew she had to talk to Matt, had to make him see that she hadn't wished he was William.

She dressed and prepared to go downstairs to face the inevitable confrontation. But at the top of the stairs she paused, one foot suspended in midair at the sound of angry voices. For a moment she thought the two agents were back, then recognized Jason's voice. When she walked into the kitchen, the two brothers were sitting across the table from each other, matching scowls on their faces. Jason was too uptight to acknowledge her entrance. Matt only gave her a quick dismissive glance that cut deep.

She would not permit him to do that to her. Pouring a cup of coffee, she pulled out the chair at the head of the table and sat sipping the fragrant brew, her gaze moving back and forth between the men. She was suddenly curious about what was going on.

"I'm not giving you fifty thousand dollars, Jason, to start an emu farm," Matt announced.

Ginny almost choked and coffee sloshed from her cup onto the tabletop, but she remained seated. She wasn't about to get up and miss anything, not after hearing that.

"Listen, Matt, you might be the firstborn and inherited everything, but thirty-five percent of the vineyard's profits are mine."

"And ten percent goes to your mother," Matt said. "I'm well aware of that, and you'll get your money. What I'm telling you, Jason, is that things aren't going to be the same around here. There'll be no more handouts for your wild schemes."

"Come on, Matt. Wild schemes?"

Matt picked up the ledgers from the chair beside him and threw them on the table. "What about the longhorns you bought? You purchased ten longhorns. Why? They're not good beef."

"A couple of South Texas ranchers I met were breeding and selling them to other ranchers—a kind of nostalgic, patriotic thing. If you're a cattle rancher in this state, you have to have a couple of longhorns. I just got into the market a little late, that's all."

"And you had to buy land to put them on and some-one to take care of them?"

"Well, sure. Dad wasn't exactly excited at the thought of having them munching on his vines. And they couldn't live off the land around the granite quarry."

"And the buffalo, Jason? You bought thirty head of buffalo from a ranch in Montana and had them shipped here."

"Okay, so I was speculating. Hey, there was a big in-terest in buffalo meat because it's low in fat, high in protein. For some stupid reason people just can't bring themselves to eat the damn beasts, and they're carriers of some disease that affects cattle fetuses, so the ranch-ers don't want them around."

Matt tapped the ledgers. "So you bought some land around Wichita Falls. Why Wichita Falls?"

Jason smiled. "Place will freeze your butt off in the winter, Matt. Buffalo are used to cold weather. Be-sides, the land was dirt cheap."

"Not so cheap when you add in the salary of a cou-ple of hands to stay on the land and take care of them."

Jason shrugged. "But the emus are a sure thing. They lay eggs that sell for two to five thousand dollars apiece. They're low in maintenance and can be kept in a rela-tively small area. Like a large corral with some shelter from the weather. Not a big expense."

"Except for the fifty thousand to buy two females and one male. No!"

"Matt," Jason growled, as Austin strolled into the kitchen still in his pajamas, his hair sticking out in all directions, "that's not fair."

Ginny motioned for Austin to be quiet, poured him some orange juice, hurriedly fixed his cold cereal and pushed it in front of him, then returned to her chair.

"Jason," Matt snarled back, "you get plenty of money from the wine sale and the granite production. And what about your own businesses?"

Jason sat up straighter. "What?"

"Do you think I don't know you're in partnership with a Ralph Johnson and his advertising company in Austin and San Antonio? You own two wine-and-cheese shops in Austin that are making money hand over fist."

"Hey, I'm a Renaissance man."

"I don't care what you are. Take the fifty thousand out of your own profits and stop trying to suck the vineyard dry." Matt leaned forward. "As matter of fact, there's going to be a drastic drop in the wine profits in the next two years. I'm switching over to champagne production."

Jason's eyes widened and his mouth worked, then he started laughing. "Texas champagne? That's ludicrous, Matt. Who's going to buy champagne, or any sparkling wine, from a Texas vineyard?"

"You, for one, will beg me to let you stock your wine shops when you taste it. If nothing else, think of the novelty, brother. *Texas Joie*. Texas Joy. Think about the ad campaign you and your buddy could come up with— if you had the account, that is. But get used to the idea, because that's the way it's going to be. No money for bird eggs out of my pockets."

Matt's smile reminded Ginny of a shark.

Jason knew when he was licked, but he wasn't about to leave Matt with the last word. He stood up to go, but stopped at the door. "Why don't we see what Dad's attorney has to say?"

"Be my guest. But, Jason, I've already looked over the will and you don't have a snowbird's chance in hell of challenging it or my authority. The will's as ironclad now as it was a hundred years ago concerning the inheritance. You contest it and you take the chance of losing everything. So do us both a favor and leave it alone."

Jason's departure left a stony silence. Austin, recognizing the tone of his father's voice, decided for once to say nothing, and he applied himself to his breakfast.

Ginny recognized that Matt's anger had nothing to do with Jason. She desperately wanted to talk to him, but knew that something so personal would have to wait until Austin was engrossed elsewhere. She couldn't take the chance of the boy eavesdropping. When she attempted to get Matt's attention, he ignored her.

Matt remembered how his father used to mete out his punishment. He would wait until the family were all seated at the table ready to eat. Once Matt's plate was set in front of him, his young stomach growling with hunger, the old bastard would announce what his punishment would be and send him from the table.

As he patiently waited for Austin to finish eating, Matt fished out a wad of money and flipped it across the table at Ginny, pretending not to see the way she flinched. "That's your salary for the week. After you fix the men their meal today, meet Austin and me at the car. I have some business in Fredericksburg and you can do some shopping. I know you can use more clothing. Also, the men don't eat here on the weekends, so you don't have to cook tomorrow or Sunday."

He turned his attention to his son. "Austin, didn't I warn you I would not tolerate any illegal computer hacking?"

Austin jerked in surprise, then glanced at Ginny. "Yes."

"And you somehow got into government records, didn't you?"

"Yes, but—"

"I know you were helping, Ginny, but I warned you. You're grounded from using your computer for a week."

Austin jumped up and in the process knocked over his chair. "You can't do that!" He jammed his tightly clenched fists on his hips. "I won't do it."

Matt glanced away from his son as if struggling to control his temper. When he looked back at Austin, his face was devoid of emotion.

All his son's anger was directed at him, and Matt sighed, the memories flooding back. "You will do it. I'm going to trust you to do it. But understand this. If you don't, I'll disconnect everything and lock it away." Matt pretended not to see the way his son's chin wobbled or notice his brave attempt to outstare his father. He also tried to keep his eyes from wandering toward Ginny, but they seemed to have a will of their own. When he saw her tears, he felt as low and mangy as Dog, and pushing back his own chair with a crash, he hurried out of the house.

All the way down the sidewalk, one thought kept repeating itself in his mind, one childish thought that made his steps even heavier. He wished someone had cried for him when his father had dealt out his harsh punishment.

CHAPTER ELEVEN

"I HATE HIM," Austin said as he kicked at a stone in his path.

"No, you don't." Ginny glanced at him and wanted to cry and smile at the same time. Austin wasn't going to allow his father to go unpunished. He'd outdone himself this morning. His hair stuck out from his head in a fuzzy, multicolored ball so that he resembled a clown.

"Do too hate him."

"Do not." They were almost at the cookhouse.

"Do too."

"No, you're just angry." She stopped and grasped his shoulder. Dog, who'd been trotting along beside them, sat down with an unhappy whine. "I'm sorry, Austin."

"You! What for?" Without realizing what he was doing, Austin absently rubbed the top of Dog's head, eliciting a tongue-lolling, tail-thumping expression of ecstasy from the animal.

"Well, if you hadn't been trying to help me, you wouldn't have committed—what is it? Computer theft? Breaking and entering? Whatever, but you wouldn't have done it, would you?"

"No." He refused to look at her, just stared at the ground between his feet, his hand still on Dog.

"Then it was my fault, wasn't it?"

"Indirectly," he whispered, then glanced up at her and grinned. "Did you see those agents' expressions when I gave them those statistics?"

"You're changing the subject. If it was my fault you got in trouble, maybe your father ought to punish me, too?" She couldn't tell him that Matt had already punished her by ignoring what had happened between them.

"He wouldn't dare." After thinking about it for a moment, Austin laughed. "Do you want me to give you a new hairstyle?" He became aware that something warm and wet was lapping at his hand and froze in fear. "Ginny, is he getting ready to bite me?"

She grinned. "Does he look like he wants to hurt you?"

Only Austin's eyes moved. "No." He experimented, touching the soft head again and smiled when Dog showed all his teeth. "He *is* smiling. I didn't believe dogs could smile, but he likes me, doesn't he?"

Ginny wanted to cry and choked back her tears. It wasn't the question, it was the boy's wonder that someone, even a dog, actually liked him.

"Hey, I like you," she said. "Actually I'm crazy about you."

"Are you?"

She'd reached the back door of the cookhouse and was about to open it when she heard something unusual. Her hand was on the screen door when she heard the sound again and looked around. Austin was sitting on the bottom step, his arms around Dog, his face buried in the thick fur, sobbing.

Ginny sat down close to him but didn't touch him. "Austin?"

Eyes awash with tears, he looked up. "I miss my mom."

He was only ten years old, and she wondered if he'd ever really had the chance to grieve for his mother. Ginny pushed a distressed Dog out of the way and gathered him in her arms and let him cry.

"He hates me, Ginny," Austin sobbed against the comfort of her chest. "Why does he hate me?"

She pulled a tissue from her shirt pocket and wiped his eyes, handing him a dry one to blow his nose. "No, he doesn't. Austin, what makes you think that?"

"He's so cold. When I do something that should make him angry, he just stares at me or walks away from me. And he's going to make me go to the local school here. I just know it." He grabbed Ginny and began to cry again. "I want my mother, Ginny. I want to go home."

She sat holding him for a long time, rocking him and waving Dog's concerned whines away, giving herself time to think of what she could say to ease his hurt. When she thought the storm of tears was finally over she said, "Well, I know for a fact that he loves you, Austin. He's too worried about you not to care. As for school, he's trying to work something out." She saw the spark of interest but didn't want to build up his hopes. "I know that for a fact, because he told me. But he's worried because he doesn't want to just send you off anywhere. He's trying to make the right decision for you and him."

"He hates me," Austin said sulkily, then blew his nose. "He won't even say anything about the way I dress or my hair."

Dog kept trying to stick his nose, or tongue, into the problem, and Ginny ordered him to sit. "You know, Austin. I think Matt's afraid."

"What?" He did a double take. "Afraid? Matt?"

"Yes, Austin. Of himself." The more she thought about it, the more she was sure she was right. "Think of just the little he's told us about his childhood. He didn't exactly have a happy loving home life, did he? Today, we have a term for what his father was. You're smart enough to know what I'm talking about. Matt's father was a child abuser. He was a tyrant, a mean-spirited man who verbally and physically abused Matt.

"He humiliated him, called him dumb and said he'd never amount to anything. He treated Matt's mother so badly she ran away and left Matt behind to endure his punishment alone, so in a way he lost his mother, too. Matt ran away from home when he was eighteen, and as far as I know he never went back or spoke to his father again."

"But how would that make Matt afraid of himself?" Austin wanted to know.

"I don't know all the psychological ins and outs, but maybe he's afraid he might be like his father, and that's why he keeps his distance."

Austin sat with his elbows on his thighs and stared out into space. "You think he might like me some?"

"Oh, I think so. He was proud of you yesterday, not only about the car, but the way you handled those FBI agents. You're good at research, so why don't you try and find out more about Matt's childhood?"

"How am I supposed to do that?" Austin gave Ginny a disgusted glance. "It's not like he'll talk to me."

"Listen, my friend. Jericho's been around here a long time. I bet if you asked him, he'd tell you anything you wanted to know."

"Well . . . maybe. I can't believe he was a Texas Ranger."

"He's got pictures and awards in his office."

"Do you know their credo, Ginny?"

She'd only heard of the Texas Rangers in passing, or maybe on television, and shook her head.

"One Riot. One Ranger," Austin said in awe.

She stood up and dusted off the seat of her jeans. "I'm going to go put the spaghetti sauce I started yesterday on to cook some more." When he began to get up, she touched his shoulder. "I'll be a moment, then I want to introduce you to someone."

They approached the barn in time to hear Jason's raised voice. Ginny reached the stall first, yanked opened the door, then stopped. Jason was trying valiantly to tighten a saddle strap around Ernestine's fat stomach, but the horse kept sidestepping around the stall.

"What're you doing to that poor animal?" she demanded.

Exasperated, he stopped what he was doing, dropped his hold on the cinch strap and watched as the horse danced away, managing to dislodge the saddle at the same time. "Well, hell. I think it's obvious to anyone with eyes that I was trying to saddle her."

"Why?" Ginny grasped the leather contraption around Ernestine's head and pulled it off, leaving only the lead rope. When the bit was slipped out of the horse's mouth, Ginny was so outraged she tossed it at Jason. "How would you like one of those jammed down your throat! Just what were you doing with her?"

Jason was taken aback, and to defuse the situation, he winked at Austin. "Hey, Einstein, tell her I was just going to ride the animal, not take her to the local slaughterhouse."

"She's pregnant."

Amusement played around his shapely mouth, then he smiled. "Yes."

"She's going to have a baby."

"So?"

"You can't ride her. You might hurt her and the baby."

Jason thought for a moment she was joking. The sounds of his laughter quickly died away when he realized that neither Ginny nor Austin saw the humor in the situation. "It's okay to ride her."

Ginny ignored Jason and stroked Ernestine between the eyes, motioning for Austin to come closer while she made the introductions. "If you get those two brushes over there and start on this side, I'll do the other."

Austin unquestionably trusted Ginny and did as he was told.

Jason couldn't believe it. They weren't going to let him ride the damn horse. "Really, Ginny. It's okay."

"Go find another horse. You're not riding Ernestine."

"It's good for her. Honest. She needs the exercise."

"We'll exercise her another way."

Jericho and Dog had been watching from the doorway, and when Jason again moved toward the horse, Dog snarled and crouched, making him pull up short. "I'd leave it be if I was you, son," Jericho said. "She done made up her mind."

"This is stupid. Call off your damn dog, Jericho."

"Ain't my dog. He never belonged to no one, 'cept maybe now he's taken to Miss Ginny and the boy. So I guess you'd better beg the lady's pardon and maybe she'll call Dog off."

Jason edged out of the stall, eyeing animals and humans with a wry grin and baffled expression. "Things have sure changed around here lately." But being a generally good-natured man, he laughed as he left the barn. Being a determined man, he wasn't willing to give up on what he wanted, and he headed for the lab, where he knew he'd find Matt. He figured now was as good a time as any to have another discussion about the finer points of raising emus.

Ginny left Jericho and Austin grooming Ernestine. She hoped that Austin would ask the older man about his father's youth and that Jericho would be willing to talk. As she walked out into the sunshine, the warm breeze brushed her cheeks and ruffled her hair, and her steps lightened. She felt the painful grip of grief, Austin's and some of her own, ease a little. The pain of what happened with Matt was a different matter.

Ginny deliberately concentrated on her duties and worked fast to have the noon meal ready on time. Spaghetti with meatballs, hot French bread, lots of garlic butter and a green salad. Seemed like a balanced meal to her, but she wondered if the men, especially the boys, would even touch the salad. It was doubtful, and she didn't intend to have anyone walk away grumbling again. She decided to try to duplicate one of William's specialties and was frantically working at it when Austin rushed in.

He skidded to a stop, sniffed the air and noticed what she was doing. "Pizza!" He dragged a tall stool over to the counter and washed his hands. "Can I help?"

Ginny couldn't find any round pizza pans and had been forced to use the large cookie sheets. The dough was spread out evenly on the pans, and she had just finished putting on the sauce. She pushed the pans in front of Austin. "Your duty is to put on all the fixin's."

"Neat." Austin held his arms straight out while Ginny tied a big dish towel around his chest to protect his clothes.

Then she busied herself, but kept a watchful eye on Austin's work. Despite his outrageous hair and dress, he was a clean, neat child. He was meticulous in his placement of the cheese, green and red peppers, pepperoni, onions and black and green olives. When he was finished and satisfied with his task, Ginny popped the three pans into the oven. Then they leaned against the counter and smiled at each other.

"How can anyone complain today, Austin? Pizza *and* spaghetti!"

Ginny was taking the pizzas out of the ovens when they both stopped to listen to sounds from the other room. "That's probably Jericho. Take a look, Austin, and then you might as well go ahead and ring the dinner bell. By the time they wash up we'll have everything on the table."

Austin jumped down off the stool and pushed open the double doors to the dining room. Immediately he let them swing shut. "Gin," he said, looking at her over his shoulder with a grin. "Better hurry up. They're all out there waiting. Matt and Jason, too."

"What?" Ginny thought he was joking and peeked through a crack in the doors. "They look hungry, don't they?" She handed Austin two hot pads. "You start taking out the pizzas and I'll set up the cart."

It was a hectic ten minutes, but when all the food was on the table and quiet prevailed, Ginny cut the small pizza Austin had made for the two of them and fixed his plate of spaghetti with sauce. He eyed the meatballs hungrily.

"They're loaded with fat," She reminded him. But he gave her such a pitiful look that she laughed and relented.

"Don't forget, we're going with Dad after lunch," he managed to say around a full mouth.

Ginny eyed his hair and ventured a suggestion. "When you finish, how about sticking your head under the faucet and washing that junk out of your hair?"

Austin gave her suggestion some thought. "Okay. Jericho let me sit on Ernestine, said I didn't weigh much. He was real nice, Gin. Showed me all his pictures and told me about some of his adventures when he was a Texas Ranger." The boy took a big bite of pizza, nodded his approval, then swallowed. "Told me some stuff about Matt, too. Things about him when he was a kid."

Ginny waited to hear more, but Austin turned his full attention to his plate. Whatever he and Jericho had talked about had made an impression on the boy, and he might need time to think it all through. But when he was ready, Ginny would be there for him if he wanted to share this newfound knowledge with her.

IN THE PAST FOUR YEARS Ginny had taught herself to read people—their body language, their facial expressions. And she was damn good at it. But Matt was a whole new ball game. He was calm and polite. He smiled at all the right moments. His gaze was direct, and as she stared at him from the back seat of the new car, she frowned. The position of the mirror allowed her an unobstructed view of his face while he drove, and all it revealed was that he was paying attention to the task at hand. Not once did he glance up to catch her watching him.

The Jeep stopped at the front gate. Austin hopped out enthusiastically and opened the gate with ease. She figured it was as good a time as any to apologize. "Matt, I want..."

He drove through the opening and stopped, then turned in his seat. Ginny started to speak again but realized his attention was on Austin as he relocked the gate.

"I don't know how you did it," he said, "but thanks for getting him to wash that crap out of his hair." Matt leaned across the seat and opened the door for his son.

So, it was going to be like that, was it? She gave the back of his head a hard stare. She'd see about that. She was not one to be so casually dismissed, even if the dismissal was smooth and cordially done. These southern gentlemen were game players. On the surface, all chivalry and charm. Oh, those graceful manners—the silky voice, the fleeting touch, the flash of a warm smile or that gleam in the eye—all designed to confuse the opposite sex. Nothing was as it seemed and she wondered how any woman ever understood them.

Ginny had been so wrapped up in her musings that she hadn't noticed that Matt kept glancing at her from the rearview mirror. Childishly, she made a face at him. When he didn't react, she had a sudden feeling of dread and slowly twisted around to look out the back window, sure she was going to see the FBI following them. Instead, she saw Dog running down the highway in hot pursuit. His tongue hung out one side of his mouth, and he was quickly losing ground.

"Matt, please stop," she said. "He might get run over."

"No." Matt increased his speed. "He'll go back home when he gets tired."

"Matt," Austin said, "what if he doesn't and keeps following us?"

Ginny couldn't stand to see how valiantly Dog was struggling to catch them. "Stop the car, Matt. Now."

He heard the anger in her voice and glanced in the rearview mirror to catch her glaring at him. "Sure, Red." It wouldn't do any good for her to see his amusement, he thought, even if he was so damn angry with her. He bit his lip and slowed down, easing the Jeep onto the shoulder of the road.

Ginny opened the door and waited. In a second Dog hurled himself through the opening and immediately planted himself on the seat beside her. He stared at Matt and growled. Ginny and Austin laughed as she reached across the panting animal and closed the door.

"I don't want him on the seat," Matt said. "Tell him to get in the back."

Dog jumped into the cargo area without Ginny telling him. He rested his chin on the back of her seat close to her shoulder, his pale gaze bouncing from Ginny to Austin as he gave them his toothy grin.

Hearing Matt's low rumbling grumble made Ginny smile, and when Austin peered around his seat at her, trying to keep a straight face, they both lost it and laughed until tears filled their eyes. Dog even thought it was amusing and started to yelp.

Try as he might, Matt couldn't remain impervious to their laughter and gave up, joining them. "He could use another bath," he said, eyeing Dog from the rearview mirror. The mention of a bath made the animal throw his head back and howl as if he was baying at the moon.

They laughed and talked all the way into Fredericksburg. When Matt dropped Ginny and Austin off in town, they were all in a good mood. Matt pointed to the bakery.

"I have to meet someone. Probably be gone awhile." He glanced at his watch. "Meet me back here in, say, two hours." As they were about to get out, Matt stopped them. "Hold on a minute. I'm not taking that animal with me. Dog wanted to be with you, so be it. You two can take care of him."

He didn't need to say anything. Dog made it perfectly clear what his preference was as he shot out the door. "Hey, Red," Matt called after Ginny. "If he bites anybody, it's your fault."

Ginny found the small town charming and was amazed to see how many people crowded the wide sidewalks. At first she resisted the lure of the shops, telling herself there couldn't be anything in them to interest her. But almost two hours later, sitting on the bench in front of the bakery shop waiting for Matt, she was taking a much-needed break.

She glanced at Austin beside her, watching as he swung his feet and greedily licked the last of the ice cream from his spoon. "Here let me have that." Taking the paper cup from him, she poured some water out of the bottle she was holding and set it down on the ground.

Dog was sitting beside the bench, surrounded by shopping bags, happily on guard duty and grinning his special smile at anyone who happened to look too long at the packages, Ginny or Austin. "Don't get used to bottled water, mutt," Ginny said as he eagerly lapped up the drink. "At two dollars a pop, you're not likely to get it again."

Austin wiped his mouth with the back of his hand, then pulled out the kaleidoscope Ginny had bought him and held it up to one eye. "Do you know who Matt was meeting?" He handed her the kaleidoscope. "Here, take a look."

"Matt didn't tell me anything." She twisted the end and sighed. "Beautiful, isn't it? Like a rainbow."

"Well, actually, it's only bits and pieces of colored glass..."

"Austin, don't ruin it for me." She loved the sound of his laughter, young and filled with joy. Without thinking she leaned over and kissed his cheek. The sweet softness reminded her of Beth, and by the sudden tears in Austin's eyes she knew he was thinking of his mom.

Ginny quickly turned her head, not wanting Austin to see that she noticed his tears or that her own eyes were shining a little too brightly. She stared off down the street. They'd had a great time. The shops were a treasure trove of everything imaginable—fashionable clothes from country-style broom dresses to leather jackets and jeans, jams and jellies, antiques, arts and crafts. She and Austin had explored them all, and she was amazed at the boy's enthusiasm and energy. He explained that his mother and Peter had loved to shop and almost always included him.

"There's Dad." Austin immediately grabbed some of the shopping bags and headed toward the car.

Matt eyed the bags being stuffed in the back, then turned his attention to Dog, who was seated beside Ginny. "Am I going to have to get a lawyer because he took a bite out of someone?"

"Dad," Austin said, but didn't correct himself this time, "you wouldn't believe it. He sat by the door of every shop we went into."

"By the looks of it, you two were in quite a few." He backed out into the street again. As he drove he listened to Austin tell him what they had done, every once in a while glancing at Ginny when she interrupted with a story of her own. They were in Two Rivers before he realized it and was amazed at how quickly time had passed. He pulled into a parking place in front of a store.

"Austin, I have to go over to the post office and pick up the mail. Why don't you show Ginny around."

Austin's happiness deflated like a pricked balloon as he and Ginny got out of the car. "Yeah, sure. Ginny, this is our hick town, Two Rivers. Five stores, a grocery, a post office, and down at the other end is a McDonald's and a fried-chicken place. Oh yes, and the general store, where the town's senior citizens meet to talk about their latest ailments or operations."

Matt slammed his door and followed them, stepping up over the high curb. "Just show her around and try acting like a human being for once."

Ginny didn't know what was going on. One minute they were talking and happy, the next they were snarling at each other like animals. Even Dog growled. "Matt, go do whatever it is you have to do," she said. "Austin, show some respect for your elders."

"Does that include him?" Austin asked, glaring at his father.

"Anyone over thirty," she snapped, and grabbed his hand. "Shut up, Dog, or you can stay in the car." The males, all three, meekly walked in their appointed directions.

The little town seemed to be bustling, too. But as Austin had said, most of the people were probably collecting social security. They wandered in and out of the shops, but after the first two, Ginny realized that the stores themselves were fronts, mere showpieces. The action was all in the back. She gave Austin's hand a tug and headed in that direction. No one would yell at her if she had a child in tow.

A small elderly man with fuzzy white hair that formed a halo around his head sat perched on a tall stool, the tools of his trade scattered around him.

"He's making a kaleidoscope, Ginny," Austin whispered in awe, and drew closer.

Without looking up, the man said, " 'Course I am. It's what I do. Don't just stand in the doorway blocking what little breeze there is. Come in and look around."

Austin and Ginny moved farther into the room, but still the old man did not look up at them. He was bent over his work, his supple hands polishing a brass tube.

"Ginny bought me a kaleidoscope in Fredericksburg." Austin's nose was almost level with the high worktable, and his eyes darted everywhere.

"Yep, that's mine. I sell them over there."

"Did you hand-polish the wood?" he wanted to know.

"Everything's hand-worked. You're young Matt's boy?" Austin nodded, and the old man turned his head and stared at him. "Hair looks okay today, but I liked it better the way you had it the other day." He turned his attention back to what he was doing, but not before he gave Ginny a quick once-over.

"Name's Charlie, boy. Come back and see me and I'll show you how I make 'em." He winked at Ginny.

Ginny murmured her thanks and pulled Austin out of the room and into the front of the store. Once they were back outside, they ambled toward the general store, the biggest building on the street. Dog tagged along behind as they window-shopped.

"Austin." Ginny stopped and stared. "Do you remember the shop with the dulcimers?"

"Yeah, they were neat. Sounded like bagpipes."

"Look in there." The window was finned with all different sizes of the fretted lap instrument from the Appalachian mountains. "They look identical to the ones we saw in Fredericksburg earlier."

"Cool," he said. "But I like the kaleidoscope better."

Wooden benches, smooth and shiny from long use, were positioned on either side of the double doors to the general store. Austin mumbled under his breath when he saw the old lady on one bench and the elderly gentleman on the other. As he and Ginny drew closer, the woman glanced up from the baby booties she was crocheting and stared hard at the boy.

"Well, Mister," she said to the elderly man. "Looky here. It's young Matt's baby with his hair clean." She returned her attention to her work.

Ginny felt Austin stiffen beside her and wanted to laugh. "You brought all this attention on yourself," she whispered. "Good afternoon," she said to the woman, then tensed at her next words.

"You the gal staying with young Matthew? Guess times have changed, but in my day—"

"Hush, Miss Sally. This ain't your day—it's theirs."

Ginny turned her attention to the man called Mister. He stopped whittling the block of wood in his hands, smiled, then spit a long stream of brown juice into a brass container. Ginny shivered with distaste. "Don't pay her no mind, you hear? She's just jealous she don't have a man."

Ginny quickly shoved Austin through the screen doors, letting them swing and thump shut behind them. "I wonder if there's anyone younger than fifty around here." No wonder Austin hated the town so much, she thought.

"Most all the young people have jobs during the summer. And I'm under fifty—not by much mind you."

Ginny glanced around, trying to find the source of the voice. She spotted a woman moving toward them from the shadowy back of the store.

"I'm Annie," the woman said. "Hello, Austin. Come on back. There's some homemade peach pie and cold milk if you'd like."

Annie was pushing fifty, Ginny thought, but she was in good shape, tall and thin, and judging by her bright intelligent gaze, she was nobody's fool. Ginny liked Annie immediately and wondered if it was because of the woman's red hair.

As if reading her thoughts, Annie touched her thick hair, piled high on her head in a tight knot. "The boys call you Red in school?"

Ginny grinned. "They tried."

"Me, too." Annie smiled. "The only one who did was Matt. Oh, he wasn't in my class, but this is a small town and everyone knows everyone else—and everyone else's business, as well. There are no secrets in Two Rivers." She eyed Ginny as she led them down the aisle to the back room of the store.

Ginny pulled up short as they walked through the doorway. Eight women of varying ages between about forty-five and seventy, the youngest being Annie, were seated around a quilting frame, each with a needle and thread in hand.

Annie quickly introduced Ginny and Austin and settled Austin at a corner table with his pie and milk. Ginny admired the quilt the women were working on.

"It's the Wedding Ring design. Very old pattern."

"It's beautiful," Ginny said, addressing the woman who appeared to be the eldest of the group.

"Rosemary's ninety-three," Annie told her, "and can outsew and outlast the rest of us."

Ginny told them about her shopping spree in Fredericksburg and how impressed she was with the town and the quality of merchandise.

"What'd you think?" Rosemary snapped. "Small towns don't sell nothing but crap?"

"Rosemary," Annie warned. "This is Matthew's lady." She apologized to Ginny. "Rosemary's very loyal to us even if she was born in Fredericksburg."

Ginny was at a loss. She had no idea what Annie was talking about, and her expression must have said as much.

"You don't know that almost everything we make is sold on consignment to the merchants in Fredericksburg," Annie explained, "along with Charlie's kaleidoscopes and Byron's dulcimers." She stopped for a moment as a noise at the front of the store caught her attention, then shrugged and continued, "I also make quilted animals, like rabbits and bears, and Miss Sally knits the clothes. Mister whittles beautiful wooden toys."

It was Ginny who recognized Dog's growl. Something was wrong. She raced out of the room, leaving Annie and the others staring after her in surprise. Almost immediately she bumped into a solid form. Strong hands grabbed her shoulders to steady her.

She glanced up and blanched. "Agent Harrison?"

"Mrs. Carney," he said in a low voice, "if you'll just come with us."

Ginny tried to pull away, but by now the other agent was at her side and had a firm grasp on her arm. "Let go of me!" She was confused by their silence as they tried to hustle her out of the store. They'd only gone a few feet when she realized they were trying to take her against her will and yelled, "Austin, get Matt!"

She dug her heels in the floor, the soles of her running shoes sticking to the wood as if they'd suddenly been nailed there. The jarring action loosened Agent Wilson's grip enough that she twisted her arm free and lashed out, striking him in the nose.

Ginny couldn't say what happened next, but everything was total chaos. A sound loud enough to make the dead sit up and cover their ears reverberated throughout the store.

Austin, a milk mustache still outlining his upper lip, shot out of his chair and managed to grasp Agent Harrison around his leg and hold on for dear life, letting go only when Dog appeared.

Dog flew threw the screen door and clamped his teeth on Agent Harrison's arm with such force that the agent collapsed to his knees. His gaze locked with a pair of pale predatory eyes and he froze, terrified of moving lest the beast take his entire arm off.

Matt heard the alarm bell sound and, like most of the other townspeople, ran to the general store. He had a bad feeling about the alarm and was hoping that Austin hadn't gotten hurt when he caught sight of the scuffle taking place inside the general store. He stormed through the screen doors and skidded to a stop. If he hadn't been so angry, he would have laughed.

Dog had secured Agent Harrison and the man was frozen with terror—and rightly so, Matt thought. He'd seen Dog bring down a wild pig and it wasn't a pretty sight.

Matt's attention was drawn to the other hapless agent. Unlike his partner, he was still standing, but precariously. His nose was bleeding and dribbling down onto his white shirt. A ten-year-old boy had a death grip around his knees, rendering him immobile.

Matt gazed at Ginny and the other ladies surrounding the terrified agent. Each woman had a weapon, ranging from a can of beans to a rolling pin. Since Ginny was nursing her right hand, he assumed she'd been the one to deliver the bloody nose. Matt's eyes watered. He knew the situation was a serious one, but he could hardly keep from laughing, so ludicrous was the scene.

When Sheriff Argus dashed in, he couldn't believe what he was seeing. Everyone was laughing, except for the agents and Dog. After a moment, he realized since he was the law, he'd better take things in hand. He asked Ginny to call off Dog. When the agents tried to talk their way out of their predicament, he just gave them one of his unblinking stares and they fell silent.

Argus ordered them out of his county, threatening to lodge a complaint with their supervisor if they ever tried anything like this again. Then he made sure everyone else was in good shape, worrying that the older ladies might need some assistance. But he should have known better. They were all taking "just a thimbleful" of one-hundred-year-old bourbon. Then he turned to Ginny.

"Having you around's sure exciting. Do you think that's going to do it for the day?"

"That's it for the year, Argus," Matt answered for her. "Now if you don't mind, I want to take my family home."

Family. To Ginny they were the most wonderful words in the world. Her eyes filled with tears as she swallowed around the lump in her throat.

"Don't you dare," Matt whispered next to her ear.

CHAPTER TWELVE

MATT LEANED against the stone fence, his legs crossed in front of him, a cloud of steam from a mug of hot coffee warming his face. There was a coolness in the morning air and he shivered. He was shirtless and shoeless, wearing an old pair of jeans that hung loosely on his hips, but not as loosely as they had before. His black hair was hanging free, tickling his shoulders. After taking a tentative sip of the coffee, then cursing when he scalded his tongue, he set the mug down, took a rubber band from his wrist and pulled his hair back in a ponytail. Maybe it was time to get a haircut.

He'd never been a morning person before, but there was something so peaceful about listening to the land waking up. Birds chattered and fussed at him from the oak tree, and he thought a couple of bird feeders might be nice. Then he laughed at himself. Who would have thought the most important thing on his mind was some silly little birds?

Matt glanced back at the house, finding beauty in the red granite stones. Though the stone was really more of a rose pink, the Van der Bollen quarry had been selling it for years as red granite, the only color of its kind in Texas.

Matt's sigh was a serene sound, coming from deep inside him. He'd always hated the house. Now he knew it wasn't the stone, mortar and wood he despised, but the people who'd inhabited it. He'd even hated himself for too many years. But now there was only a kind of emptiness where all that hate, regret and sorrow had been. A hollowness just waiting to be filled up. His thoughts made him uncomfortable, and he turned his attention to the fields of vines.

His summers in France had taught him about the land, the soil, the grapes. The Van der Bollen land, the entire vineyard, was on the slope of a valley and had a south and southeast exposure that provided just the right amount of sun, as well as protection from winter frost. The soil was almost identical to that of Épernay and Reims—an exceptionally rich soil with the major element chalk, to throw off excess moisture.

His ancestor, old Joseph, had known all about wine and the proper soil. He'd found his paradise and fought fiercely for every square inch of it. He'd cleared the land of rocks and stones. He'd built a home and raised a family. He'd fought Indians, unscrupulous men and squatters who attempted to take his land from him. Old Joseph had been an ambitious man, a man of vision, and he had obtained other land outside the valley: the two quarries and acres and acres of fertile farmland, now planted with peach trees.

Matt admired Joseph for all he'd accomplished. Hell, he hated to admit it, but he even admired his father for his tenacity and unwavering dedication to the land and the wine. Matt thought the vineyard was probably the only thing his father had felt deeply about or truly loved.

Matt had felt that way, also, but he'd given it up, run away to become a policeman and made a new life for himself. But there was always that yearning deep inside him, a craving to dig his hands into the earth, to plant and nurture the succulent grapes. The pull had been almost unbearable at times, and on the oddest occasions he'd find himself actually contemplating returning, until memories of his father would surface with such clarity they'd make him cringe, and he knew the contempt and hatred he'd have to contend with. If anything, he'd learned early in his police career that life was too precious and too short to waste.

Matt sighed again. He'd never been one to daydream, to reflect on the past, but lately so much had changed. *He'd* changed. He sipped his coffee, now almost cool, and focused his wandering attention back on the vineyard. The grapes were filling out, becoming plump with juice. It wouldn't be long now before they'd ripen, their skins almost popping open they'd be so full.

Then the place would be as busy as a stirred anthill with the seasonal pickers. One group was assigned to pick nothing but the red grapes, the *blancs de noirs*. Another picked only the precious *blancs de blancs,* or white grapes, and the third group the delicate Pinot *noirs,* the red grapes that made the purest gold wine. Then there'd be the processing and fermentation stages, the blending process, and when things had settled down for everyone else, there would still be long hours of work for him.

His pleasurable thoughts were disturbed as he remembered the reason he'd risen so early. Jericho, with a straight face, had told him what Ginny had been doing. Jason confirmed the old man's story, but Matt thought they were both putting him on. He heard the footfalls draw nearer now, but he still wasn't convinced and waited to see for himself.

Ginny rounded the curve in the driveway and headed toward the house. Dog was running happily beside her.

Her hand was slippery with sweat and she took a firmer grip on the rope, then glanced over her shoulder at Ernestine. She was worried that she might be going too fast for the pregnant mare, but when she checked, Ernestine wasn't even breathing hard. She noticed Dog wasn't panting any more than usual, either, and she grumbled breathlessly to herself. It appeared she was the only one who was truly exerting herself.

"'Morning," Matt called out as he fought to keep a straight face. "Have a nice run this morning?"

Ginny slowed and veered from her path to the barn. "Well, I'm exhausted, but these two don't seem to be even winded."

Matt nodded. "Ernestine's a quarter horse, so she's used to running. As for that animal—" he faked a glare at Dog "—there's no telling about him. He's such a mixed breed, more wolf than German shepherd, maybe a drop or two of greyhound there, too." He looked at Ginny curiously. "Mind telling me why Ernestine's running behind you? Horses are for riding, Ginny."

"Not when she's pregnant. Besides, Jason said she needed exercise."

"I see. And you thought jogging with you would be good for her?"

"Yes. But I called your local veterinarian to make sure it wouldn't hurt her."

That did it. Matt nodded again and quickly headed for the house before he insulted her by bursting out laughing. He could well imagine what the townsfolk had thought when the vet told them about Ernestine's new fitness routine. Once in the house he turned to see Ginny leading the mare to the barn. He wondered why no one in town had mentioned this little tidbit to him. But of course he knew the reason. In the past three weeks, ever since the FBI had tried forcibly to remove Ginny from the general store, the town had taken to her as if she'd lived among them all her life.

Ginny had begun to venture off the vineyard, making visits to the general store, even Fredericksburg. But she never left the place without Dog at her side. The folks in town had become accustomed to having an animal they once feared and despised in their midst. They'd even come to like him, but Dog's loyalties were to Ginny first, then Austin, and he only tolerated everyone else.

Matt was happy to see her begin to live again. What surprised him was that she'd made fast friends with Annie and the quilting group, even though the women were much older than she was. Even Austin, whom Ginny often took with her, seemed to enjoy these trips to town. It took a little investigating to discover that his son was not spending his time with a gaggle of old ladies but was learning to make kaleidoscopes with Charlie or being taught to play the dulcimer by Byron, Charlie's brother. Matt only wished his son would take an interest in the vineyard.

Matt was in the process of pouring himself another cup of coffee and stopped. He set the pot down hard on the burner. The thought had hit too close to home, and memories of his father washed over him like a sickness. There had been lecture after lecture about the business. That was all he'd ever had in common with his father—a love for the business. And here he was wishing for the same kind of relationship with his son. It was unthinkable. It was unforgivable. He'd made a promise to himself long before Austin was born that he'd never do that to a child. That was why he'd never wanted children in the first place. . . .

Picking up a dish towel, Matt dabbed at his damp face. When the wave of revulsion passed, he made it to the nearest chair and sat down. Just thinking that he might be like his father in any way made him feel sick to his stomach.

GINNY STOOD BACK and shook herself like Dog. She'd washed down Ernestine and brushed her. Then she'd turned her attention to Dog. This time he knew what to expect, and when she'd finished, she was as wet as he was. She turned off the hose, emptied the metal tub and headed for the house and her own bath.

God, she felt good. Her feeling had nothing to do with the morning exercise, either. She was free. For the first time in four years she was no longer looking over her shoulder or worrying about what she was saying or to whom she was saying it. Even her problems with Matt had faded away. Oh, she'd never been able to talk to him about what had happened between them, but after the incident at the general store three weeks ago, it seemed to have been forgotten.

No one had moved her from the bedroom, but the door between them had remained firmly shut. He'd never referred to that night, and since he was no longer angry at her, she decided to let the situation slide. It was easier that way. Easier than having to examine and expose emotions she wasn't even sure of herself. Though the bedroom door was shut, it hadn't locked out the memories that came to her late at night when her will was weak.

Matt wasn't around when she entered the house, and she immediately made her way upstairs, detouring to Austin's room to give him a wake-up call. When she returned to the kitchen after her bath, she was surprised to find Austin already there. Usually it took three wake-up calls. Sometimes, when she was in a hurry to be finished with the day's chores, she had to bodily drag him out of bed.

Austin glanced up from his bowl of cereal, saw her stagger in shock and laughed. "Matt asked me to be up and dressed early."

She poured herself a cup of coffee, eyeing Austin's blue-and-white-striped cotton dress shirt and navy gabardine slacks. He was a handsome child, she thought, with a sense of style. His dark hair was clean and neatly combed. His face, hands and even his fingernails were clean, she noticed. When she spotted the polished black loafers, her eyebrows shot up.

"Why?" she asked. "Are you going somewhere?"

Austin shrugged, trying to hide his excitement. "Don't know. He just said Sunday best, and it's not Sunday."

They both stared when Matt strolled in. The double-breasted, dark gray suit he was wearing was only a little loose on the shoulders. From his gleaming black alligator cowboy boots to his newly brushed charcoal gray Stetson, he looked sexy enough to make any woman over the age of thirteen drool.

Ginny was certainly not immune to his devastating good looks. Nor, she sniffed the air, his after-shave. "You're all dressed up?" She could have kicked herself—any dumb ox could see that.

Matt flipped his hat off with one hand, then twirled the brim between his fingers. He placed the Stetson on the seat of a chair, pulled out the chair beside it and sat down. He looked at Austin. "Do you remember a few weeks ago when we all went to Fredericksburg and I left you two to shop because I had a meeting with someone?"

Austin nodded, his face mirroring his confusion. "Yes, sir."

"Well, I met with Dean Halstead and a couple of regents from the University of Texas. The meeting was about you."

Austin swallowed, unable to speak.

Ginny hadn't been struck speechless like Austin, nor was she able to contain her excitement. "Why? What about Austin? What'd they say?"

Matt grinned, but his attention was on his son. "I'd already sent them all your grades, test scores, transcripts and the letters from your teachers in California. They were very impressed. Hell, I'm impressed, and I thought your mother kept me pretty well apprised of what you were doing."

"Mom did?" Austin's eyes widened.

"Sure. I paid the bills, and she sent me a copy of all your grades and accomplishments."

"She did?" He was puzzled. "I don't understand. You paid?"

"Sure, Austin. For your education, all the special classes and courses, your computer equipment, the field trips. Of course I paid."

"But why?" He was truly confused.

It was Matt's turned to look stumped. "Because you're my son." He saw the disappointment in the child's eyes and continued. "It was something I wanted to do. I couldn't be there with you..." He was on shaky ground of his own making here. "Your mom wouldn't take money when she left me. She didn't want anything from me, but I wouldn't let her cut me off from you entirely."

Austin's gaze dropped to the table. He swallowed hard and pushed his spoon and bowl around in a circle a couple of times before he could look up again. "Thanks, Dad." He ducked his head again. "What about the meeting with Dean Halstead?"

The emotion in the room almost did Ginny in, and if it hadn't been for the suspense, she would have blubbered like a baby. Instead, she reached under the table, grabbed Matt's thigh and squeezed.

"There's no doubt, Austin—" Matt's voice rose a fraction as he felt Ginny's nails dig into his flesh, then it leveled out as she loosened her grip "—they'll take you in their medical school. It's just a matter of your age and maturity."

"Medical school?" Ginny asked. "I thought it was mathematics ... or something like that."

"Well, yes," Austin said. "I believe Einstein stopped too soon in his unified-field theory to establish a merger between quantum theory and his general theory of relativity. Mass energy without the drawbacks," he quickly explained at their blank expressions. "I want to study everything, but mostly I want to be in medical research. To study deoxyribonucleic acid—DNA to you two. That's where science is headed. And if we combine that research with the continuation of Einstein's work, it will eventually affect every aspect of life as we know it. Even space travel could change."

"Well, yes." Matt glanced at Ginny to see if she was as dumbstruck as he was. He knew that Austin was a genius, and though in the past few weeks they'd grown closer, Austin had never talked to Matt about what he wanted to do. Listening to his son now made him realize just how special he was.

Ginny responded to Matt's stunned expression with one of her own. She knew, of course, that Austin was a genius, but up until now, she'd thought of him as a child, confused, angry, rebellious at being sent to live with a father he didn't know. To her he was a sad little boy who missed his mother.

"Austin," Matt said, "the meeting was to begin working out some of the problems of having a ten-year-old boy at the college."

"I don't see... If it's the money, Mom's insurance policy and the money the airline paid should be enough."

Matt shook his head. "That money is being invested for your future. As to the rest, I'll take care of it. But there are other problems, like where would you live? You can't commute from here on a daily basis. Who'd take care of you? And I won't let you go out of state to some boarding school."

Austin leaned forward eagerly. "So, bottom line, what's going to happen?"

Matt laughed, "Okay, bottom line. We're going to the university this morning. You're going to be tested, and then we'll meet with Dean Halstead and the regents. If they like you and accept you, we'll take a trip to the dean's home so you can meet his wife and family. If—and I stress if, Austin—it all works out, you're going to live with them."

Austin couldn't believe it. From the moment he'd been hauled to this godforsaken place, he'd wanted nothing more than to go home, back to Peter and California. Now here was his chance to leave and never come back, and he was feeling a kind of hollow emptiness.

"There are rules, Austin." Matt waited until he had his son's full attention. "You live with the Halsteads five days a week, but you have to come home on weekends, holidays and summer vacation. If you can't agree to that, then the whole deal is off."

Ginny thought she was going to cry.

Austin's ear-to-ear smile of happiness, his shining dark eyes and barely contained excitement were more than she could take. She shoved her chair away from the table, walked over to the sink and busied herself with the breakfast dishes.

Austin and Matt grinned at each other. "Women," Austin said.

Matt chuckled. "Well, son, I have some real bad news for you. Dean Halstead has five daughters, from two to fifteen. So you best ask Ginny for all the advice she can give you. But I promise you it will never be enough to make you any smarter where they're concerned."

Ginny managed to contain the serious flood of tears until they'd left, then sat down and had a good cry. She even broke Matt's strict rule and allowed Dog into the house for company.

Finally, after she'd shed tears for Matt and Austin, she cried for herself for the first time in four years. Cried for her own loss, because no matter how much she wanted her child and husband back, they were gone forever. The memories all came back to her like a movie, starting from the moment she met William, through their years of happiness together, to the bombing of the car.

Then, like a movie, it ended. She could no longer clearly see William or Beth's features. They'd faded away. She would always love them, she would always feel an ache for them. But for the first time she realized she could go on without them. They would have wanted her to.

Her heart heavy with emotion, she rose from the table. She had a meal to fix for a bunch of hungry men.

IT WAS GETTING DARK and she was getting worried.

How many times had she stood at the back door and stared fixedly down the drive, sure she'd heard the sound of Matt's car, only to be mistaken?

"Walking the floor won't make them get here any faster," Jason said.

Ginny spun around and glared at Matt's brother. He'd joined the men for lunch, followed her back to the house and in general had managed to make a nuisance of himself. She thought he'd leave when Annie showed up, but no such luck. He was, she had to admit, an endearing man, but he kept insisting she was acting like a mother hen.

Ginny caught Annie shaking her head at Jason. "Okay, you two. There's something going on here. Jason's been acting like he's my best buddy ever since lunch. And, Annie—" her eyes narrowed a fraction "—you told me you were going to San Antonio today. What's up?"

Jason fidgeted in his chair. "Hey, I just thought you'd like my charming company for a while. Do you and Austin want to come watch the pickers tomorrow?"

Ginny shook her head in confusion. "What does one thing have to do with the other? And what are pickers?"

Annie laughed. "They harvest the peach crop, working their way through the county. It's quite something to see for the first time."

Ginny returned to her chair, pushed aside the legal papers she and Annie had been working on and placed her elbows on the tabletop. Resting her chin on her fists, she stared across the table at Jason and Annie. "He told you not to leave me alone, didn't he?"

"He who?" Jason grinned.

"I may be rusty, Jason, but I'm still an attorney. I can spot a liar in a rainstorm with a wet paper bag over his head."

"I resent that," Jason said.

"Oh, be quiet, Jason," Annie admonished. "You were never good at lying. Even crazy Miss Sally could tell when you were telling a whopper." Annie smiled at Ginny. "The jig is up, handsome. She's wise to us. Yes, Matt asked us all to keep an eye on you."

"All?" Ginny asked.

"Jason, Jericho," Annie said, looking suddenly uncomfortable.

"Oh, hell," Jason snapped. "Everyone in town has been looking out for you."

Ginny was struck speechless. But not for long. "Why, for heaven's sake?" Jason found something of great interest on the ceiling and her gaze shifted to Annie. "Why?"

"Matt and Argus felt it was necessary—in case someone showed up again."

Ginny thought about it for a moment. "You're probably right. The FBI wasn't exactly happy with me when I refused to sign their release absolving the government of any responsibility concerning my case. I made it perfectly clear that I do hold them totally responsible and will until the person who killed my family is caught.''

''Well, there's the rub— Ouch!'' Jason stared at Annie and bent down to massage his aching shin. ''What?''

''Big mouth,'' Annie mumbled.

''Okay, you two. Out with it.''

Annie wanted desperately to strangle Jason Van der Bollen, and her look warned him to be quiet. ''I think you should ask Matt or Argus about this, Ginny.''

''But they're not here and I'm asking you. Spit it out.''

''Look—'' Jason began.

''You've said enough, Jason.'' Annie picked up the half-empty bottle of wine and refilled her glass and Ginny's, deliberately ignoring Jason's. ''You really ought to talk to Matt, but I can see you're not going to wait.'' She took a breath. ''From what little I know, it seems Jericho started it all.''

Ginny frowned. ''Explain.''

''You do know about him, don't you? I mean, that he was a famous Texas Ranger?''

''Tracked a serial killer,'' Jason broke in, ''for three straight years over eight Texas counties. The sicko had a thing for young girls—did unspeakable things to them before he finally killed them. You know, way back then a serial killer was almost unheard-of. Jericho was the first lawman to recognize the similarities between the killings. Like Texas Rangers are supposed to, he never gave up looking—he just kept coming till he found his man. When he did, he didn't say a word to the guy, just shot him and walked calmly away. And never looked back. Almost went up on charges, but the governor wouldn't hear of it and gave Jericho a commendation, instead."

"Thank you, Jason," Annie said sarcastically. "I couldn't have told the story without you." She pushed the wine bottle out of his reach. "Anyway, seems Jericho did a lot of things for a lot of people and made friends in high places. After the FBI tried to take you out of the general store, Jericho told Argus he was going to call in some markers. Seems once he did, all hell started breaking loose." Annie pushed the wine bottle a little farther from Jason's outstretched arm. "The attorney general—ours, that is—called the governor of Massachusetts and the mayor of Boston and asked them to check on the status of the bombing that killed your child and husband."

Jason couldn't help himself and took over the story. "Boston's chief of police called our attorney general and told him they weren't working the case because he thought the feds still were. When he was advised of the situation, he said he'd pull the file personally and take care of it."

After a long silence Ginny asked the obvious. "So, the Boston police have reopened the case and started a full investigation?"

Annie shot a look at Jason, and this time he closed his mouth. "Ginny," Annie said, "when they know where you are, that you're no longer under federal protection..."

"I see. Do Matt and Argus think I'm in danger?" A look of horror crossed her face. "Is my being here putting Matt or Austin in danger?"

"No!" Annie and Jason shouted.

"Look, talk to Matt, Ginny." Annie started gathering up the papers they'd been working on. "You don't have long to wait. He's here now."

Ginny jumped up and went to the door, holding it open as Matt walked in with Austin in his arms. "What's wrong?" Then she relaxed when she noticed how Austin's arms were wrapped around his father's neck and the way his small legs dangled like limp noodles.

"He's asleep. Poor little guy's all tuckered out. He's had a long day." Matt kept moving toward the stairs.

Ginny followed him, thinking that Austin wasn't the only one who'd had a hard day. Matt look tired, his face drawn with fatigue and his limp more pronounced. But there was something different about him, even though he was exhausted. A look of pride. "His PJs are in the first drawer of the dresser," she told him.

Matt stopped and half turned toward her. "I have to undress him?"

"Matt, you can't put the child to bed with his clothes on. He won't get a good night's sleep." Matt looked as if he wanted to protest and hand the duty over to her but she quickly returned to the kitchen.

"Don't either of you dare laugh!"

Annie picked up her purse and the papers. "I wouldn't think of it," she said, "because I'm going home. Oh, but Lordy, Lordy, would I love to be a fly on the wall up there right now. I undressed *my* children when they were dead to the world. Then I got wise and tucked them in clothes and all." She waved good-night to the two of them and headed for her car.

"I don't see what's taking Matt so long," Jason said.

"That's because you've never tried to undress a sleeping child before."

"I don't know about that. Is it the same as undressing a woman who's passed out?"

Ginny gave him a hard look until she realized by his grin that he was joking. "Good night, Jason."

"Oh, no—you're not getting rid of me that easily. I've been waiting to have a word with big brother." He gave her one of his most charming smiles. "Did you think I was staying just to protect you?"

They were trading friendly insults when they heard the slow uneven tread of Matt's footsteps on the stairs. Jason got up, opened the refrigerator and pulled out a bottle of Matt's private stock of wine. He was pouring a glass when Matt made it to the closest chair and flopped down.

"You could have warned me what a job that was going to be. Skinning an eel would've been easier." He took the glass Jason handed him, then leaned his head back and closed his eyes.

"How did it go?" She didn't care how tired he was. She wanted to know what had happened at the university.

"Fine." He opened his eyes and looked at Ginny. "Sorry. He was great. Remember my telling you he was ten going on forty? Well, you should have seem him with the Halstead girls. I don't think I could have been prouder of him. He was a perfect little gentleman. But I'll tell you this, I give him two weeks with those girls and he'll be ten going on a hundred. They're just itching to get at him."

Matt and Jason laughed and Ginny frowned. It must be some male thing, she decided.

"How did he do on the test?" Ginny asked. "What did the dean say? Are they going to allow him to go there?"

Matt glanced at Jason, the bottle still in his hand. "Pour Ginny some, will you, and you have a glass with us." Matt took a deep breath and sighed. "The professors who tested Austin were astounded at his knowledge and comprehension, especially in science." He yanked the rubber band from his ponytail, letting his hair fall free. "They're going to accept him all right. I don't think I've ever seen ten grown men so excited over a small boy. I just didn't realize how intelligent he is. I mean, I know he's a genius, but the scope of his mind is beyond me."

"Did you feed him?" Ginny asked. "Did you eat?"

Matt laughed. "Yes. We were treated royally." He yawned and glanced at his watch, surprised to see it was only nine o'clock. It felt like midnight. He looked at Jason. "Thanks for staying."

Jason nodded. "Ginny knows why Annie and I were here, though. Guessed, then dragged the whole story out of us."

Matt chuckled, too damn tired to care. "Figures."

Jason headed for the door, ready to leave, then stopped. "Say, Matt, what about llamas? There's a great market for their wool, and I understand their poop is a first-class fertilizer—rich, odorless."

Matt was so tired he thought he must be hearing things. "Llamas' what?" Then he saw the laughter on his brother's handsome face and picked up the wine bottle, pretending to aim it at him. Jason disappeared into the black night.

Matt turned to Ginny. "Did he say poop?"

"Odorless poop."

Matt shook his head, pushed back his chair and slowly got up. "I'm going to bed." Then he did something he'd told himself he wasn't going to do. He leaned down and gently kissed her on the cheek. "Don't worry so much, Red. We have everything under control."

As he climbed the stairs, he wondered if he was right. Lately, nothing seemed to be going as he thought it should. That included his feelings for Ginny.

CHAPTER THIRTEEN

WARM BREATH tickled her ear and lured her from a deep sleep.

Slowly, she opened her eyes to find Matt leaning over her, his mouth near and inviting.

"Wake up, Red," he murmured. She looked so tempting, all warm and sleepy, but he backed away, determined he wasn't going to be first to initiate anything this time.

Ginny sat up, pushed the hair back from her face and said, "Is something wrong?" In his haste, it looked as if Matt had only taken time to hurriedly slip on a pair of gray sweat pants and throw on a shirt, leaving it unbuttoned and hanging open. His appearance alarmed her. "Austin? Has something happened to him?"

"Everything's fine. I tried to wake him, but it was like trying to wake the dead."

Ginny rubbed her eyes. "You have to drag him out of bed and stand him up. What's wrong, Matt?"

Matt shook his head, wishing he could sleep the sleep of the innocent. "Ernestine's about to drop her foal, and I thought you'd like to be there."

"I would. I do." She started to throw off the covers, then stopped and looked at Matt, but he'd already turned away and was heading for the door.

"There's a cup of coffee waiting downstairs, so hurry up."

Like Matt, she was in too big a rush to think about clothes and grabbed the first thing handy, a pair of sweatpants. She was about to change her top but decided his shirt would serve for a trip to the barn.

She stuck her bare feet into her running shoes without tying them and checked to make sure she was all buttoned up as she sprinted down the stairs to the kitchen. Matt met her at the door, handed her a large mug of steaming coffee, and together they left the house. Dog eagerly followed, bumping the side of her leg as he tried to snap at her loose shoelaces until she finally paid some attention to him.

She was surprised at the damp nip in the air and shivered. It was so dark. The stars were hidden by dense clouds, and the air was fragrant with approaching rain. The only light to guide them was the illumination from the barn ahead.

When Ginny stumbled over a protruding tree root, Matt grasped her arm. Instead of letting go, he moved closer and wrapped his arm around her shoulders. Just to help, he told himself, to keep her from falling on her face.

"What time is it?"

"Around three-thirty, I think."

As they stepped into the shelter of the barn, a warmth wrapped around them. Still Matt held her to his side, loath to let go of the serenity he felt when she was in his arms.

They approached the stall, and it was Ginny who broke the spell as she hurried to the door. "Matt! She's gone."

Jericho stepped out of the darkness, an old Winchester rifle held securely in his crossed arms. "Cleaned out the third stall and moved her there 'cause it's bigger."

Matt eyed the rifle, and he and Jericho nodded to each other.

"I'm off to bed, now that you're here to watch over her."

Ginny was surprised that Jericho was leaving. She knew he cared as much about Ernestine as she did. "You're not staying?"

"Naw. I've seen her do this three times before. She's an old hand at it. Besides, vet said she was in excellent health." He grinned, then ducked his head. "Must have been all that fresh air and early-morning jogging." He winked at Ginny and melted soundlessly into the darkness.

"Does he live here at the vineyard? I know he has the office in here. I don't believe he ever said."

Matt pointed to the open stall door and they headed in that direction. "There's a stone cottage a distance up behind the main house and off an old road," he said. "The cottage sits on the ledge overlooking the spot where the Pedernales and Llano rivers cross. Jericho's lived there off and on for as long as I can remember."

"Do you know why he always comes back here to the vineyard?"

"No. He only spoke of his past once to me and that was to tell me he owed the family a debt he could only repay with his life. I tried for years to find out what kept him here until one time he looked me straight in the eye and said some things were best left alone."

"He owed your father? I had a feeling Jericho didn't particularly like him."

"I meant my grandfather. He and Jericho were great buddies. I'm sure there're a lot of skeletons in their closets. Jericho held my father in the utmost contempt. He despised him, and my father reciprocated the feeling, but he never once asked the old man to leave the property, not even after Grandfather passed away.''

She decided to mull over the mystery when she had more time. Her attention was drawn to Ernestine now. She would have walked right up to the horse as she always did, but Matt grabbed her arm and held her still.

''Give her a minute, Ginny. She's nervous and in pain. Let her get used to having company.'' He followed the direction of Ernestine's nervous gaze, noticing the way her ears lay flat against her head when she spotted Dog at Ginny's heels. He ordered Dog out of the barn.

The stall was big and warm, with a thick layer of fresh hay covering the floor. To the left was another smaller stall that opened into the bigger one, with bales of hay stacked around the wall. Some of the bales had tumbled over and come undone, carpeting the floor with the fragrant hay. Matt carefully eased in that direction, pulling Ginny along beside him. They sat down and leaned against one of the broken bales, all the while keeping a watchful eye on Ernestine, monitoring her mood by the movement of her ears.

Ginny followed Matt, her attention never wavering from her four-legged friend. She noticed the way Ernestine's coat glistened with perspiration, the way she quivered. ''Matt, she's shivering. Get her a blanket.''

Matt smiled as he reminded himself that Ginny was, after all, a city girl. ''She's having a contraction. I bet it won't be long now before she lies down.''

A quiet settled around them, disturbed occasionally by Ernestine's labored breathing. Matt lay back on the pile of hay and stared up at the ceiling. "Was Beth's birth hard?"

Ginny looked over her shoulder at Matt. His question startled her, causing memories to resurface. She smiled. "Beth was born at three o'clock in the morning after six hours of labor. Was it a hard birth? I can't remember. I was so happy when she was born, happy she was healthy, that any pain I'd had giving birth didn't matter."

"I never understood that—about women forgetting all that pain. I still remember every second I hurt when I was shot. How can you forget?"

Ginny looked at Ernestine and had a feeling they were going to be here longer than Matt had predicted. She pushed some hay together in a semblance of a pillow and lay down beside him. "I don't understand it, either, but there it is. I don't remember."

"How about William? Was he there for Beth's birth?"

Ginny laughed. "William wouldn't even clean out the Thanksgiving turkey. He stayed far away from the delivery room. Were you there for Austin's?"

"No. I was young and stupid and didn't want any kids." He rolled over on his side and looked down at Ginny. "Do you know that little guy kept five professors, all with letters after their names that I couldn't even decipher, enthralled with his theories for almost an hour? Ginny, what he was talking about was so far over my head, so far over anything I'll ever understand. It was mind-boggling. And he's not just smart, Ginny. He has manners and honest respect for people. He's..."

"Special," Ginny said helpfully.

"Yeah, and he's my son," Matt said proudly, almost reverently. "Amazing, isn't it? Because it sure as hell amazes me."

Ginny wanted to smile, but she kept her face expressionless and closed her eyes. "What you mean is that you're astonished at how much you care for him, right?"

Matt shook his head. "You know, I tried not to care. I certainly didn't want to."

"Why would you *not* want to love him, Matt?"

"You know some of my background. Figure it out for yourself."

She felt him start to pull away from her and opened her eyes only to see that he'd actually moved closer—too close. Now, she thought, was as good a time as any to have that talk with him.

She reached up, brushed his hair away from the side of his face and secured it behind his ear. When he didn't flinch, she lightly touched his cheek with the tips of her fingers. "When we made love—after we made love—I..."

Matt lowered his head, not wanting to hear what she had to say. He was shocked when she suddenly wrapped her arms around his neck, then flipped him over on his back, using her weight to hold him still.

"You're going to listen this time, Matthew Bolt." She watched the desire and amusement drain from his face. "Don't even think of getting up and leaving or I'll sic Dog on you." He looked as if he wanted to say something, make a smart or hurtful remark, and she pressed her finger across his lips. "Shut up. Matt, I hurt you and I'm sorry. Believe me, I was not comparing you to William, and I wasn't thinking about him while we were making love—well, not the way you think.

"What I was crying about..." Matt wasn't making this easy. He just stared at her with that empty look in his eyes. "Matt, I thought I'd never want anyone but William. That I could never care for another man."

Matt moved as if he wanted to get up, and she leaned down harder on him. "I wanted you desperately and I never confused you with William. Never wished you were him. How could I? All I could think about was you and the way you made me feel. And you did make me feel, Matt. No one has ever made me feel like that before.

"But afterward I felt guilty. Like I'd somehow been unfaithful. That's when I became upset. I tried to see William's face, to remind myself of the life we had together. But he's gone, Matt. He will always be a wonderful part of my past, I'll have happy memories of our time together, but I'm alive. I can't live in the past. It's over...."

Matt hadn't known he'd been holding his breath until he felt the pain in his chest and the sudden lightheadedness. Or maybe he hadn't been holding his breath, he thought. Maybe the pain was the cracking of that thick, protective shell around his heart. Whatever it was, it hurt—a combination of the worst and best pain he'd ever felt.

Ginny kissed him, softly, sweetly, as her tears splashed down on his face. She drew back and wiped them away. "I'm sorry. I know how you hate them."

Matt slid his fingers through her hair. "I hate them because I associate them with my own pain, something I don't deal with too well." He pulled her down so that her lips were close to his. "I'm not noted for dealing well with long-term relationships, either, Red."

Ginny wanted nothing more than to feel his mouth on hers. "But that was the old Matt, wasn't it?"

He chuckled and shook his head. "I guess. Maybe. I don't know."

"Why don't we just see what happens," she suggested. "After you make love to me again, that is. I've thought about nothing else since that night."

Matt kissed her, long and deep, and in so doing managed to roll her over in the thick fresh hay. He slid his hands up beneath her shirt, and the heat of her warmed him deep inside.

For a second Ginny moved her head sideways, away from his mouth. "Listen."

Matt lifted his head and smiled. The rain was coming down hard on the barn's tin roof, the drumming a welcoming sound. "Do you know I had sex for the first time in this barn?" He worked diligently at getting her sweatpants off, then followed with his own.

"How old were you?" she whispered against his lips.

"I'll never tell."

She shifted her hips tantalizingly against his. "How old?"

"Old enough that she didn't have any complaints." He chuckled when Ginny tried to move away. "Thirteen. Now be quiet."

Matt made long, slow love to her, both of them savoring their closeness, their fragrant bed, the sound of the rain overhead and their joy in each other. Afterward, she was so relaxed she could have lain there all day, but a sudden sound made her realize they weren't alone.

Ginny started grabbing for her clothes, then stopped. "Matt. Matt!" She reached over and tapped him on the chest. "Oh, Matt, look!"

Ernestine was shivering and shaking and her coat was gleaming as if it had been oiled. "Something's wrong, Matt. Why isn't she lying down?"

"She's fine, Ginny." They both stopped trying to dress and watched. "Some horses lie down, some stand up. It all depends on what Mother Nature dictates at the time." As they stood in the open doorway, still naked and warm from their lovemaking, Matt wrapped his arms around Ginny and held her tightly against his chest.

Ginny watched the mare's efforts, saw her pain and remembered how she herself had felt giving birth. She watched as a new life slipped into the world from the warmth and security of the mother's womb. She watched as Ernestine sniffed, licked and nuzzled her foal. Tears flooded her eyes and slowly trickled down her cheeks as she remembered holding Beth, still wet from the birth, in her arms.

Matt felt the warm tears on his arm and knew immediately what Ginny was thinking. He ached for her, but all he could do was swallow around the lump in his throat and hold her tighter against him.

The tiny, colt struggling to stand on its wobbly legs made Ginny laugh softly. Matt relaxed but continued to hold her awhile longer, knowing the real world was going to intrude all too soon on their happiness. He kissed her lightly on her cheek.

"Come on, let's leave them alone." He picked up their clothes, handed Ginny hers and began to dress.

"Can I pet him?"

Matt shook his head. "Later. Give Ernestine some time alone with her son and him some time to gain strength." Matt glanced at Ginny and laughed. "Don't look so disappointed." Then he began to pick the pieces of hay out of wildly tangled hair. "I'll tell you something—you'd better dust yourself off. If we run into Jericho or one of the other hands, there won't be any doubt what we've been up to."

Ginny eyed him and smiled. "Take a little of your own advice. The way you look with that silly grin plastered on your face, anyone could guess immediately what you've been doing."

Matt grabbed Ginny's hand and they ran out of the barn and into the morning. Dawn was just breaking through the darkness, pushing its way through the shrinking clouds and painting the sky with narrow fingers of fire. It had stopped raining, and the thick grass was spongy under their feet. The air smelled freshly washed.

Ginny felt alive. She and Matt had solved their difficulties. They'd made love and it had been better than before. A new life had been born and... A thought flitted across her mind like a hummingbird. She wanted to say something to Matt but decided she didn't know how he'd react. They'd made love, sweetly, passionately, but without protection. Suddenly the idea of another new life filled her to overflowing with so many emotions that she couldn't move.

Matt noticed Ginny's strange expression and saw her eyes fill with tears. Gathering her in his arms, he swung her around in a circle. "Don't go all emotional on me. Just enjoy the fact that we're alive for this beautiful day."

Ginny grabbed his shoulders and held on as he whirled her around, laughing along with him. Anyone watching them would think they'd gone crazy. Maybe she *was* crazy, she thought, because suddenly she realized that, more than anything, she did want another baby, maybe even babies. Thirty-two wasn't too old to have lots of them.

She was so lost in her fantasies that she didn't realize they'd reached the kitchen. The shock of her wet bare feet on the cold floor jolted her back to reality. "Matt, where are my shoes?"

He gazed down at his own bare feet. "With mine, I suspect." He gathered her in his arms and whispered, "Let's sneak upstairs and have a shower together. I still have these crazy dreams about me bathing you that first day."

"You have to go get our shoes, Matt. They're a dead giveaway to anyone who sees them."

Matt glanced through the screen door. Dog had followed them and sat dejectedly on the stoop. "Go fetch Ginny's shoes, you mangy mutt," he said as his hands wandered beneath her shirt and cupped her breasts. Dog grinned and lay down.

"Matt, please. You can't let anyone find them. I'd die of embarrassment." She laughed as his scowl deepened. "And the way we left the hay where we lay—kick it around."

He groaned dramatically, then dropped his hands. Dog moved aside only long enough to let Matt out the door, then he slipped into the house before the screen door slammed shut. He headed straight for Ginny, his tail swishing the air like a beater and his backside wiggling.

MATT FINISHED his breakfast, placed his plate in the sink and returned to the table with the coffeepot. He refilled Ginny's mug, then his own. "What were all those legal-looking papers Annie had with her last night? What are you two up to?"

Ginny took a sip of coffee. "Matt, did you know the town's been selling their crafts to merchants in Fredericksburg and at the most ridiculously low prices? They're practically giving their things away, compared to the markup. I told Annie the townsfolk ought to set up a business of their own, sell their own merchandise."

"They didn't go for that, did they?"

"No."

"Let me tell you something. They need the money, always have, but they don't want strangers tramping through their town. So they sell low and end up with a little extra cash to supplement their social security."

"But, Matt, they can do much better. I explained to Annie that I used to be a corporate attorney in Boston and explained the benefits of the town setting up their own company by incorporating, that they'd all earn a lot more money. They could set their own prices, and if the merchants wanted their goods, and believe me, they do, then they'll meet the town's prices. Everyone could draw salaries, not enough to affect their retirement income, but a lot more than they're getting now. The earnings could be used for supplies and expenses. They could air-condition their workshops, work in comfort."

"Sounds good," Matt said. "What'd they say?"

"Actually, once I explained everything, they all agreed to do it."

"But you're not licensed in Texas. How are you going to handle it for them?"

"Do you know Parnel Hoffmann-Bonn?"

Matt groaned. "Ginny, he's the town drunk. Spends most of his time sleeping it off in Argus's jail."

"But a fully licensed attorney in good standing with the Texas Bar. I checked him out." She saw Matt's doubtful expression. "He may be a drunk, Matt, but he's a nice man. A little sad, but very sweet. I'll do all the paperwork under his name and signature, and we'll pay him a fee."

Matt suddenly realized something important about his Ginny. She was one of those people who saw good in just about everyone. He wished he'd known her when she was younger. No wonder William Carney had latched on to her.

"Have you given any thought about applying to the Texas Bar Association for your license?" he asked.

"Miss Rosemary said she'd insist upon it if I stayed. She isn't too happy about having to depend on Parnel for anything."

"*If* you stay?" Matt felt as though he'd been kicked in the gut.

Ginny didn't answer him directly. "Matt, Jason and Annie told me what Jericho did about starting up the investigation in Boston again. Do you think there'll be any repercussions from that?"

"Nothing to give you cause for leaving." Fear suddenly gripped him. "You're not thinking of leaving, are you, Ginny? You made a promise to me, remember?"

"That I would never just run off, that I'd tell you first? Yes, I remember, and I'll keep my word. But, Matt, I've been pretty naive, haven't I. To think I wasn't endangering anyone but myself. I remember how easy it was for them to kill William and Beth, and I worry about you and Austin."

Matt reached out and grasped her hand. "Listen to me, Ginny. You're safe here and no harm's going to come to Austin or me. Ever since Jericho made that telephone call, we've had everything under control.''

All of a sudden she wanted to cry, but bit her lip, instead. ''We?''

''Me. Argus and Jericho. The boys. Everyone's on the alert for any trouble.''

She remembered the rifle Jericho had with him in the barn. ''Then you *are* expecting something?''

Matt shrugged. He didn't want to upset her, but he had to be honest. ''When the Boston police reopened your case, they realized they had enough evidence to start a pretty good investigation. Expert bombers leave what we call fingerprints, Ginny. They're a specialized breed and they're also superstitious. They use the same timers and explosives and other devices for each bomb they plant, and if they have a record, which most of them do, then they're fairly easy to trace. I don't think the police are going to have any trouble identifying the killer, but they want him to finger the man who gave the orders, the man with enough money to pay the bill. That'll be the hard part.''

Ginny nodded. ''There's a 'but' in your voice, Matt. But what?''

''A full investigation puts your name right out there for anyone to see. There are cops on the take everywhere. It only takes one quarter and one call for your location to be known.''

She was too quiet, he thought, and it scared him. He could almost see the wheels in her mind churning, weighing the pros and cons of staying. He didn't know exactly where the two of them were headed, but he did know one thing for sure—he wasn't going to lose her until he found out.

Ginny shivered. The thought of losing Matt and Austin the way she had lost William and Beth was too painful to consider. She was a fool, she realized now, and she ought to leave. But she could no longer deny the reality of what had happened to her, what she had allowed to happen. She'd done the unthinkable, the unforgivable. She had fallen passionately in love with Matt. And Austin—she loved him as if he were her own.

It didn't matter how Matt felt about her—she had found a home here. She had found peace. Ginny squeezed Matt's hand. "I'm staying." Yet even as she said the words, she knew she would only stay as long as the people she loved were safe.

"You're not leaving!" Austin yelled from the doorway, his voice hoarse with sleep and fear. He rushed at her, grabbed her shoulders. "You can't leave me. Please."

"I'm staying. Honestly, Austin. I'm not going anywhere."

"Promise me!" he demanded.

"That's enough, son," Matt said.

"It's not," he shot back at his father. "Ginny keeps her promises. Promise me, Ginny."

She couldn't stand seeing the fear and desperation in his young face. "I promise, Austin."

He relaxed and sat down, rubbing his face. When he glanced down at himself, he noticed the way his pajama top was misbuttoned. His cheeks burned. "Who undressed me last night?"

Ginny bit her lip. "Your dad." She saw his shoulders sag in relief and quickly got up to get some orange juice.

By the time she had Austin's breakfast on the table he was talking a mile a minute, telling her every detail of his meeting at the university.

"They're going to take me, Ginny. And the University of Texas is better than I'd hoped. It has a top-rated science-and-research department. Their medical school is tops, too. I tell you," he said around a mouthful of cereal, "I was impressed."

Matt laughed. "Of course you were. They fawned all over their child prodigy." He realized how that sounded and tried to smooth it over. "They'll get megabuck donations from their alumni because of the interest your being there will generate." By now both Ginny and Austin were glaring at him. "Son, they loved you. They want you because you'll contribute so much to their school." He wasn't getting anywhere. "Austin, you're a genius, so don't play dumb. You know damn well money and prestige are big motivators." He decided to give it one more try. "I was damn well impressed and very proud of you, son."

Austin blinked. "You were?"

"You bet."

Ginny decided not to intervene in the awkward silence that sprang up between father and son.

It was Austin who spoke first. "When do the pickers start, Dad?"

Matt blinked, partly in confusion at the change of subject and partly because his son had so freely called him Dad.

Austin took his father's silence like most children would—assumed he was about to be told *no*.

"Today's Saturday," he explained quickly, "and Uncle Jason mentioned that he'd take Ginny and me to see the peach pickers this morning. What time do they start?"

Matt looked at his watch and grinned. "He did, did he? To take you, he'd have to be dressed and up here already. What do you think the chances are that your uncle Jason's an early riser?''

''What's that you're saying about early risers, brother?'' Jason demanded as he came through the back door.

A deep throaty growl sounded, and everyone looked around to see where Dog was.

Ginny bent over and peered under her chair. Dog's eyes were pleading, and with a grin she quickly sat up, trying to shield him with her legs. But the rhythmic thumping of his tail was a dead giveaway.

Matt shoved open the screen door. ''Out,'' he ordered.

Dog tucked his tail, hunched his back pitifully, gave one soulful glance to Ginny and Austin, then bared his teeth and growled at Matt as he passed him on the way out.

''I said no dogs in the house.''

Ginny nodded dutifully, but she made the mistake of glancing at Austin, and they both burst out laughing. The two of them raced from the room to get dressed.

Matt just shook his head at Jason.

''I tell you, Matt,'' Jason said, taking advantage of the fact that he had his brother alone for a few minutes, ''you're making a mistake about the emus. I just found out there's a huge market in the cosmetic industry for emu oil. Good for women's skin or something. You know how much women spend on cosmetics?''

''Jason, have you ever seen the skin of an emu?'' Matt asked.

''Sure.''

''I rest my case.''

Ginny and Austin shot up the rest of the stairs, stumbling over each other and laughing so hard they didn't even attempt to hide the fact they'd been eavesdropping.

CHAPTER FOURTEEN

MATT WANTED to spend some time alone with Ginny and arranged for Austin to ride over to the orchard with Jason. There was a moment's panic on Jason's part when Austin insisted on taking Dog with them.

Even Dog resisted, but at Austin's urging he reluctantly gave in and hopped into the back seat of the small car. However, he kept a close watch on Ginny from the rear window as they drove down the long driveway.

When Matt climbed back in the car after locking the gate, Jason and Austin were already speeding down the highway. Matt leaned over and kissed Ginny, then said against her lips, "I've been wanting to do that all morning—and more. But we don't ever seem to be alone."

She grinned. "I know, and it won't get any better." She caressed his cheek. "Though I must admit, the thought of having to be creative has a certain appeal. This is a big place, Matt. Just think about it."

Matt closed his eyes and groaned, then with a hard quick kiss he straightened up. "We better get going."

They didn't have far to go before the traffic on the highway slowed with the increased numbers of buses and trucks. Matt looked for an opening in the long line of parked cars at the side of the road, and when he found a space, he maneuvered the Jeep in with ease.

Ginny tried to hide her smile as they crossed the highway. Men, she thought.

"What do you find so amusing, Red?"

"You. You make fun of me for talking to Dog, yet you actually patted the hood of your car just now as if it had feelings."

"Well, it does." He chuckled. "You saw how easy she handled?"

"She?"

"Sure. Didn't you know all complicated, ornery and unpredictable things are referred to as 'she'? Ships. Cars. Boats."

Ginny increased her steps and hurried ahead of him. "Stop calling me Red," she hollered over her shoulder.

Matt was enjoying the view of tight jeans and a firm behind too much to hurry. It was the sound of his son's voice that roused him from his pleasant thoughts. He lengthened his stride, caught up with Ginny and steered her to one of the orchard gates.

"Hey, Dad! Ginny," Austin called. "Look at all these trucks lined up. Uncle Jason says, depending on the crop, there'll be at least twenty loads."

Austin's face seemed to light up from inside with happiness, and Ginny felt such joy to see him this way. She walked beside the three men, allowing them to explain everything to her.

Trucks were indeed parked around the perimeter of the orchard, awaiting their cargo of peaches, which would then be delivered to a warehouse to be hand-sorted, cleaned, sized and gently wrapped for shipping.

"Where's Dog?" Ginny asked, then felt a cold wet nose touch her hand and looked down. "My God, Dog, what happened to you?"

"Uncle Jason tried to lock him in the car," Austin explained, "but Dog escaped. I think he rolled in the mud to pay him back."

"That vicious mutt is not riding anywhere in my car like that."

Matt glanced at Ginny and knew he'd lost the argument before it even started. "He can ride back with us. Come on, I'll show you around."

Ginny was amazed at the magnitude of the operation. All the fruit was picked by hand. They walked down a long row of trees, each one surrounded by two to four pickers, depending on how heavy the tree was with peaches. The pickers wore canvas bags attached by a strap over their shoulders. After carefully plucking the peaches from the tree with both hands, they gently placed them in the bags. When the bags were full, they were taken by other workers to a cleared area, where the peaches were unpacked from the bags with care, placed in wooden crates and loaded on trucks. When a truck was full it took off to the warehouse. Everything was timed like clockwork and no one paid any attention to the onlookers.

Ginny was puzzled that such small trees bore such large lush fruit. "Are they a kind of dwarf tree, Matt? How many are there?"

"About five hundred here, and we have a couple more orchards." He plucked a peach from a limb overhead and handed it to Ginny. "There's nothing like the taste of ripe fruit straight from the tree and warm from the sun." He watched her, smiling at her expression of pure pleasure as she bit into the firm flesh. Sweet juice ran down her chin, and he ached to kiss her. "The trees are pretty much regular size," he said in answer to her first question. "We just prune them a little differently because we handpick them, instead of using machinery."

"They sort of look like an umbrella turned inside out."

Matt nodded. "That's the way we prune them, cutting the tops to control the height, then pruning out some of the middle branches to allow the sun through, though not too much. The pruning's an art and a science in itself."

Ginny stepped out of the way of some men carrying crates. She'd noticed that most of the pickers were Latinos, both men and women. Every once in a while she'd catch one of them giving her a shy glance. When she smiled, she received somber looks, a quick nod or a tipped hat in return. She looked at Matt. "Do they live around here?"

"They're migrant workers, Ginny. They follow the seasons and work all over the state. They're usually not treated very well, but Two Rivers has a good program. We set up the campgrounds with tents and make sure the workers have two good hot meals a day." He guided her out of the way of another group of men. "If you've wondered where most of the townsfolk have been these past few days, they were setting up the camp and taking turns cooking meals."

"Your mother was a migrant worker, wasn't she?"

"Yes. But back then it was mostly blacks and Indians."

Austin ventured a question. "Is my grandmother still living, Dad?"

"No. She died of tuberculosis right before you were born. But you have a couple of great-uncles and cousins."

"You found her after she left here?" Ginny asked. "You forgave her?"

"I found her after I became a cop, and yes, I forgave her. How could I not? Ginny, she was one of the sweetest people I've ever known."

He was a little uncomfortable talking about his mother and her family because he'd ignored them for so many years. When he finally had made contact with them, the relationship was awkward and strained. But Austin had a right to know about his heritage.

"She was a soft-spoken, softhearted and genuinely good person. Her family loved her and protected her because they believed that, like her mother before her, she was touched with wisdom." He gave an embarrassed smile.

"Do you mean, Dad, that she was a wisewoman or a medicine woman?"

Matt smiled at Austin, but there was a sadness in his eyes. "No, son. She was too young to be considered a true wisewoman, but if she'd lived, I'm sure that's what she would've become. I remember asking an uncle once how a woman so wise and wonderful could leave her only child with a monster. He told me it was the one thing that haunted my mother. That she grieved and worried over her decision, but sometimes, he said, to become wise, a person must suffer great pain and loss. And she knew I was strong.

"It took me a couple of meetings with her to realize that if my father hadn't killed her with one of his beatings, she would have withered and died living here with him and Grandfather. Her family said my father would have sucked her spirit and wisdom from her. They were right. She was too soft and sweet and trusting to have stayed."

"But couldn't she have taken you with her, Dad?"

"I asked the same question, son. First of all, my father would have hunted her down like a dog, not because he wanted me, but because she'd taken something that was his. Second, she told me she had nothing to offer me, that she wanted better for me than what was offered children on the reservation."

"You think I might meet them, my cousins and great-uncles, someday?" Austin asked.

"Sure." Matt fell silent and watched his brother and Austin wander a few rows over, where Jason started up a conversation with some of the men. His explanations seemed to have satisfied Austin for the moment, but he knew that, given his son's curiosity, there would be more questions to come.

"Jason really likes Austin, you know," Ginny said.

"Yeah. It took me a while to learn that Jason jokes a lot, and most of his harebrained schemes are just his way of needling me, but he's not so bad. You like him, too, don't you?"

"Yes, I do. I think he'd like to be a lot closer to you, Matt. If you'd let him."

"Let him?" Matt looked startled.

"You can be kind of forbidding, Matthew Bolt." She grasped his hand. "It must have been your training as a cop that makes you scowl so fiercely." They were almost at the end of the row of trees. Some of the truck engines were idling, anticipating departure, and the noise made conversation almost impossible.

Matt touched her arm, yelling in her ear that he'd be right back. Ginny tried to answer, then gave up and waved him away. She watched him as he crossed to speak to a group of men, but her attention was distracted by a couple of pickers working a tree nearby. They didn't looked much older than Austin.

She could never say what had made her twist around. A change in the sound of the truck engines? A premonition that something wasn't right? Whatever it was, an alarm went off in her head, warning her she was in danger. She spun around and was instantly paralyzed with fear.

Coming directly at her, out of control, was one of the trucks. As it bumped over the dirt ridge surrounding the orchard, the empty wooden crates in the back went flying into the air.

Ginny couldn't move. She could only watch in horror as the truck drew nearer.

When the front end of the truck plunged back down to the ground, the tires bounced and dirt sprayed in all directions. She never saw Dog, never heard the screaming as people realized what was happening. Out of nowhere, a flying ball of muscle and bone crashed into her chest, knocking the breath out of her, lifting her off her feet and sending her reeling backward. But not far enough—the fender grazed her hip and hit Dog, miraculously spinning them both out of the path of the heavy tires.

Ginny lay on the ground with her eyes wide open, staring up at the sky, fighting for breath. She could hear more screaming as people scattered, and then the crashing and splintering of wood, followed by an eerie silence. She became aware of the heaviness on her chest and the muddy fur grasped in her hands.

"Dog," she whispered and was answered by a swipe of his tongue. "Are you hurt?" she asked him as if he would answer. When she moved her hands, he whined in pain.

Matt was the first to get to her. He'd watched, rigid with terror, too far away to do anything. All he could see was a truck careering toward Ginny, then Ginny flying through the air. When he reached her, he fell to his knees, wanting to gather her in his arms but afraid to move her. He leaned over her and saw that her eyes were open.

"Ginny?"

"Don't touch Dog, Matt. I think he's hurt."

"Dog?" He looked at the animal half lying on Ginny's chest. Dog was staring back at Matt with a watchful wariness.

"Ginny, can you move?"

"No."

He squeezed his eyes shut, imagining the worst of injuries.

"If I move, I'll hurt Dog."

People were beginning to gather around. He ordered one of the men he knew to call the sheriff, then waved the others angrily away. When Ginny grasped his hand, he looked back down at her. "I'm not hurt, Matt," she said. "Honestly. But I'm very worried about Dog. Please see if he's bleeding anywhere."

When he gently probed Dog, he was relieved to tell Ginny the animal wasn't bleeding, not externally at least, but there was something definitely wrong with him.

"Get a board, Matt," Ginny said, "and we'll slide him onto it and take him to the vet."

He'd always been cool and calm in emergency situations. He'd quelled riots and faced down killers with guns pointed at his heart. Now he thought he was going crazy. He couldn't have made a decision if his life depended on it. Then he looked across Ginny and Dog into the eyes of his son, saw the terrible pain and fear there, and understood everything.

"She's okay, Austin."

"You're lying. If she was all right, she'd be moving."

Ginny opened her eyes and turned her head. "Austin, don't speak to your father like that." She didn't want to tell anyone how badly her hip hurt. "Dog saved my life, Austin. I don't know how he knew what was happening, but he must have realized the truck was a danger to me. He knocked me out of the way, but I think he was hit, too."

"Too?" Matt demanded. "I thought you said you weren't hurt."

"Well, not badly. Just bruised, I think," she said, trying to reassure both father and son.

Someone arrived with a makeshift litter, and Ginny helped ease Dog off her chest and onto the board, all the time talking to him in a low voice. Then it was her turn, and with Matt's help, she managed to ease herself to her feet.

"See, I'm fine," she assured them. "I'm going to be as sore as the devil tomorrow, but I'll be okay." Her legs were shaking so badly she wondered how long she was going to be able to stand and was seriously considering stretching out beside Dog when Sheriff Argus and the ambulance attendant arrived.

Argus took a quick look around and sized up the situation. He'd been briefed all the way to the scene by several truck drivers with mobile phones. He didn't like what he'd heard one bit. He was relieved when he saw Ginny standing, looking pale but otherwise in good shape.

"Sheriff, I'm so glad you're here. Please tell that ambulance driver to take Dog to the vet. Now. Can't he see it's an emergency?"

Argus glanced at Matt, who appeared surprisingly meek and unwilling to interfere. Then he looked at the embarrassed ambulance driver. He wasn't sure what was going on, but it was up to him to take charge.

"Preston, what's the problem here?" the sheriff asked. "Can't you see you have a patient to transport?" He held up his hand to stop the driver's protest. "Now, please."

Ginny insisted on going along, and after a short discussion she was helped into the back of the van. Matt followed, giving orders to Jason to stick around and find out what happened, whether anyone else was injured and to make sure Austin got home safely.

An hour later Dog was carried into the house like royalty. Austin had made him a soft bed of neatly folded blankets, which he was gently eased onto. Dog glanced at the bowl of water and food, then grinned and closed his eyes.

"Dog," Ginny said, "is going to be fine. He has some badly bruised ribs and a big bump on his head. The vet said he'll be as good as new in a few days." She eased her own tired body onto a chair.

"I still don't understand why he can't stay in the barn," Matt grumbled, but his question was ignored by everyone, including his traitorous brother. Matt put his head in his hands. Never again, he vowed to himself, would he interfere with a woman on a mission—especially one concerning the welfare of a child, or an animal who'd saved her life.

Ginny carefully stood up. "I'm going to soak in a nice hot tub."

She was neck-deep in the fragrant water, just about to drift off, when Matt knocked and without waiting walked in. "I just wanted to see if you were still among the living."

She opened one eye, then closed it. "I've only been in here about fifteen minutes."

"Try forty-five."

"Well, I'm not ready to get out, so go away."

Matt pulled over a spindly little vanity stool beside the big claw-footed tub and gingerly sat down. He stared at the thick layer of fluffy bubbles, thought of all the naked pink flesh underneath and cleared his throat. This wasn't the time, he told himself.

"I just wanted to check and see how you're doing," he said.

"Liar," she whispered.

Matt got up to leave, then bent down and kissed her forehead. "Enjoy yourself. Just don't fall asleep." When he returned to the kitchen, Argus had arrived and was the only one there. "Where is everybody?"

"Jason and Austin had some whispered conversation, then Jason said he had things to do and Austin just disappeared out the door a few minutes ago." Argus glanced at the kitchen clock and shook his head. "Ten o'clock and it feels like midnight. Man, I'm getting too old for this. It wasn't an accident, Matt."

"I figured as much." Matt poured them both a cup of coffee. "I think I vaguely remember seeing someone bailing out of the cab of that truck."

"Gas pedal was wedged down with a stick."

"That was stupid, wasn't it, announcing themselves like that."

"I think the plan was that the stick would be dislodged to make it look like an accident, and if it didn't work the first time, they'd have time for another shot."

Matt agreed. "What do you suggest I do, Argus? Someone's after Ginny and I can't lose her."

Argus didn't even try to hide his smile.

"Has your heart ever stopped beating?" Matt said. "Mine did this morning."

"That happens when you care about someone. Is this thing with Ginny serious?"

Matt rubbed his face tiredly. "I don't know what the hell it is. I'm just not ready to lose her, not like that."

"She could leave."

Matt shook his head. "How are your two boys with a shotgun and some real responsibility?"

"Do you have to ask? They're my boys."

"What about Roberto and Gomez—would they be willing to help?"

"For Ginny, I think you can count them in and maybe a few of their family members, too."

Matt nodded. "I think Van der Bollen vineyards is about to become an armed camp for a while."

Argus stood and picked up his hat. "Officially I never heard that."

"How about unofficially?"

"Whatever it takes. You can count me in." He settled his hat comfortably on his head. "What about Ginny? Are you going to tell her? I mean, you can get by with Jericho walking around with his old Winchester, but when she sees the rest of them armed, she's going to ask questions."

"I'll tell her when that happens."

Argus paused at the door and glanced at Dog. "I heard he's a real hero, saved Ginny's life. Is he going to be all right?"

Matt gave Dog a hard look and received a half-hearted canine grin in return. "He's going to be fine. And if I find out you're faking it, mutt, I'll kick your scrawny butt out of here so fast..." A couple of weak thumps from Dog's tail made him feel ashamed of himself. After Argus left, he refilled Dog's water bowl, covered him with part of the blanket and gave him a pat on the head.

Ginny's movements down the stairs were slow, precise. Her hip had the beginnings of a bruise the size of a melon, and even after a hot bath, just about every muscle in her body hurt. But she knew if she didn't keep moving, if she allowed herself to relax, she might never get up again.

"Did I hear Argus's voice?" She asked as she moved around the kitchen.

"Why don't you sit down?" Matt asked.

"Actually I'm hungry and thought I'd get lunch started. What would you like?"

"What I would like is for you to sit down. You make me hurt just watching you try to move around. Are you sure you don't need to see a doctor?"

"Matt, if I sit down, it's a good bet I won't get up again for a while. And no," she snapped, then softened her tone, "I don't need a doctor for bruises."

She had a damn doctor for that animal, he thought sourly, but he was learning and wisely kept his thoughts to himself. He would have to tell her about the attempt on her life—which he was sure she suspected—but not until after he'd talked with the men.

He got up from his chair. "I have to go see Jericho and give some orders to the men. I'll be back in time for lunch."

Ginny nodded. "Where's Austin?"

"Around."

"Around?" she asked, just as the screen door slammed shut. "What kind of answer is that?" But Matt was gone and her question was left hanging in the air.

"You know, Dog," Ginny said, turning toward the animal. "You better be as sore as me, or Matt will boot you out of here." His eyes followed her every move but he didn't lift his head or even give her one of his grins. She squatted down beside him and stroked his head.

When the telephone rang, it took her a long time to stand up and reach it. When she did, there was silence on the other end, and she thought the caller had hung up. Immediately the phone rang again. Ginny looked in confusion at the receiver in her hand as it continued to ring, then realized she had the wrong phone. She slammed down the receiver and hurried over to the vineyard phone on the countertop.

"Matt?" she asked.

"If you ever want to see the boy alive again, come to the wine cellar now. Come alone. And don't tell anyone about this call."

Ginny stared at the receiver, then a hard shiver shook her and she slowly hung up. Well, that answered a lot of her questions, she thought as she poked her feet into her shoes and quickly tied them. She'd had her doubts about this morning's accident, but like an ostrich with its head in the sand, she refused to face the truth. The truth would have ruined all her plans.

Confusion, doubt, her own fear almost stole her courage. For a split second she was numb. Her head was suddenly filled with images of William and Beth, and the pain was unbearable. Then everything changed. The only emotion she felt was a barely controlled rage that someone would threaten to harm a ten-year-old boy.

The screen door banged open under her fist, and Ginny ran across the yard, heading directly for the wine cellar. When she got there, she was breathless, her body shrieking with pain, but she didn't stop. The heavy double doors were wide open, beckoning, and she rushed in. The darkness and cold made her slow down.

"Austin!" she called. "Austin, answer me!" A noise sounded from within, and she headed through the second set of doors. But before she walked into that black hole, she remembered the main light switch and flipped it on. The pale watery light from the low-wattage bulbs illuminated the interior, and she stepped inside.

"Austin," she called again.

When she received no answer, she started walking between the rows of oak casks. It was colder than she remembered, and she started shivering. She heard something behind her and swung around.

"Who's there?" She squinted into the darkness. Had she seen something move?

A figure stepped out from behind an oak cask. "Hello, Ginny."

She tried to discern the person's feature's, but the shadows were too deep. Something about the voice was vaguely familiar. "Where's Austin? If you've hurt him..."

"Is that the kid's name? He's fine."

That voice. She knew that voice. The only thing she could think to do was keep him talking, try to identify him.

"You almost injured innocent people this morning. That wasn't very smart. You made the local sheriff mad."

A snort of contempt was the response she got. "Small-town law, no more than a security guard."

Oh, God, that voice. She knew it, but from where? "Listen, you have me. Let Austin go."

"And lose the edge? I don't think so, Gin."

It was the nickname that did it. She stopped breathing for a moment, then her rage boiled over and she started walking toward the shadowy figure. "Damn you to hell, Tony Coldwell. You tell me where Austin is this minute." She stopped only when she got close enough to see the gun he held pointed at her.

Anthony Coldwell, Jr., was two years younger than she was, and from the moment his father had married her mother, Tony, Jr., had tried to put his hands on her. The last time she'd been home, he'd almost raped her, but the butler had heard her screams and intervened. Because of Junior and his father, she'd finally stopped going home altogether.

"You're still a vile creature, Junior."

"And you're still a smart-mouth stuck-up bitch."

She sighed. Junior was a sneak and a bully, but she couldn't see him killing anyone face-to-face. "What do you think you're doing here?"

"I'm going to stop you from railroading my father again."

"Again?"

"Because of pressure on the Boston cops, they've arrested a guy who fingered Dad as the man behind the bombing—the man with the money."

Ginny took a steadying breath. "That car bomb killed William and Beth, Junior. Their bodies were scattered all over the neighbors' yards. And your father ordered it. It was supposed to have been me, a way to shut me up about the money laundering."

Junior was shaking his head. "Lies. Dad might have been laundering money, but not murder, not Dad. If this guy's statement sticks, they'll retry Dad for double murder. He'll never get out of prison, never be eligible for parole."

He hadn't heard a word she'd said. He truly believed his father was innocent and so was far more dangerous than she'd first thought. "Junior, tell me were Austin is. Enough people have suffered."

"Not quite enough."

Ginny watched him raise the gun and realized he was taking aim. There was no time left, no place to run. And besides, she was damn tired of running.

"Junior, if you pull that trigger, you're going to end up in prison—and not the country club your father's in. You're a pretty man, Junior, and I hear that prisoners like pretty boys."

She heard an ominous click and held her breath.

AS MUCH AS HE HATED to admit it, Matt thought, his father had picked good men to work for him. Fiercely loyal, they were all willing to do anything necessary to keep Miss Ginny safe. Roberto had told him that he would call in five of his cousins from Austin and they could be there in an hour. Matt decided to wait before enlisting outside help, but he told Roberto to alert his cousins. If needed, he wanted them fast.

Billy Bob and Wayne could barely contain their excitement, and at first Matt had reservations about them, but they were, after all, Argus's boys and he was willing to overlook their enthusiasm. He attributed it to their age and the fact that nothing exciting ever happened around Two Rivers.

As he walked up the path to the main house, his mind was a million miles away. It wasn't until he was almost at the back door that he realized Dog was barking nonstop. The sound, a kind of wailing, sent chills up his spine.

Matt sprinted up the porch and yanked on the door, but it was locked. He pressed his head against the screen and saw that the hook had slipped into the metal eye, something that happened when the door was slammed. Ginny had asked him a couple of times to fix it.

Without a second's thought, he punched his elbow through the screen, stuck his hand in and flipped the latch. Dog was already pushing on the door. He backed out of the way and would have gone in, but Dog pulled on his pant leg.

Matt glanced down at him. "You better be right, Dog, because if she's in that house, hurt, and I don't get to her, your hide won't be worth two cents." He let Dog have the lead as he pulled out the small revolver he'd been carrying since the accident that morning and clicked off the safety.

It was obvious from Dog's stiff-legged gait that every step was painful, but Matt couldn't carry him. As he ran, he bellowed for Jericho, for anyone within hearing distance.

When Dog lay down, panting fast and hard, by the heavy double doors of the wine cellar, Matt reached down and tugged one ear. "Let me be the hero this time, fellow," he whispered. He took off his boots and made his way quietly through the main room. Once he'd eased through the second set of doors, he kept to the deep shadows made by the large casks. He knew every inch of the cellar and could moved around it blindfolded.

Voices reached him and he immediately recognized one as Ginny's. He knew where they were and edged down behind the racks of bottles, moving soundlessly over the floor.

He could hear them clearly now, but he paid little attention to the words, noting only that they were arrogant and threatening. A cop could gauge a lot about a suspect just from his tone of voice.

He stopped. He'd come too far. All he could see was the man's extended arm and the pointed revolver. Matt cursed silently. He hadn't fired a gun in a while, and he couldn't afford to be off even a fraction of an inch. He crouched, extended his gun arm and used his other hand for support.

Matt heard the change in the man's voice in an instant. God, he wasn't ready. His heart pounded in his chest so hard it hurt. He knew his hands were shaking, then suddenly he calmed, his aim steady. He fired.

THERE WAS NOWHERE to go. Ginny had to face Junior, hoping he was bluffing, but when she heard that click, she knew he was going to shoot her. Her mind went surprisingly blank. When she heard the sound of a shot she flinched. She waited for pain and the ensuing darkness. But all she was aware of was Junior falling to his knees and screaming as he held his injured hand. It didn't take a rocket scientist to realize she was still alive.

Matt came running up beside her, then watched with awe and satisfaction as Ginny walked around the man, kicking and cursing him. Matt leaned his shoulder against a wine rack and smiled, figuring this was the best therapy in the world. When she saw Matt, Ginny pointed to Junior. "This miserable excuse for a human being is Anthony Coldwell, Jr.—Tony's son. He caused the accident this morning."

She grabbed the front of Junior's shirt and shoved him back against the wine rack. "Where's Austin?"

"I don't know anything about the kid. I just saw him come in here and used him to get you down here."

Matt raised his gun once more. "Tell me where my son is."

"I swear I don't know," Junior pleaded. "I've got to get to a hospital. I'm bleeding to death."

None too gently, Matt pulled the man's injured hand up and shook it. "The bullet went right through. See." The arm went limp as Junior crumpled to the floor. Matt glanced over at Ginny. "He fainted."

"Matt, do you believe him about Austin?"

"Yeah. I do." He cocked his head, heard Dog's wild barking and the sound of raised voices. "I think the troops have arrived." Matt grabbed Ginny in his arms and kissed her hard. "Crazy female. What the hell were you doing coming here alone without telling me?"

"Because the voice on the phone said if I didn't, I'd never see Austin alive again. Oh, Matt, where is he?"

For the moment, it was a question with no answer.

CHAPTER FIFTEEN

MATT LOOKED AROUND the wine cellar, a bad feeling in the pit of his stomach. When he saw Jericho with Dog in his arms, and the rest of the men, he sighed. He'd hoped Austin would be with the old man. Then he spotted Argus.

"Austin's missing," he said to him. "That scum told Ginny he had him. Now he's saying he only saw Austin go into the cellar." Matt bit his lip and glanced over his shoulder. "Your radio working in the patrol car?"

"Sure. Why?"

"Go see if you can track down my brother."

Argus pulled out a cellular phone. "I can do better than that. I saw his car at the orchard when I passed. Jason's got a car phone."

Ginny caressed Dog's head then looked over at Matt. "What does Jason have to do with Austin's disappearance?"

"I hope nothing, but I've got this feeling." He motioned for everyone to be quiet when Argus began talking. "Ask Jason if he and Austin were talking about the cave paintings today?"

Argus did as Matt asked, then nodded.

Matt cursed loud and long, then turned and headed toward the back of the cave. "The guy on the floor is Anthony Coldwell, Jr. Take care of him, will you, Argus? I'm going to fetch my son."

Ginny wasn't about to let him go alone, not in the black mood he was in. "What's the matter, Matt?" He didn't answer her, but snatched up a flashlight from a nearby shelf and continued walking. Ginny grabbed one for herself. "Matt..."

"Dammit, Ginny, the caves back here are dangerous, unstable. My father should have had them sealed off years ago." He lengthened his stride. "Sound carries in here. If he's in here he should have heard our voices, certainly the gunshot, and he would have come to see what was going on."

"What makes you think Austin's in here?"

"Because ever since Jason mentioned the cave paintings, he's been asking questions about them. I told him..."

Matt was scaring her. Shining the light around, Ginny noted that, unlike the main cellar, the walls and ceiling here were rough limestone with jagged, protruding edges. When they came to a fork in the cavern, Matt veered right and had to hunch over a little as the long tunnel narrowed and the ceiling lowered.

"What did you tell him?" she asked.

"Nothing. Just that they were dangerous and he was to stay away from them."

"And you think a ten-year-boy with his intellect and curiosity would accept that explanation?"

"I was very clear about him staying away from the caves."

"I'm sure you were," she murmured. "But it wasn't very smart of you."

She was so busy thinking about what Matt had done that she wasn't watching her footing, and she stumbled over a scattering of rocks on the floor.

Matt stopped and asked in a low voice, "Are you all right?"

"Fine," she answered, wondering why they were being so quiet. "Tell me something. When you were a boy and your father ordered you not to do something you really wanted to do, that it was dangerous, how did you react?"

Matt didn't answer right away, then cursed under his breath. "Dammit, that's no excuse for disobeying my orders, Ginny. The caves with the paintings are collapsing."

She sighed. Men were so buttheaded sometimes.

He quickly swung the beam of the flashlight around, noting that the wall was giving way and the amount of rubble on the sandy floor was increasing. "It's getting worse. Why don't you go back."

"No."

"Then try not to touch the walls." They both stood paralyzed for a second at the sound of rocks tumbling to the floor somewhere deep within the cave. Matt took off at a more frantic pace. "Be careful, Ginny."

She followed Matt for what seemed a mile. The passage became so low at times that Matt was almost bent double, then at other times the ceiling rose majestically and the wall receded into small chambers on either side of them.

Matt pointed to a tunnel so narrow they'd have to move through it sideways. "This tunnel curves a bit, then opens into a cave at the other end," he told her. "I want you to stay here."

"No, Matt. I'm coming with you."

"Dammit, Ginny. Do you ever listen to anyone?"

"Yes. But not this time, not when it concerns Austin."

Matt directed the beam of the flashlight down the tunnel. He was about to move on when he stopped. A rumble of voices reached them. It was eerie how some of the words were easily understood and others seemed to echo around the rock formations, turning into moans or whispers. He was sure the voices were coming from Argus and the men in the wine cellar. Still, he shivered at the ghostly sounds.

"This is the most fascinating place I've ever been in and the scariest," he whispered. Taking a deep breath to steady his nerves, he said, "Let's go."

Ginny hesitated. The voices had unnerved her. But then she thought of Austin, alone, frightened and possibly hurt, and she turned sideways to take that first reluctant step.

They edged their way carefully through the narrow tunnel, and just when she thought she couldn't stand the closeness any longer, the wall curved. Suddenly they stepped into a huge chamber where the limestone was a brilliant white, so bright that their flashlights made dirty yellow pools of light against it. The cavern was as high as a two-story house and the walls were rough in places with deep gouges. The floor was soft and sandy, scattered with rocks and boulders.

Ginny was so fascinated she almost forgot the reason they were here. She grabbed Matt's arm, realizing that he, too, had stopped. "It's beautiful," she breathed.

Matt swept his light across the cave floor. "Beautiful, but deadly." The beam of his light caught a set of small footprints in the white sand.

Ginny shone the narrow beam of her light around the cave, enthralled by the few markings she saw on the walls. Matt touched her shoulder to get her attention, and she followed him farther into the depths of the cavern. She felt a quick rush of relief when they finally spotted a glow of light behind a large boulder. They stepped around the rock and both halted.

Austin was sitting cross-legged on the floor of the cave, a sketch pad in his lap. His flashlight was stuck in the ground so the light was directed toward the facing wall, and he glanced from the wall to his pad as he sketched the cave paintings. He was so focused on his work that he didn't hear their approach.

Ginny turned from Austin to Matt. She knew he was very angry at his son, but she'd attributed much of his quietness, almost coldness, to his fear. Now she wasn't sure how he was going to react.

"Get up, Austin," Matt said, his voice calm, emotionless.

Ginny bit her lip. Austin's face and clothes were dusted with the fine white limestone powder that covered the floor, making him look as ghostly as the spirits he was drawing.

Austin jumped as if he'd been jabbed with an electrical prod. "Dad, Ginny, look!" He all but shouted in his excitement. "I'm sure those paintings aren't Indian!"

"Austin, go back to the house."

Austin was too wound up to hear the controlled fury in his father's voice. "Ginny, I think these are much, much older. Did you know that the French found a new cave near the town of Vallon-Pont d'Arc in the Ardeche River Canyon?" He hopped up, yanked the flashlight from the ground and began playing the light across the wall. "They estimate those new finds from about 20,000 B.C. to 17,000 B.C.—"

"Austin," Matt said again, his voice quiet.

"Older than the Altamira in Spain and Lascaux in France."

"Austin."

"There are some animals here—a couple of mammoths, I think. And cats—big cats I know weren't in this area. Oh, and, Ginny, there are some handprints, big and small." Austin finally became aware that something was wrong, and his flood of words began to slow. "I think this cave was used for religious reasons—maybe for animal or even human sacrifices—"

"Get to the house. Now, Austin." Matt took a couple of steps forward, then backtracked so sharply he almost stumbled.

"What'd I do?" Austin was suddenly scared.

Matt's tight control began to slip. "Pick up your flashlight and get out of here—now."

"I don't see..." Austin glanced with pleading eyes at Ginny, but she only shook her head and motioned furtively for him to do as his father said. He squatted down to gather up his drawings and was shocked motionless when Matt grabbed his arm and hauled him back up.

Matt abruptly released the thin arm as if it had burned a whole through his hand. "Didn't you hear me? Leave those and get out of here!"

Ginny watched Austin's eyes fill with tears, more at the tone of Matt's voice than the actual words. She motioned again for him to go, and this time he did, running toward the cave opening, the light in his hand bouncing erratically over the walls.

Then she turned to face Matt. "What's wrong with you? There was no call to talk to him like that and make him leave his work behind."

Matt's stiffly held shoulders seemed to sag. He looked shattered, confused. "God," he said, "I never wanted kids."

Ginny heard a far-off sob and twisted around to see Austin standing by the cave opening, his eyes filled with pain. The next instant he was gone.

"Have you lost all your senses? He heard that."

As if in a daze, Matt looked at Ginny. "What?"

"Austin—he heard you say you didn't want kids."

Matt shuddered. "Well, I didn't. Can't you see why?"

"What are you talking about?"

The day's events had been too much for him, full of emotions he'd never felt equipped to handle. "My goddamn temper—just like my father's. I was so angry I wanted to shake that boy."

Everything in him seemed to give way, and he collapsed into a sitting position on the cave floor, folded his arms across his knees and rested his head on them.

She could see he was upset and confused. "But you did nothing more than raise your voice and yank him up by the arm."

"Dammit, Ginny. All the way down here I was so scared something might happen to him. I was imagining a cave-in and him trapped beneath the rock. I really lost it, didn't I?"

Ginny bit her lip. She wanted to cry and laugh at the same time. "You're his father, Matt, and you love him. Of course you were scared to death. That's a normal reaction." When Matt lifted his head and looked at her, she was surprised to see the fear still in his eyes. "What's the matter?"

"I know all too well what a father's love can do to a boy. I made a promise to myself years ago that I'd never abuse a child of mine. For that reason, I didn't want children and never intended to have any. I still feel the same, but..." Matt shook his head in total confusion. "I love Austin. He's a great kid. And knowing that, I still almost struck him."

"But you didn't." Ginny knelt down beside him and stroked his head. Poor Matt, she thought, confronted for the first time in his life with something he couldn't control, much less truly understand. But that was what love was all about, she thought—unpredictable and irrational. Her heart ached for him.

"Listen to me, Matt. From what I can see, you're not anything like your father. He was mean-spirited and a bully. He had to have control—whether it was over a softhearted woman or a young boy who couldn't fight back. That's not like you, Matt. How can you even think you're remotely like him? Sure, you got angry at Austin. You even lost your temper. But you didn't strike him. Dammit, even if you thought about shaking him, that's natural. But what matters is that you didn't."

Matt was quiet for a long moment, then he shuddered deeply as if a sudden weight had been lifted. He reached out for Ginny, wrapped his arms around her waist and rested his head against her stomach. His shoulders began to tremble, then shake, and for the first time in too many years to remember, he wept.

Ginny held him until the emotional storm had calmed. She didn't bother to hide her own tears.

When he finally released her, Matt wiped his face with his shirtsleeve and looked away in embarrassment. He retrieved his flashlight from the ground and aimed the beam of light on Austin's sketch pad.

"Look at these, Ginny," he said, picking up the pad and flipping through it. "He's good. These are first-rate." He carefully straightened some of the loose pages. I used to sit here by the hour drawing, too. But I was never as good as this. Funny, I got rid of everything that reminded me of home, except my drawings. I still have them."

"Why don't you show them to him?" she asked as he struggled to his feet.

"No, they're amateurish compared to these."

Ginny wanted to shake him and told him so, laughing. Even she could lose her temper when pushed too far. "We have to find Austin, Matt. You have to talk to him now. Don't let it go another minute."

"Ginny, what am I going to say to him? Of course I'll apologize for my temper, but..."

"Be totally honest with Austin, Matt. Explain to him why you said those things—how you feel."

He didn't acknowledge hearing her but headed toward the tunnel that led out of the cave.

By the time they reached the wine cellars, Matt's limp was more pronounced than ever, and Ginny tried repeatedly to get him to stop and rest. But he seemed oblivious to her concerns, as if he was totally focused on planning his strategy with Austin. She wanted to warn him not to depend too much on his own plans, that children had a way of playing havoc with the best-laid ones.

No one remained in the main wine cellar, and as they finally stepped outside, the noonday sun blazed down on them. Ginny was shocked to realize that it was still daytime. She felt as if they'd been in the caves for hours.

She closed her eyes and turned her face up to the warm rays, inhaling the fresh, rainwashed air. She wanted nothing more than to enjoy the fact that she was alive and Matt and Austin were safe. She wanted to ignore the growing doubts that were threatening her newly acquired peace of mind.

"Everything shipshape, boss?" Jericho asked as they passed him.

Matt ignored the old man's question and continued to limp toward the house. Ginny stopped only for a second to ask if he'd seen Austin and to give Dog a pat.

"Boy ran past us, real upset. He was heading for the house."

"Thanks, Jericho." Ginny took off after Matt at a run. It wasn't that she didn't trust him to say the right things, but men like Matt often had trouble expressing their feelings. She intended to make sure that didn't happen, even if she had to lock the two in Austin's room until Matt talked to his son.

By the time she reached the back door she could hear Matt at the top of the stairs and cursed under her breath. She wanted to give him some advice in dealing with a hurt and angry child, but she was too late.

Ginny leaned against the wall outside Austin's room, then slid down and sat on the floor. She wouldn't think of interfering, but she wanted to make sure things were resolved between them, and eavesdropping was the only way. Wrapping her arms around her bent legs, she rested her head on her knees, closed her eyes and said a silent prayer.

Matt stopped at the foot of Austin's bed. His son was sprawled across the bedspread, crying, his sobs loud and heartbreaking to Matt's ears. He swallowed, then put down Austin's sketch pad and another envelope he'd retrieved from a hall cabinet.

"Austin," he said softly, and watched the way his son's body went perfectly still. The sobbing halted.

Austin sat up, wiped his eyes, then twisted around to face his father.

Matt flinched. Austin's face was still dusted with the white limestone powder, making the tear tracks stand out like red welts on his skin. There was so much hate in those eyes so like his own. For the first time Matt realized just how much Austin was like him at that age— tough. But was that necessarily a good thing? It had served him well because of his father. Austin deserved better. He deserved a father who loved him and respected him. He needed a loving family to build his life around. Austin needed what he had never had.

"I love you, son." It was the only thing Matt could think to say that made any sense.

Austin had steeled himself for ranting and raving, maybe a spanking, some sort of horrible punishment, and he was ready for it. The quiet declaration surprised him. There was something different about his father, the way he was looking at him. As if... as if he really meant what he said.

Matt took his son's silence as a blessing. He remembered his confrontations with his own father and the fact that he couldn't and wouldn't keep his mouth shut. It had always got him in more trouble.

"I should never have talked to you like I did in the cave but, Austin, I was so scared something might have happened to you."

"You wouldn't have really cared if I died." Austin wasn't about to let go of his hurt pride so easily. "You never wanted me. Isn't that what you said?"

Matt sighed and sat down on the side of the bed. "You're wrong. I would never want you dead. But you're right about what I said. It's not that I didn't want you, Austin. I just never wanted children."

Damn. He knew he wasn't saying the right things and wished Ginny would stop her eavesdropping and come to his rescue. How could he make Austin understand that what he'd done was for his own welfare?

"Austin, you're smart. You know far more about the world than I did at your age. You know about the terrible things some parents do to their children—the abuse, both mental and physical. A lot of those damaged children grow up to be just like their parents."

Austin nodded, skeptical, waiting for the trap he thought his father was setting for him.

"As a cop I saw things—such horrible things done to children it would make you sick. At trial time, so many of those parents who hurt their children would tell their own horror stories about their youth. I was one of those children, Austin. My father, for whatever twisted reason, found great pleasure in abusing me."

"He beat you?" Austin asked.

"Yes. Frequently. Repeatedly. And there was verbal abuse, the belittling. I know what I went through, what I suffered. I could never stand the thought of making a child of mine suffer like that. So I decided long ago never to have children. Your mother was a wonderful woman, but I made her very unhappy about the way I felt. After you were born, she left me and moved away. I never got the chance to see if I could even be a good father. Now that I have the chance I'm scared."

The thought that his father, this big stern man, could be frightened of him confused Austin. "But you never hit me or belittled me."

"No, I haven't, have I?" He tried to smile, but his lips felt stiff. "And you've certainly pushed me, haven't you?"

"Yes, sir."

"I couldn't stand the thought of hurting you. It would break my heart, Austin, if I did. I couldn't live with myself, wouldn't want to."

A light suddenly went off in Austin's head, and he beamed. "You really do love me, don't you?"

Matt chuckled. "Surprised me, too, but yes, I do."

Just as quickly Austin grew serious. "Do you think Jason was abused, too?"

Matt shook his head. "I don't think so. His mother, Delta, was—still is—a strong woman who handled my father differently." Austin seemed relieved. "Will you forgive me for the way I acted today, son?"

Austin nodded, sniffed a couple of times, then grabbed a tissue and blew his nose noisily. "I'm sorry I disobeyed you." Then he did the one thing he'd most wanted to do—he threw his arms around his father.

For a second Matt hesitated, but the incredible feeling of Austin's arms around his neck was too much; every restraint, every wall he'd built around himself, crumbled. He wrapped his arms around his son and held him close. There was a lump in his throat the size of a basketball, and when Austin pulled slightly away he made no attempt to hide his tears.

"I love you, Dad," Austin whispered, then bounced back with resiliency to ask excitedly. "About the cave—have you ever thought of calling the archaeology department at the university? Someone should see those cave drawings, document them, before they're destroyed." He sat down again and gave Matt a stern look.

"I know what you mean, Austin, but I can't have hordes of people traipsing through the wine cellar. It'll ruin the delicate balance of the atmosphere." Matt gave Austin his sketch pad and a thick manila envelope.

"These aren't as good as yours, but I did them years ago when the wall paintings were in even better condition."

Austin spread his father's drawings across his bed, marveling at the detail. He glanced up when he felt the side of the bed dip. He watched in puzzlement as Matt put his fingers to his lips. With exaggerated steps on tiptoe, like a cartoon character, his father moved silently to the door, opened it and glanced down the hall.

"What're you doing?" Austin asked.

"Just making sure our eavesdropper has left. You didn't really think Ginny was going to allow us to be alone together without her supervision, did you?"

Austin giggled. "No."

Matt returned to the bed and sat, absently rubbing his sore leg. "Austin, we have a problem. I need your help." He told his son about what had happened in the wine cellar and about the son of Anthony Coldwell. "She's going to leave us, Austin."

"No, she wouldn't do that. She promised."

"She promised only to tell me. That she wouldn't just run off without talking to me first. I know she's planning right now to slip away."

"But, Dad, why? She loves it here. She loves *us.*"

"That's just it. She cares too much and would never put us in danger. After this morning and the incident at the orchard, and then that guy showing up, she's scared it could happen again and we might be hurt."

Austin looked as though he might cry, and Matt felt close to tears himself. The thought of losing Ginny was inconceivable. "We have to think of something, son. Something to make her feel safe so she'll want to stay."

"Marry her, Dad. Then she can't leave us."

Matt was so startled he almost choked. When he could speak he said, "What did you say?"

Austin's grin was impish, his dark eyes alight with laughter. "Marry Ginny. She wouldn't leave then."

Ah, he thought, it was so simple in a child's mind. Matt played with the corner of one of his drawings, wondering if maybe Austin knew more than he should.

"Dad! You do want to marry her, don't you?"

"Yes." There he'd said it. And he felt relieved for doing so, even if it was to his ten-year-old son. Then disappointment settled over him. "She won't do it, Austin, even as wonderful a catch as I am." His son laughed. "If Ginny thinks her being here is going to put you or me in any danger, she'll bolt."

Austin jumped off the bed and began pacing the bedroom floor. "Then we'll have to come up with a plan to make her realize she's safe here."

Matt stretched out on the bed and watched as the brilliant mind of his son started planning their strategy. It had been a long rigorous morning and he'd almost fallen asleep when Austin's exuberant shout jolted him awake.

"I've got it, Dad! The perfect plan."

GINNY'S TEARS were coming fast and hard, and she had to bite her knuckle to keep from sobbing out loud. She eased up from her position outside Austin's bedroom door. Everything had worked out. The relief that washed over her left her weak with emotion, and she had to struggle to stand.

Once in her own bedroom, she began to pack some of her clothes, deciding what she should take with her and what she'd have to leave behind. That she was leaving was a foregone conclusion. Her troubles had followed her, and she could not risk exposing Matt and Austin—or any of the other men—to such danger.

She was going to have to break her promise to Matt and Austin and leave without telling them. But when? When was a good time to go? The thought that she would never see them again was like a physical blow, and she doubled over in pain. Never see Matt again? How had it happened that she'd fallen so deeply in love with him? And Austin? She wouldn't even allow herself to think about Austin.

And then there was Jericho and the hired hands. In the past few days she'd started lowering their fat intake without them even noticing. What was going to happen to them now? And Dog. Who else could love an ugly bad-tempered beast that grinned—and had saved her life on more than one occasion.

Ginny sat on the end of the bed, her arms limp between her legs, her body racked with sobs. How could she leave them when she loved them so much? Then her resolve returned. She stopped crying and sat up straight. If she had to go, it would be quickly.

She would leave the next night, she thought, and no one would be the wiser until she was far away from here.

CHAPTER SIXTEEN

SOMETHING WAS UP.

Matt and Austin had been acting strangely since the previous afternoon—whispered conferences, private phone calls, a series of trips back and forth to town on the flimsiest of pretexts.

Ginny watched them now as they walked into the kitchen after another one of these mysterious errands in town. She eyed them suspiciously and received such unbelievably innocent looks in return that warnings pealed in her head like Sunday-morning church bells.

She went over to the counter and started putting together sandwiches for lunch while Matt talked in low tones on the phone. Austin stuck to her side like a leech, following her every movement, asking questions about yesterday's events, telling her what he'd found out about the cave paintings. He was talking a blue streak, and Ginny seriously considered taping his mouth shut. Even Dog had had enough and lay curled up on his bed in the corner of the kitchen, his eyes closed.

She set the plate of pimento-cheese sandwiches and a bag of potato chips on the table, hoping the food would silence him.

Austin glanced at his hands and hurried to the sink. Passing his father on the way, he gave him an exasperated look and jerked his head toward the table. It was exhausting, trying to keep Ginny distracted. "Ginny, do you ever want to marry and have more children?"

Ginny had just taken a sip of her soft drink and almost choked. "Someday maybe."

Austin dried his hands and stood beside her chair. "I bet you were a good mother to Beth. You're not too old to have more, you know. I've read where older women in their late thirties are having babies."

"I'm only thirty-two, Austin."

"You see? That's not too old, is it?"

What was he up to? she wondered. All this talk about marriage and babies was making her nervous, and she was tense enough about leaving tonight. She jumped in surprise when Austin suddenly wrapped his arms around her neck and hugged her. She closed her eyes tight. Oh, God, how could she leave him? There was something frantic about his hold on her, and she grasped his shoulders and eased him gently away so she could look at him.

"What's wrong, Austin?"

"Nothing. I just wanted you to know I love you."

He was killing her, she thought. Her heart ached with longing and the realization that her leaving was going to hurt not only her but others, as well. "I love you, too." If he didn't quit patting her on the shoulder and looking at her with those big dark eyes, she was going to start bawling.

Matt hung the phone up and sat down at the table. As he reached for a sandwich he caught Austin's glance, winked and nodded, then smiled at his son's sigh of relief.

"Okay, you two." Ginny set her glass down with a loud thump. "There's something funny going on." If she'd accomplished anything while here, it was to help bring father and son together. It would make it easier for her once she left, knowing they'd have each other.

Matt grinned. "I was just talking to Argus. After he locked Junior up, he made a few phone calls to Boston. It's kind of a crazy situation, but the guy who made and planted the bomb is more than willing to testify against Tony Coldwell. With the promise of a more lenient sentence, he signed a very detailed confession. Ginny, your stepfather was the only man behind the bombing. It's all over but for Coldwell's retrial on two counts of murder. And I doubt you'll even have to testify. As for Junior, the Texas court will deal with him. He won't get off lightly for what he tried to do, I promise you that."

She faked a happy smile. "That's wonderful."

"But you're still worried, right?"

"Matt..." She wasn't hungry any longer and pushed her plate aside. "I just don't think it's all that simple. Tony might have ordered and paid for the bombing, but he was laundering drug money, and I've been told that drug lords have a pretty long arm when it comes to revenge."

He couldn't argue with her there. "But they're not interested in you, never have been. As soon as Tony was caught, they pulled in their horns and slipped away quietly in the night. They might have lain low for a week or so, but you can rest assured they quickly found somebody else more than willing to launder their money for them. Believe me, Ginny, they don't want any attention directed their way. There'll be no retaliation."

"You're sure? Sure enough to bet Austin's life or yours on it?"

Well, that confirmed it, he thought. She was going to skip, all right. It was time to unfold the plan. "Austin and I discussed your problem and came up with an idea."

"Dad!"

"Well, actually," Matt went on, "Austin came up with a plan. I ran it by Argus and he thinks it'll work."

"Of course it'll work," Austin said, his scowl as fierce as Matt's. "Tell her what it is."

"Maybe you'd like to do that," Matt said.

"No. You wouldn't let me talk to the sheriff, so you'd better do it."

Ginny's gaze bounced from one to the other and she couldn't help smiling. They were so alike it was scary.

"Thank you," Matt said, then returned his attention to Ginny. "We know you're thinking about leaving, Ginny, but that's not necessary."

"I told Dad he should marry you and make you stay."

"Austin, I'm doing this and I'll thank you to be quiet."

For a moment she couldn't breathe and her heart began to race. "And what did your dad say to that?"

"This isn't the time, Austin," Matt growled.

"He said he would, but that you wouldn't agree to it."

Ginny gazed at Matt. "He said that, did he?"

"Oh, yeah," Austin continued, ignoring the fierce looks directed at him. "I told him you loved me—and him, too."

She was a little amused that Austin had put himself first in the affection lineup. But now it was her turn to be a little apprehensive about where he was leading them.

"Maybe you should let your father tell me about this plan of yours," she said.

"Sure." Austin looked from one to the other. "I told Dad you're not too old yet to have babies."

"Thank you," she said, thinking she'd like to muzzle the boy. Her cheeks were on fire and she wanted to laugh and cry at the same time. When she glanced at Matt, it appeared he was thinking the same thing, and they both avoided looking at Austin.

Matt cleared his throat. "At first we entertained the idea of going public with your story—newspaper and television coverage. Tell everyone what happened to you. We'd pull the fangs, so to speak, out of anyone who might secretly be interested in your whereabouts and put a burr under the FBI all at the same time. But we decided not to draw any undue attention to you right now. So we'll set that plan on the back burner and use it only when needed." Matt glanced at his watch, then deliberately took a moment to munch on his sandwich and some chips.

Ginny's heart was beating fast, her palms damp. If there was any hope, the slightest chance that she could stay and they'd be safe, she was willing to listen. Her apprehension made her tense. She was going to be a nervous wreck if Matt didn't hurry up. For a second she was seriously considering pouring his drink in his lap to rouse him from his silence.

Matt took one look at Ginny's expression and set down his glass. "Austin's always making fun of Two Rivers, saying a person can't burp without everyone knowing it. Well, he told me we ought to use that to our advantage, and he's right." Matt was proud of his son and showed it.

Ginny had had enough. "I don't have the foggiest idea what you're talking about."

"I put the plan to Argus and he's sure it'll work."

"How about telling me?" she said, finally realizing what was going on as the telephone rang and Matt and Austin both jumped. They'd been playing for time.

Matt grinned and gave Austin a thumbs-up. When he returned to the table he was smiling like the cat that caught the canary. "It's all set up."

Austin hooted with joy.

When Dog barked his agreement they all searched for him. Ginny glanced under her chair and laughed. "You're feeling better, Dog?"

"Tell her, Dad." Austin's young voice rang with happiness. "Tell her everything now."

Matt sighed. He'd been worried that everyone wouldn't go along with the plan. "I think we can do better than that. Let's go show her."

Ginny didn't like the mystery and let her feelings be known, but between Matt, Austin and Dog, she was ushered to the car. Before she could make any more protest, they were speeding down the driveway. They wouldn't answer her questions, only laughed at her smoldering anger.

Two Rivers had a deserted air about it, even for a Sunday. When Matt parked the Jeep in front of the general store, Ginny noted that Miss Sally and Mister were absent from their usual places on the benches. Matt, Austin and Dog were out of the car before she could even open her door. They were so pleased with themselves that their barely concealed excitement was contagious, and she quickly bounded over the high curb.

Matt held open the door of the store and motioned for her to enter. She paused directly in front of him, giving him an assessing look. His dark eyes sparkled just a bit too brightly, and the smile he tried to hide kept peeking out around the corners of his mouth.

"You're far too pleased with yourself," she whispered for his ears only, "and that could get you in all kinds of trouble later."

Confusion slowed her steps, then stopped them altogether when she thought they were interrupting a town meeting. Miss Rosemary and Miss Sally, the eldest of the group, were seated at a table in the back of the store, along with everyone else she'd met from the town and some she had yet to meet. Everyone was holding a drink.

As if on cue, Miss Rosemary and Miss Sally raised their glasses of amber liquid. "Welcome to Two Rivers, Ginny," Miss Sally said. "We look forward to a long and happy friendship."

Ginny bit her lip and choked back the sobs that threatened to erupt. They were all trying to break her heart by making her feel special and loved. She wanted to say something, explain that it was appreciated, but all for naught. She wasn't going to stay.

Like a magician, Miss Rosemary hushed Miss Sally with a wave of her cane. "Argus and Matthew told us of your troubles, and you must know that as a town we all stick together. So, my dear child, your problems have become ours, and we take our duties as good neighbors and friends most seriously. Argus, you're better with all the official details. Please tell her the rest."

Argus bowed gallantly to Miss Rosemary, then smiled at a baffled Ginny. "It was Austin's idea." There were murmurs among the group, and Austin puffed out his chest in pride. "He reminded us of something we kinda take for granted. As in all small towns, we know just about everything there is to know about each other. We know who comes and goes and when. There's only one main road through Two Rivers, and it's not widely traveled by strangers.''

Miss Rosemary thumped her cane on the floor. "Get on with it, boy. Can't you see Ginny's about to faint with curiosity?''

"Yes, ma'am,'' Argus said apologetically. "The thing is, Ginny, we had a town meeting yesterday afternoon and decided to close Two Rivers to strangers. We're not blocking off the highway or anything, but we're all going to keep a more vigilant eye on everyone. Our first line of defense is Foster Schneider, who lives at one end of town, and Tom Klein, who lives at the other end. They don't miss anyone passing. When a vehicle goes by they're not familiar with, they'll set up the alarm.''

Miss Rosemary banged her cane once more. "You're the longest-winded boy I've ever met. Step back, Argus, I'll finish this.'' She cleared her throat. "Thing is, child, no one's going to get to you, young Matthew or Austin. We have a system in place, an alarm. Mister got a friend of his with the highway department to furnish us with some radio thingamajigs. We can all listen and talk on them. So you're quite safe here now and can go on with your life. We've all come to love you. We want you to stay, child. Please say you will.''

It was too much. Ginny turned her face into Matt's chest and cried. Matt's arms wrapped around her and he held her close, trying hard to control his own emotions. He felt Austin leaning against his side and dropped one arm and hugged him. When Dog nipped at his ankle, he glanced down at the ugly face and said, "Sorry, pal, you'll get a pat later.''

Everyone was as teary-eyed as Ginny, and then they all started to laugh and passed around the bottle of bourbon again, giving Matt and his new family time to regain their composure.

Ginny dried her eyes on Matt's shirt. "I don't know what to say. Thank you, everyone. Austin, you're a genius."

Jason joined them and kissed her lightly on the cheek. "Of course Einstein's a genius. He's my nephew." He took Austin by the shoulder and steered him away from Matt and Ginny. "Have I told you about my emu project, Austin?"

Ginny smiled, then turned to Matt, her expression serious. "Do you really think it could work?"

"Yes." He paused. "You were going to leave without telling me, weren't you, Ginny."

There was no sense lying. "It was for you and Austin that I was leaving."

He allowed himself to relax. "Was leaving? You did say *was?*"

"Oh, Matt, I want to stay. So you really think this crazy plan will work."

"It's only crazy to you because you haven't been in a small town long enough to know how it operates. I promise you it'll work."

The sound of static, and a garbled voice came over the radio receiver, bringing an immediate hush to the room. Foster Schneider warned of an incoming car.

Ginny watched in confusion as Argus and some of the other men left the store to station themselves around town. Then the rest of the townspeople dispersed to a previously assigned position. Clouds had covered the sky, and the day was darkening. A gusty wind picked up leaves and scattered them down the length of the main street. Ginny and Austin stood to one side of the store door, watching as headlights appeared at the end of the street and slowed for the first stop sign.

"Look," Austin said, pointing. Two cars parked on opposite sides of the street backed out into the road, moving slowly until their bumpers touched and were blocking the unknown car. Argus ambled toward the driver's side and leaned down.

Ginny sensed Matt beside her and glanced up to find him silently laughing. "What?"

She followed the direction of his gaze and her mouth dropped open in surprise. The car had been surrounded with men from the town, each casually carrying a lethal-looking rifle in his hands. Whoever was in the car could no longer go forward and, because of the weapons trained on him, couldn't back up, either.

Argus broke away from the group and walked back to the general store. "Ginny, Agent Harrison and his boss, Agent Fry, would like a word with you." He tried hard to contain his amusement that their plan had worked as he followed Matt and Ginny down the street. "You should have seen their faces when they realized they'd driven into a trap."

As they approached the car, Agent Harrison started to get out on the passenger side, until Mister shoved it shut with the butt of his rifle. He spit a long stream of brown juice onto the ground and gave the agent a cross-eyed stare. "No need to get out, son. You won't be staying."

Ginny stood by the car and nodded to the new agent when he introduced himself. They still had the ability to make her uncomfortable and, admittedly, scared. She reached out and grabbed Matt and Austin's hands and held on for dear life.

"Mrs. Carney, would you mind telling me what's going on here?" The agent glanced around at the men surrounding his car. "I only came to have a word with you—" he laughed a little nervously "—not to arrest you. Or start a war."

"Agent Fry, what could we possibly have left to say to each other? I thought I made myself clear to Agent Harrison when I told him that I wasn't going back into the program. That I'm taking my life back."

"He filled us in and also told us you weren't going to change your mind, but I thought I should give it a try." He glanced around again, shrugged, then started to laugh. "You've made some good friends, Mrs. Carney. I wish you luck." He gave the sheriff a respectful nod and put the car into reverse so he could turn around.

They all stood in the street and watched the taillights of the car disappear. Austin was the first to speak. "It worked," he marveled. "It really worked."

Matt shook hands with a couple of the men, then turned to Ginny. and Austin. "Let's go home."

Dog heartily agreed and bounded for the Jeep. He sat by the door and waited, grinning hugely, watching his new family approach with a bright gleam in his eerie eyes.

"He's getting a little too familiar with my car, Ginny," Matt said. "Tell him the back seat is not exclusively his territory, and his claim on a corner of the kitchen is over. No dogs in the house. Do I make myself clear?"

MATT STOOD under the shower, letting the hot water beat relentlessly down on his head. It'd been a hell of a weekend, the longest in his life, he thought, and he was damn glad it was over. He turned his face up and let the water pour over him, then shifted his weight, cursing the weakness in his leg.

"You should do something about that," Ginny said as she slipped in behind him, pulling the shower door firmly shut.

She was as unpredictable as the wind, he thought.

"Physical therapy would help strengthen the muscles." She slid her hand over his hip and down his thigh, lightly touching the angry red scar. "And it wouldn't hurt so much."

"Is that right?" He started to turn around, but she pressed against him, her arms moving around his waist.

"I thought I'd help you bathe, since you can barely stand."

"I see." His heart was suddenly in his throat. "I do seem to be having trouble."

"How about a shampoo? Grab the shower head." Before he could answer she squirted his head with shampoo and began to gently scrub. Just when he thought he might close his eyes and nod off, she thrust his head back under the stream of water, jarring him from his dreams.

Soapy hands began to roam over his body, strong hands that made him catch his breath. He was so relaxed and felt so good that he wondered why he hadn't talked her into this before.

"Was what Austin said this afternoon true?" Matt rolled his head, feeling the tension melt from his neck and shoulders.

"Austin doesn't tell lies."

Something in the tone of her voice made him pause. Matt closed his eyes. "Well . . . *do* you love me?"

She moved her hands across his chest, down to his stomach, and pulled him back against her. She gave him a straight-out honest answer. "Yes." When he attempted to turn around, she stopped him. "There's something else you have to know."

He didn't like the sound of that and prepared himself for the worst.

"Do you remember Austin telling me that I wasn't too old to have babies?"

"Yes." He held his breath.

"I'd like to have babies, Matt. But if you don't, please tell me now."

Matt slowly let his breath out with relief. "I'm not opposed to babies. Do you think, if that is a possibility, we ought to get married soon?"

Ginny rubbed her cheek against his smooth back. "Very soon, I should say."

"Will you let go of your death grip on me so I can turn around and kiss you?"

She laughed and did as he asked.

When he finally let her go, he gathered her face between his hands and looked deeply into her eyes. "I love you, Ginny." He kissed her slowly and sweetly. "But I'm not William—never will be."

"I love you, Matthew Bolt. And I need you."

He felt the truth of her words in his heart. "So. You think you're ready to take on father and son."

"Yes, and anyone else that unexpectedly comes along." She smiled a secret little smile that made her eyes light up from within. William and Beth would understand, she thought, and would give them their blessing.